ROOT ROT

& OTHER GRIM TALES

ALSO BY SARAH READ

The Bone Weaver's Orchard

Out of Water

ROOT ROT
& OTHER GRIM TALES

Sarah Read

Root Rot & Other Grim Tales
Copyright © 2023 by Sarah Read
Print ISBN: 979-8988128625

Cover & Interior Illustrations by Thomas Brown
Book Design by Todd Keisling | Dullington Design Co.

"The Hope Chest" previously appeared in *Black Static* #72, November 2019, reprint Ellen Datlow's *Best Horror of the Year* Volume 12, September 2020; "That's for Remembrance" previously appeared in *Menacing Hedge* Summer 2017; "Wish Wash" previously appeared in *The Hideous Book of Hidden Horrors*, 2022; "Root Rot" previously appeared in *Humans are the Problem: A Monster Anthology*, 2021; "Into the Wood" previously appeared in *Pareidolia* anthology from Black Shuck Books, July 2019; "Bloody Bon Secours" previously appeared in *Violent Vixens*, August 2021; "Diamond Saw" previously appeared in *Black Static* #71, September 2019; "When Auntie's Due" previously appeared in *Mother*, 2022; "Seeing Stones" previously appeared in *The Bad Book*, July 2021; "Death Plate Seating for 1,000" previously appeared in *Thirteen Haunted Houses*, 2022; "The Inn of the Fates" previously appeared in *Under Twin Suns*, June 2021; "Trouble with Fate" previously appeared in *We Are Wolves*, winter 2020; "The Terror Bay Resort Experience" previously appeared in *The Wicked Library*, 2022; "The Time That is Left" previously appeared in *Shadow Atlas*, 2021

All other stories are original to this collection.

No part of this work may be reproduced or transmitted in any form or by any means without permission, except for inclusion of brief quotations with attribution in a review or report. Requests for reproduction or related information should be addressed to the Contact page at www.badhandbooks.com.

The stories and poetry within this anthology are works of fiction. All characters, products, corporations, institutions, and/or entities in this book are either products of the respective authors' imaginations or, if real, used fictitiously without intent to describe actual characteristics.

Bad Hand Books
www.badhandbooks.com

For those who swim. There is always another shore.

TABLE OF CONTENTS

The Hope Chest 9

That's for Remembrance 29

Wish Wash 37

Root Rot 55

Into the Wood 71

Pelts 83

Bloody Bon Secours 93

Diamond Saw 105

When Auntie's Due 119

Seeing Stones 135

Death Plate Seating for 1,000 151

Inn of the Fates 167

Trouble with Fate 179

The Terror Bay Resort Experience 191

Skydivers 217

The Time That is Left 235

The Pescadoor 249

The Ballad of Lady Lithium 293

Acknowledgments 303

About the Author 305

Content Warnings 307

THE HOPE CHEST

Hannah walked the half mile from the bus stop, but Grandma didn't meet her at the bus, or on the road, or on the porch. Or in the house. Her mother sat alone at the table, with her hands clutched around a glass of ice water as if it were keeping her warm.

By the time Hannah was close enough to smell that it wasn't water, she was close enough to see that her mother had been crying and that the ice in the glass shook. That her sleeves were soaked to the elbow as if the tears had been a tide, or the glass had spilled and spilled.

"Where's Grandma?"

"Just 'where's grandma?' You're not going to ask me what's wrong?"

It was an eggshell day. A choke-back-the-lump-in-your-throat-and-bite-your-tongue day.

"What's wrong?" Hannah whispered. It was difficult for her to ask with her throat full and her tongue between her teeth.

"Grandma's gone. She got … very sick. She's at the hospital. You can't go see her."

Hannah's stomach twisted and her cheeks pricked with ice needles. "Why? I want to go! I need to see her."

Her mother shook her head once, but then looked sick from the motion and stopped, squeezed her eyes shut.

"I want to be with her."

"No visitors allowed. What if it's contagious? If you get too close to Grandma, you'll die. Is that what you want?"

Hannah shook her head slowly, the motion pulling at all the knots twisting down her throat to her heart. "Is she going to die?"

Her mother said nothing. Took a drink. The insides of her hands looked bright red through the glass.

Hannah stepped backwards, eggshells underfoot, even inside her shoes.

It was important to know when to disappear.

"I was stuck here with her all day. Aren't you afraid I'm going to die, too?"

Hannah was halfway down the hall before the glass hit the wall.

Grandma's dress form stood in the corner of the attic, set to her measurements. Bust, waist, hips, shoulders, neck, height. The hidden network of cranks twisted the padded surfaces into the exact shape of her, the shape of the hole in the house where she should have been.

The air swirled with dust, rafters dotted with cobwebs and desiccated bees. Shelves of fabric and the feathery crepe of pattern paper lined the walls in a small labyrinth through the attic space.

In the corner sat an antique sewing machine, cast iron set into the dry wood of a desk. The missing drawer knobs had been replaced with brightly colored buttons.

Hannah rested her forehead against the padded curve of the dress form's shoulder. Up close, she could see tiny holes in the fabric, small scars left by decades of pinpricks as dress after dress had been draped over the figure.

Hannah breathed, in out in out, and calmed the shake in her chest.

Between the curved plates of canvas, deep inside the form's chest, was the network of metal bones and cranks, stiff, rusted.

Hannah looked away. She didn't like to see inside the thing, as if it were Grandma herself laid open.

Have the doctors opened her? Are her insides exposed, examined?

She stepped away from the dress form and over to the cedar hope chest on the far wall. The humidity in the attic had warped the wood so that one side of the lid gaped like parted lips. She heaved it open, the hinges groaning and raising a cloud of dust.

Tissue paper lay over the stack of fabric inside. There were curtains, handkerchiefs and a tablecloth, all treasured, but beneath them—greater treasures.

Hannah pulled the sky-blue satin dress out from beneath the stack of crisp linens. She carried it over to the dress form.

The buttons were small and difficult to manage, but she opened it enough to slip it over the form and smooth it down, and fastened it up the back. It was beautiful. It was Grandma. It even smelled like her. Hannah buried her face into the familiar shoulder. She wrapped her arms around the form. It hugged just like Grandma.

"No, we can't go to the craft store. We've got hospital bills," her mother said.

They'd cashed Grandma's pension check. Hannah didn't think hospitals took cash.

Liquor stores did, though.

She helped her mother carry the sloshing boxes into the house, then disappeared into the attic as her mother settled in.

Grandma's dress form stood in front of the sewing machine. The small wooden chair lay on its side on the wide floorboards.

Hannah tiptoed across the dusty boards and righted the chair.

The form faced the machine, its buttoned sleeve cuffs resting on the table. A tangle of thread trailed from the bobbin like a cobweb. The thread was bright green, the color of emeralds or Astroturf.

Hannah scanned the rows of cubbyhole shelves. There was a bolt of fabric that exactly matched the thread. She pulled it free and carried it to the cutting table, unspooled it a few turns, and cut a yard exactly as her grandmother had showed her.

She carried the soft cotton to the machine and moved Grandma's form aside, then pulled up the chair so she could reach the treadle. She untangled the bobbin and threaded the needle.

Hannah only knew how to sew one thing: a pillowcase, but she'd made enough of them that she thought she could remember how, even without Grandma here to help.

Maybe she'd feel better with something handmade, from home. Maybe it would help her heal faster, come home sooner.

She ran a tight seam down the edge of the fabric and the needle stitched through the meat of her finger.

She yelped and stood, knocking the chair back. As she pulled away, the thread trailing from her finger pulled against the fabric and puckered her stitches. Blood ran down her wrist as she snipped the thread and pulled it through her wound.

Her breath hitched and she ran to the dress form and threw her arms around its waist, sobbing into the lace at its front.

Her sobs slowed and she leaned away, feeling silly, ashamed. Her blood left a smear on the blue satin of her grandmother's best dress.

Hannah gaped at the stain in horror.

Cold water, she remembered. That was for getting blood out.

She wrapped her finger in a strip of scrap muslin and worked at the tiny row of buttons at the back of the dress.

Hannah raced the dress down the attic stairs and held it under a stream of cold water in the bathroom sink. The water diluted the blood, turning the blue a dingy brown, spreading the stain further in creeping sepia. She kept rinsing till the whole dress had soaked up the water like a thick, heavy sponge.

When it looked clean, Hannah laid the dress in the bathtub. A glint caught her eye and she saw Grandma's glasses curled in the soap dish. They were bent, no longer face-shaped, but Hannah took them and put them in her pocket, hoped she could add them to the form. Grandma couldn't see without her glasses.

Her finger had bled through her soaked bandage. She peeled off the cloth. In the stark light of the bathroom, she could see how dirty the fabric had been.

She tossed the strip into the trash and rinsed the cut, grinding her teeth at the sting, wondering if enough cold water could wash all of the blood from her, if her insides were stained that awful brown.

The needle had punched a ragged hole right through her fingertip. She smeared it with ointment and wrapped a Band-Aid around it.

She looked down at the dress in the tub. It was like Grandma lay there, deflated and empty.

She didn't want to see the bones of the form again. Didn't want to see that skin of it riddled with needle holes, like her finger.

She slipped into the hallway and walked to her grandmother's bedroom.

Her mother's door, next to it, was open a crack. The TV light flickered over the row of bottles on the bedside table. The light shone off her mother's glasses so that Hannah couldn't tell if her eyes were open or not.

Hannah hurried past and ducked into her grandmother's bedroom.

The bed was unmade. Grandma always made her bed, right after her morning bath.

Hannah stared at the depression in the pillow. The pillowcase was patterned with bright green leaves and red ladybugs. They had made it together.

Hannah was still determined to finish a new one.

She went to the closet door and pulled it open.

The smell of her grandmother floated free as if escaping a cage. Tears sprang to Hannah's eyes as she ran her hand over the row of drab everyday dresses.

She pulled down a yellow one that she remembered from an Easter picnic. There was a hat, somewhere, to match. The form would look better with a hat.

She dug through the boxes on the closet shelf till she found it, and the cream shoes to go with.

Then she went to the wooden box where her grandmother kept her modest collection of jewels. She lifted the lid. "Claire de Lune" began to play across the empty red velvet cushions. She snapped the lid shut.

A crash sounded from the next room.

Hannah's breath froze. She rushed to the closet and stepped inside, burrowing her way to the back. She pulled the yellow dress over her face and held her breath.

Her mother burst into the room. "Hannah!"

Hannah huddled, fingernails digging into the shoes clutched in her hand.

The music box began to play again. Then there was a crash and the music slowed, deepened, stopped.

Her mother's steps stormed out and the door slammed.

The wire hangers chimed softly as Hannah shook in place.

She waited. Long enough for her mother to settle, to finish another glass, to sleep.

Hannah slipped out of her hiding place.

The jewelry box lay smashed on the floor. There were no jewels. Hannah knelt by the pieces and ran her fingers over the nap of the velvet. In the plush of carpet, she saw a small sparkle. A single earring, just a plain gold orb, winked at her from the carpet strands.

Hannah pulled it free. She pinched it in her good fingers and hurried back up to the attic.

It was as if the past had come again.

Grandma's form stood under her wide hat, her Easter dress falling in tiers of yellow polyester, showing only a few inches of the support post, and then the scuffed cream pumps.

Hannah set back to work on her grandmother's pillowcase. Just as she snapped the last thread, a scream rose through the floorboards.

Hannah raced for the stairs, clutching the green fabric in her fist.

Her mother stood in the hall, gripping the bathroom doorframe and panting. She spun to face Hannah. "Did you put that there?"

Hannah stared at her mother's hand and nodded, afraid to trust her voice. *Who else could have?* she wanted to ask. *There's no one else here.*

"What the hell were you thinking?"

There were no eggshells left to walk on, only fine white powder and torn soft membrane.

"I found it. In the attic. It was dirty, so… I washed it." A near-enough almost-truth.

"What the hell were you doing in the attic?"

Hannah squeezed her fists and felt the cotton against her palm. She held the pillowcase out. "I made this for Grandma. To help her feel better."

Her mother covered her face with her hands. Hannah thought she might be crying, but when the hands came away, the face beneath was angry.

Her mother snatched the pillowcase from her. "From that dusty old attic? It would make her sicker." She whipped the fabric across Hannah's face.

It stung. It tasted of dust.

Her mother stomped off toward the living room.

Hannah stood in the hall. She remembered how the dress had looked, for a moment, as if someone lay in the tub. Hannah understood why her mother had screamed.

"I'm going to work!" her mother called out. The front door slammed.

Hannah didn't feel like an Easter picnic anymore.

She slipped back into Grandma's bedroom, stepped over the broken pieces of jewelry box, and went to the closet.

Something grey, maybe. Or black. She pulled a somber dress from a hanger, then a few others. Maybe Grandma would like to decide what she wore. Maybe her mood wasn't as bleak as Hannah's.

She filled her arms with dresses and carried them slowly up the attic steps.

She hung them from the rafters and went back for more, then everything from the drawers, the shoes, all the hats.

Grandma could wear whatever she wanted. She must miss her clothes.

Hannah brought the thick, brown, wool duffel coat up last and laid it across the floorboards. She crawled on top of it and closed her eyes. The wool itched the stinging spot on her cheek, but she pressed her face in closer. She smelled snowmen and Christmas shopping and ice skating hidden in its fibers. She fell asleep, holding Grandma's hand, gliding across a mirror pond.

She woke to the sound of a car door slamming.

She crawled out from under an old scrap-sewn quilt and peered through the fly-specked glass of the attic window.

Her mother was home, loading her arms with large bags from the trunk of the car. Hannah watched as she struggled up the front steps and though the door.

Hannah turned away from the window.

Grandma had chosen a black dress.

Hannah ran over and hugged the form. "You're as sad as me," she whispered into the dark fabric. The form hugged her back.

There was a commotion downstairs, the tumbling of a half-dozen large bags.

"Hannah!"

Hannah squeezed the form tighter. She wanted to kiss her, but there was no face. She would make one, she decided. It's what Grandma would have done.

"Hannah!"

Her mother's voice had grown closer, nearing the attic stairs. Hannah didn't want her to come up, to see, to start smashing things.

She let go of the form and hurried down the stairs.

Her mother was in Grandma's room. The pieces of jewelry box

were gone. The bed was covered in paper bags printed with sharp logos. Bright fabrics and sleek boxes spilled from inside.

Her mother pointed to the empty closet. "Where are my mother's clothes?"

Hannah chewed her lip. "I … packed them," she said. "In case she wants them."

Her mother shook her head. "She has to wear the hospital clothes. You know that, right?"

Hannah nodded.

"Whatever. You actually did me a favor this time." Her mother grabbed a fistful of hangers, then dumped the contents of the bags onto the covers and began slipping shirts onto the hangers.

"Did you get her new clothes?" Hannah asked. "For when she comes home?"

"These are mine. She always makes her own ugly clothes."

Hannah flinched.

"I'm staying here, now." She hung the clothes up, tags fluttering from the cuffs. "Here, do me another favor." She handed Hannah a brown paper bag. "Clean the bathroom."

Hannah peered into the bag and saw a bottle of bleach cleaner and a package of sponges.

"But it is clean, I just … "

"I didn't ask if it was clean. I told you to clean it."

Her good mood was fading fast.

Hannah took the bag to the bathroom, closed the door, and latched the lock.

She gasped at the sight of a blue body in the tub, choked on the scream in her throat. She squeezed her eyes shut and opened them, and the body was a dress again.

Hannah lifted the dress from the tub. It was still wet on the underside. She draped the dress over the towel rack, wet-side-out so it could finish drying, and turned back to the bathtub.

The dress had left a damp outline of a body at the bottom of the tub. Hannah shivered. She pulled a sponge from the package and wiped and scrubbed, but she could still see the outline of something lying there.

Even Grandma had struggled to sew spheres. The shape Hannah affixed to the top of the form was not entirely like a head. The muslin was too pale, and the scraps she had used to stuff it showed through as if she were looking at a ghost.

Hannah took a marking pencil from the button-pull drawer and sketched a face onto the fabric. She placed a hat on top to hide the unnatural bulges. A black hat, to match the dress.

She filled two gloves with more scraps and fastened them to the ends of the cuffs with straight pins.

She pushed the post of the single gold earring through the center of Grandma's right eye. Grandma's eyes always twinkled.

Hannah admired her work. It was Grandma—the form of her, so close that Hannah's nose began to tickle and her eyes stung.

She hugged the form and kissed her cheek.

Grandma's kisses smelled like pencil clay, and the pins in the cuffs stuck her when they hugged, but Hannah's heart was lighter when she went to bed.

If Hannah could, herself, make a Grandma, then surely the doctors could make her whole again.

When Hannah woke, her mother had already left for work. There were waffles on the table, still steaming and pooling with butter and syrup. Bacon curled beside them.

Hannah rushed to the table and began to fill her mouth before she even looked at the clock.

She had an hour before the bus would come. She slowed her chewing.

"Grandma?"

She walked down the hall, peering into each room.

Grandma lay in her bed, her form under the scrap quilt from the attic. Hannah rushed to her and threw her arms over her.

Grandma hugged her back, the cuff pins dragging across Hannah's skin.

"I don't want to go to school today, Grandma, I want to stay here with you."

Grandma squeezed her tighter.

"Will you call me in sick?"

Grandma was silent.

I haven't given her a tongue.

The graphite line of Grandma's mouth twisted, but it couldn't open.

"I'll fix it, Grandma, I'll be right back."

Hannah raced to the attic. She grabbed a seam-ripper, a needle and thread, and a short length of red ribbon, then hurried back to the bedroom and leaned over Grandma's form.

She poked the seam ripper into the corner of Grandma's mouth and tore across the pencil line. The muslin sprang back, and the scrap stuffing began to spill from the opening. Hannah stuffed it back inside. She slipped the ribbon between the frayed lips and stitched it in place.

THE HOPE CHEST

The tongue flopped against the round muslin chin. The frayed lips wriggled to keep the mass of scraps inside. It looked like speech, but no sound came.

Hannah frowned. She didn't know what else Grandma needed in order to speak. Inside parts, of which Hannah had no knowledge.

"It's okay, Grandma, we can look it up."

Grandma's old books filled the walls of the office in the basement. Hannah had browsed through them all at one time or another. The ones that looked the most boring—uniform black covers with plain white print across a dozen identical volumes all along the bottom shelf—were the best ones.

Hannah didn't know quite what she was looking for. Or how, exactly, to spell it. So she pulled out the first volume and began to flip through.

Grandma chose the last volume. Her gloved finger slipped through the pages as the silent fabric of her mouth moved, and colorful threads from the frayed edges of the scraps sprinkled down across the paper.

By the time Grandma handed her the book, the bus had long since come and gone.

The page Grandma held open to her had a black line drawing and a greyscale photo of something that looked both slimy and stringy.

"Vo-cal c-ords," Hannah read. This was the piece Grandma needed to talk. Hannah had never seen anything that looked like the picture. The book said it was a structure in the throat, but Hannah wasn't even certain that the form had a throat. The head was just a ball, closed off, and the neck of the form was sealed on top.

It would be a lot of work. It was going to be difficult and take a long time, but she had to do it.

Grandma needed a voice. Grandma had something to say.

Hannah hadn't finished by the time her mother came home. She left Grandma with a half-carved hole through her neck when her mother called to her from the kitchen.

Her mother stood with the phone to her ear. She slammed the receiver down. "Why is there a message from the school saying you didn't show up? And what is this mess?"

Hannah's throat clenched so hard she couldn't speak. *Vocal cords.* Hers were trapped in the nervous knot of her neck. She had forgotten about her need to call in sick. Forgotten about her waffles.

Her neck hurt. "I have a sore throat," she croaked. A sort-of truth.

"You should have told me so I could call. Now I'm in trouble. That means you're in trouble." Her mother's voice was creeping louder, well into the range where Hannah knew it was time to disappear. To the attic, the woods, the back of a closet—anywhere. But she was pinned down by her mother's angry stare. If she bolted, this time she'd be chased. Some animal sense in her knew it. A prey instinct.

She stood—a statue, facing the oncoming storm of her mother's rage.

Even with her eyes fixed open, she didn't see the plate coming. The sound of it shattering against the wall and scattering across the floor registered before the pain bloomed on the side of her face.

It came to her slowly, like a thaw. *Hurts.*

It occupied the fullness of her mind, save for a small, indifferent piece of her which registered the pain of her mother's satisfied expression. It was difficult to tell which pain was worse.

One of them would heal.

But the catharsis had uncoiled the spring of her mother's heels and it was safe, now, something told her, to run.

She did.

Up the attic stairs as a voice chased her, "Come back here and clean this up!" and into the close heat of the attic, to the hope chest.

Hannah curled inside and pulled Grandma's most precious linens over her before tipping the lid shut.

She couldn't hear anything anymore. There were no footsteps pounding the stairs, only the pounding in her cheekbone. It stung with every beat of her heart and ached in between. She counted each beat till they slowed, till there was more ache than sting.

Time does not pass in the hope chest. That is its purpose. A capsule, preserving the best things.

Hannah lifted the lid, feeling older, anyway, and climbed out of the chest when enough time had passed.

The sun had sunk lower, and cut through the attic window at an angle that hid everything in contrast. All bright and black, with no familiar shapes.

No familiar form.

Grandma.

She wasn't there—not on the broad cutting table where she'd left her, not by the sewing machine or in the rows of fabric.

Hannah's heart raced again, bringing the sting in her face back afresh.

She forced herself to move slowly, against her panic, down the stairs.

The hall was quiet. The doorway to Grandma's room set mostly closed, the soft light from the bedside lamp showing in a stripe against the doorjamb.

Hannah pressed her eye to the crack, wondering if her grandmother had gone to bed. The wood of the door hurt against the swelling of her cheek.

Only her mother was there, curled on the mattress.

Hannah crept down the hall.

She peered into the bathroom and caught a flash of her reflection in the mirror. She gasped. The form of her face was wrong, the shape unfamiliar, the color strange. She flipped on the light.

Her cheek swelled red and purple, taut as a ripe berry, as if the scraps beneath her skin were showing through.

But her eye was drawn away to the figure in the bathtub. She screamed.

Grandma was there—her form bent into the tub, glasses askew, ribbon tongue rolling from her mouth, which was split wide, wide, wider than Hannah had carved it. Rags spilled from her torn mouth. The unfinished hole in her throat gaped, voiceless.

Hannah screamed for them both.

Her mother came running, stopped behind her, and gasped so deeply Hannah felt a pull at her own lungs. Then she screamed, too.

Hannah felt fingers in her hair tighten into a fist.

"Did you do this?"

"No!"

"What the hell do you think you're playing at?"

The hand in her hair pushed her further into the bathroom, the loud voice driving her forward.

Her feet gave, and she shrieked as the hand suspended her by her hair, briefly, before allowing her to fall.

She heard the slam of a cupboard and felt a roughness scrape past her teeth, tasted bitterness. Her mother rammed the sponge into her mouth.

"Clean it up! Clean this trash away and scrub the tub. Get every trace of her out of there!"

The sponge dammed the sob in the back of Hannah's throat.

The door slammed shut behind her.

She coughed the sponge out of her mouth and vomited over it. She pinched the vomit-covered sponge, stood on shaking legs, and rinsed the sick off it in the sink. And she wondered how anything could ever be cleaned with a dirty sponge.

Every trace, every last stray thread from a frayed edge, was tucked safely away in the attic again.

If Grandma wants a bath, I'll bring her a basin upstairs. It's safer.

The fiberglass of the tub shone white, save for the rust stain that never moved no matter what effort Hannah applied.

"What the hell is that smell?"

The taste of the sponge rose again in Hannah's throat. She turned and looked at her mother standing in the doorway. Her eyes were ringed in red and the lines of her face cut deep.

"Look at you. You're filthy and you stink."

Hannah could no longer smell anything but bleach. Her mother reached for an ornate glass bottle in the cabinet that Hannah had never seen before, and sprayed a fragrant, expensive cloud into the air.

"I think … " Her mother chewed at a lip that already looked raw. "I think you'd better take a bath," she whispered. Her hands flexed.

Hannah's animal mind wanted her to run, but there was nowhere to go. Mother stood in the only doorway, a look in her eye that set Hannah's rabbit heart racing.

"Turn on the water."

Hannah didn't move. Her mother reached past her and twisted the knob all the way to hot.

"Stand up. Get those filthy clothes off and get in the tub."

Her mother's voice shook, Hannah thought, or else the water beat the sound right out of the air, drowning her voice in the rust-stained basin.

"Get in, Hannah." The voice came firm, then, steadied on anger.

Hannah looked at the water and saw her shadow there, the form of herself, an exact copy pressed to that white depth, stained there, permanent, like the rust. And Grandma's shadow beneath hers, stuck there. Trapped.

"I … don't want to go in there." Hannah squeezed her voice past the lump in her throat.

Her mother advanced into the room and grabbed the short hairs at the back of Hannah's neck, lifting her to stand.

"I said get that stinking filthy ass of yours into the tub this second!"

She pushed Hannah toward the water.

Hannah twisted and saw, over her mother's shoulder, Grandma's familiar form in the bathroom doorway. She cried out, a yelp of pain, a call for help.

Her mother's eyes tracked hers.

The fist at the back of her head loosened and she slid free. Hannah backed away till her hand plunged into the steaming water. She pulled it out and clutched her soaked sleeve to her chest.

Her mother began to turn, mouth stretching wide, ready to birth a tirade.

Her mouth froze open when she saw the figure standing there. Grandma's exact form, but her mouth torn too wide and spilling rags.

The limp-glove hand rose to the mouth and pulled free a fistful of bright scraps. The hand shot forward and crammed the rags into Mother's gaping mouth.

The other glove rose and reached again past the ribbon tongue to the scraps inside and pulled more free, and pushed them into Mother's trapped shout.

The glove hands picked and plucked every scrap of fiber from inside the muslin shell till it hung limp as wet hair over the form's neck.

Mother stood, stiff and overstuffed, plump with scraps that strained at her seams.

Grandma pulled a crooked needle and a length of black thread from a tuck in her dress, and whip-stitched Mother's lips shut to keep the rags from spilling out.

They dressed Mother in her new clothes and stood her form in the corner of the living room. Her tall, familiar shape had a view of the mailbox, where Hannah collected the letters.

"Your check is here, Grandma! It came again!"

They could live well, just the two of them, on what Grandma received.

"Do you want to go to the craft store and get some new buttons?"

"Yes," Grandma said, her voice as soft as old linen.

That's for Remembrance

Gramma Rosemary's hands shake and her lips quiver all the time now, so that if it weren't for the light in her white eyes I'd think she was wracked with grief. And she is, I suppose, when she remembers to be.

Her lips, hanging flaccid from the folds in her face, are so soft I almost can't feel them against my palm as they gather the pile of pills I hold up for her. We both hate this part, but if she tries to do it herself, she drops them all into the deep, awful carpet and we never see them again. Best for us both just to take a momentary leave from pride.

I hand her one of the cups of cold tea collected on the table and hope it's one from today.

"Thank you, sweet Susie," she says, and takes her minute to raise her eyes again—to remind herself that what she can't do now has no reflection on all the things that she has done. Her face smoothes when that firmness returns—when she remembers who she is.

And I flip open my sketchbook and settle in, hunker down so I'm not swept away in her tide of memories. And I don't mind, really.

Sure, it's two hours—at least—of my day tossed under the relentless roll of her stories. But I get my homework done, and Gramma Rosemary's happy, and Mom is relieved and grateful, and never complains about the out-of-state art school tuition. It's cheaper than in-state plus a home nursing service. A good deal for both of us, and best of all for Gramma Rosemary.

Her conversations always begin the same way. "Do you remember?" she'll ask. And, queen of nostalgia as she is, you would think that what would follow is an account of a thing that really happened. But that's not the case anymore.

Ever since the cataracts turned her eyes as white as Grampa Thomas's barn cat's, she tells tales of times that never were, says, "I remember. I remember," smiles, and pours another cup of tea and sets it right next to the others—tepid and un-drunk.

I'm halfway through my sketch when I see her cat eyes are locked on me, and not on the middle-distance of memory.

"Do you still wear your purple wings?" she asks, flapping her twisted hands in the air.

"No, Gramma," I say. I remember how the wings smelled when they burned, the plastic mesh melting into a shell of ashy enamel.

"That's a shame. You were so good in them. I remember when you'd never take them off."

I try not to remember it. A Halloween costume at age four that I didn't take off till I was nine—when it stopped working.

"Do you remember the time you wore them into the barn and found Grampa Thomas there? Hanging from a beam. You flew right up and tried to lift him, but you were too small. And it was too late."

"Gramma, Grampa Thomas died before I was born. He was *your* grandfather. James was my grandfather. Don't you remember James?"

"Oh yes, Thomas was mine. I remember, now. Such a sad man. He never should have hid near those civilians. He drew the fire straight to that poor girl. His guilt was never quiet after that."

"Gramma, that was the documentary we watched. Gettysburg."

"Yes, I remember. You were so pretty there, in your purple wings, over the battlefield like an angel."

It's times like this when I want to run. I wish I could run into her memories—be back in the times when things were better. I set down my sketchbook and give her a big hug. Her smell is different now, but there's a whisper of her better scent, there on her neck. It's the smell of those good times, when the hugs were just for hugs and not for comfort. I remember it. It's the fabric softener in her blouses, her lipstick and hairspray—how her lips smelled like her neck, her cheek, because her perfume was kept with her makeup and it all came together to be the smell of her. All that is still there, under the sweet-sour smell of dementia.

"You ought to put your wings on, sweet Susan," she says. "Just because you couldn't pull him out of the sky, or out of the fire of the crash, and you can't pull him out of the ground, now—that doesn't mean they don't work. Thomas would want you to wear your wings."

"James, Gramma. James, not Thomas."

I stand outside her door the next day, hesitating. I miss her so badly I want to run to her, but the *her* that I miss isn't in there anymore. But it isn't much better out here. The weeds are choking out the perennial lilies she used to pamper. The lawn is shaggy. *I could fix this*, I think. *I should fix this. Bring back the world I remember. Make it*

like new again. But the knot in my stomach makes my hands heavy and it's all I can do just to lift one to the doorknob.

The parlor is covered in china teacups cradled in small saucers. Framed pictures are slid back on their doilies to make room for more small place settings.

"Gramma Ros?"

"Hi, dear."

She's there, on the sofa—almost invisible in a floral suit that blends with the upholstery, the wallpaper, the lampshade. The suit hangs from her diminishing frame like a curtain. She hasn't worn it since James was alive to drive her to midnight mass.

My chest feels tight as my eyes trace the lines where she's tried to put on makeup. Her cloudy eyes and shaking hands have painted a wide grimace across her face. A teacup rattles in her fingers.

"Don't gape, dear. Have a seat."

Sit? Or call Mom, call the doctor? But my knees are bending as if they belong to nine-year-old me, incapable of ignoring Gramma's directive. I reach for a cup of tea.

"Not that one—that's Joe's. It's not tea in there, of course." She sighs and adds sugar to her own cup. I see a cloud of granules swirling in the cold liquid. My blood's as cold as the tea.

Joe's. It's whisky, then. I drink it anyway. Gramma clucks her tongue, but we both know Joe owes me a whisky.

"Are you feeling okay, Gramma?" I can't keep the shake out of my voice, but she's staring at the chair next to me and doesn't seem to notice. I lose count of the teacups. She's been in the storage shed, clearly. I see her mother's apple pattern, and her grandmother's gold-rim china, more that I don't recognize. Two hundred years of teacups, at least, and I wonder how many dead relatives she's remembered into the room.

"I'm fine. But I've been talking with Joe, James, and Thomas. And we're concerned about you." She nods at the empty seats.

"Oh, Gramma Ros." *This is the beginning of the end, then.* My face is too heavy, and it drops into my hands. I'm rupturing from that tight knot in my gut—the fracture is stealing up my neck like a split seam. When it reaches my mouth, it breaks out of me, splitting the air with a wail. My palms are already soaked with tears.

"Oh, honey!" I can't hear her get closer, but I can smell her. That smell of better times off-gassing from her old suit, overwhelming the smell of sweat and diapers.

I'm expecting her arm around me, but instead she's pushing something onto my lap—a box wrapped in ragged paper bags.

I wipe my eyes clear, and she's beaming at me—her red, smeared smile so broad that I can see how her back teeth have gone slate grey. She's taking my hands and guiding them to the package. My fingers smudge the paper, all tears and graphite. I imagine my face doesn't look much better.

The paper rips like old cloth, sending up clouds of attic-scented dust. Under the paper is a warped Macy's box, the Christmas-red foil letters peeling away from the white cardboard. I slide my fingers under the lid. The yellowed Scotch tape cracks like an eggshell. Underneath is a mound of blue tulle mesh, pressed into the shape of the box.

Gramma's lipstick mouth is hanging, now, shaking, as she looks from the box to me. I'm afraid to touch the fabric. My fingers are frozen, pinching the cardboard. Gramma Ros reaches in and pulls out the pair of wings and shakes them, unfolding the yards of lace.

"These were meant to be your mother's," she says. She untangles the two elastic arm loops and holds them out. "Do you remember that Halloween?"

I'm trying not to. Fighting it. Squeezing my eyes shut and holding onto that dust smell—the smell of things getting old, being forgotten.

"She wanted to go with you around the neighborhood. I know she did. She's the one who suggested the matching costumes."

The old box slides off my lap. It's how I know I'm standing.

"Gramma, I don't want to." My voice is nine again.

For a moment, the hazel in her eyes shows through the cataracts. "You were five minutes too late to save Thomas. Five seconds too late for James. And you're *ten years* too late for Joe. You've pulled your head out of the clouds and buried your feet so deep into the ground that if you don't fly straight up this very moment, it'll be too late for you, too."

The heat in my face breaks my reverie, and my hands are shaking worse than hers. "I couldn't have saved any of them! Not if I had a thousand wings. Whether it's five minutes on the end of a rope, five seconds in a tailspin, or ten years on the neck of a bottle—none of that is enough time. Putting on a costume won't help!"

Her eyelids are the color of the sky the day his plane fell. Her mouth, held tight, the color of the blood smeared across the car window. She rubs her thumb over the elastic. The straps are frayed with age. They look as though they'd snap if I stretched them.

"I'm not talking about them, anymore, sweet Susan. I already said—it's too late. Always late. I'm talking about you."

This isn't what I came here to do. I came to study art. To build a future and leave the past behind me. I squeeze my eyes shut, but when I do, I remember—the feel of the air dragging at my wings, the texture of the fabric pinched between my fingers, the squeeze of the elastic straps as I chased his car. I thought they would make me faster. I thought I could catch him and somehow keep the car on the road.

I thought maybe the rapid blowing of his toxic whisky breath would catch in my wings, an updraft I could use to lift us from the twisted metal. But it blew clear through them. As if they weren't even there.

Gramma Rosemary's skeletal hand cups my chin. "I remember. I remember. Your memories are your wings, sweet Susan. They'll lift you, if you let them. Or they'll drag behind you like a net, getting heavier the more you carry. The worst thing you can do is forget."

The worst thing. It hits me then, how hard she fights against the ever-growing emptiness in her mind. The holes in her net, memories running out like an hourglass. I watch them swirl in the clouds of her eyes, and I feel the scrape of old elastic along my arms.

The wings are heavy at first. So many burdens, so many memories. I remember. I remember the way Thomas danced—not in the air on the end of a rope, but across the floor, a smile creeping out from under his mustache. I remember the childlike glee on James's face every time he prepped his plane for flight. And I remember the apology in Joe's eyes as I tried to pull him through the broken car window. I remember, and my heart rises.

I'm holding Gramma Ros, cradled in my arms like she used to hold me. I can smell her hair, the way it smells just like her blush, like her clothes, like better times. I remember those times, and I lift us both.

WISH WASH

I could hear my mom's voice inside my head, "You should get better friends" as we walked away from Joey's dad's truck into the woods, Joey swinging his dad's axe, me keeping far enough back.

Thing is, we were never friends, me and Joey. But I thought we could be, if I was cool enough. If I could prove it. Which is how I ended up in the woods alone at night with Joey, his father's stolen axe catching the beam from my flashlight, his father's stolen car disappearing behind the trees.

"I can't even see this trail you're talking about," Joey said.

"It's a deer path. I followed it out here last summer when I got that buck." It was my only claim to fame, that buck. The only thing that got Joey to notice me in any way that wasn't knocking me over or throwing me down by my neck: the twelve-point buck I scored on the first day of break. I'd bagged it right here in these woods. I don't know why I told Joey I'd been poaching, or where I'd found it. I don't know why I told him I only got it because it got its rack all tangled up in the most twisted tree I ever saw. All I know is that while I was talking, Joey was listening, so I didn't stop.

And now it's the first day of summer break again. The sun is set behind the tops of the trees. And Joey's dad's all passed out on his sagging sofa, and unlikely to miss his truck for a few hours. Or his axe. He'd have missed his gun, though, Joey said, even in his sleep, and he didn't dare pick it off his sleeping pa. And for that I've been whispering prayers of thanks to the trees for the past thirty minutes. But as Joey put it, if a buck's all caught up in a tree, a gun's just cheating anyway. My face heated at that. I didn't see how an axe was any more noble, if the animal is trapped. But it made sense to Joey, and I kept my mouth shut. Joey's never been too smart. What he lacked in brains he made up for in force of will.

"Get ahead of me. I'll follow you," he said.

I pushed past him, my feet sinking into undergrowth along the side of the trail. I could feel the axe behind me as much as I could feel Joey. It quickened my pace, and before long, we had stepped into the circle of low growth that surrounded the twisted tree. No saplings had survived in its shadow, though its trunk was not any larger than a man's chest. Its writhing path through the air gave it wide berth.

I swept the flashlight beam over the ground till I found the spot. A few large bones still lay scattered where I had butchered the deer. I couldn't carry much, and I didn't want to get caught, so I'd just taken the rack and choice cuts, left the rest for nature. And they'd taken their chance on most of it. Only the pieces too heavy to drag or too small to bother with remained.

Joey grabbed the light from my hand and swung the beam over the rest of the tree, searching for another prize deer. My heart leapt when we spotted one, its tawny coat hanging slack from its frame, antlers caught up in the tree just as the other had been. This one was already dead, though. And had been a while.

The axe flashed in the beam, and just as I gasped to shout *no*, the forest silence was cut through with a tearing sound and my mouth filled with the taste of rotten game. I bent and heaved all over my own shoes. Between the sounds of my own heaves, I heard Joey coughing, too, and the axe still swinging.

I staggered back from the puddle I'd made and sat hard on the ground. Finally my gut stopped clenching and the axe stopped swinging, and the beam of light hit my face like a gunshot. I lifted a hand to block the glow, and saw Joey there, holding his prize up to show me—the rack chopped messily from the dead deer.

"Who else have you told about this old tree?" He set the rack on the ground between us.

I shrugged. I told everyone about the deer, everyone. But I'd said I got in in season. I couldn't remember who else I'd told about the tree, the dirty part of the story, that I'd slaughtered a trapped animal.

"So it's our little secret, yeah?"

I shrugged again, too tired and humiliated to want to feel cool anymore, even to Joey Spencer.

He huffed. "You know what they say about keeping a secret? Two can keep a secret if one of them is dead." He swung the axe at me, playfully. Something wet hit my face.

My stomach cramped again and I folded down over my knees.

Joey laughed and turned back to the tree. "Damn tree keeps killing our deer. Twisted devil thing." He swung the axe again, this time with purpose and a broad stance, and all the power of his ninth-grade varsity swing, and he hit the tree with a thwack like he was bringing all the runners home.

The whole tree shuddered, showering us in dry bark shaken from its dead limbs and twigs dried to tinder.

I pushed myself into a crabwalk and scrambled back from the clearing as the axe hit again and again, and Joey circled the tree taking notches out of its narrow trunk.

Finally he stood back, panting. The tree groaned. It seemed to moan and stretch like a long sleeper, before falling away, taking the nearby pines with it.

Joey picked up the flashlight and shined it over the ruin of the tree. The light disappeared into its hollow center, as if it were the source of all the forest's shadows.

"Whoa." Joey leaned in over the hollow. Then jumped back, just as a hand as twisted as the tree had been, as pale as the scattered deer bones, appeared over the ragged edge of wood.

An old man's face, lined and bearded, followed the hand, then the rest of him as he tumbled out of the tree and onto the forest floor.

The old man's body lay in a shaking heap, a sound as dry as old twigs and hollow as old bones barking from the tangle of limbs and long hair. "You've freed me." The pile of man rearranged itself, untangled its limbs like a fallen marionette pulled upright. His skin was sallow and flaky as birch bark, his beard hanging like Spanish moss.

Joey dropped the axe.

The old man turned to the sound with a crackle of stiff joints. His eyes glittered like black marble through the haze of dust surrounding him. "To repay your kind deed, I offer you abundance." He held his twisted hands open, one toward each of us.

My eyes traced his empty palm, then followed the shaggy sinew of his arm back toward those black eyes.

"A what?" Joey asked.

40

The old man tilted his head and a clump of hair fell from his skull to the forest floor.

I stood slowly, legs like cold water, and the old man turned to me.

"I can see that you are two gentlemen of distinction. So tell me how it is that two fine benefactors such as yourselves have come to free me from my prison?" The old man reached up to the shattered edge of the tree stump and broke off a handful of splinters, rubbing them between his fingers before bringing them to a grey tongue that darted out of his beard.

"Well, Casey here said he caught himself a big buck at this tree, so we came to see if we could get any more. We figured this tree caught and killed enough deer, and didn't want anyone else learning what an easy pick it was. So I cut it down."

I could still tase the rotten game in my throat, the vomit in the back of my nose. The fallen tree had pummeled the remains of the deer, branches scattering the rot.

The old man's nose twitched above his beard and he grinned. "My little revenge on Artemis, yes," he said. "I remember that buck. You left it here." He looked straight at me, his black eyes flashing the yellow of a wasp's coat.

"It was more than I could carry," I said, looking away from his gaze, staring at my pile of sick.

"And yet you came back?" The old man's eyes squeezed shut like knots on a tree. He ran his fingers through his beard and pulled a twig free, kept pulling till the twig was as long as a walking stick. He leaned on it. "What a fool am I to be freed by fools."

"Excuse me?" Joey's brow twisted and he took a step toward the man. I knew that step. Knew the way he could step into a swing that would probably kill the old man.

"So we're not in trouble?" I asked.

"Not with me," the man said. "And the tree is mine and the land is mine."

"I thought this was county land," Joey said.

"Oh I've been here far longer than the county. Though I've been sleeping so long I suppose I've been forgotten. I think they'll find if they examine the records that this patch of land never quite makes it into the books." He traced a shape in the dirt that it was too dark to see, dragging his stick across the forest floor.

"You were sleeping in the tree?" Joey leaned over the hollow stump and scooped out a fist of rotted wood dust and dry beetles. "That does not look comfortable."

The old man smiled, his mouth a dark hollow like the tree's. "My dear boy, it was not. And that is why you shall both have a reward."

Joey grinned in a way I hadn't seen him do since my older sister Emily's skirt went up in the wind at recess. A manic lust that most reasonable folk took as a warning. The old man didn't heed it. "What kind of a reward?"

"A wish," the man said. "It's the custom. One for each of you."

My shoulders had relaxed some, now that the man seemed happy, and Joey had dropped his axe. I began to hold onto the prospect that we might make it out of the woods after all.

"A wish? For what?" Joey looked to me as if I might have an answer.

"For whatever you want," said the man.

"So we just tell you, and you get it for us?"

"In a manner of speaking, yes." The man tapped his walking stick into the ground as if planting it.

Joey frowned in thought. "You go first, Casey. I have to think."

"I don't know," I said. Five minutes ago, I'd have wished to be back at home, in bed. But if he meant it… If he really would give us anything we wanted… "What do people usually wish for?"

The old man lifted his stick free and drove it into the ground again impatiently. "Gold, usually. Health, long life. Revenge."

Joey looked at me and grinned. My blood went cold. "I know!" he said, nearly catching his foot on the axe blade as he stepped toward me. "I wish for Casey's wish! There. Now I've got two wishes. And he's got none."

The old man and I looked at each other in silence, me in confusion, him with a glint of trouble in his black wasp eyes.

The man leaned on his stick again and turned his gaze on Joey, eyes flashing yellow. "Well, you've just used your wish. So that's still just one."

Joey's face fell, but recovered when he realized he'd at least deprived me of mine. "But none for this loser. It was me who cut your evil old tree down, anyway."

Heat rose in my throat again, not bile but rage. I'd told him my secrets. Led him to the tree. For what? To have him beat me again. Not with his fists, this time, but with his stupid mouth.

The man laughed, a sound like a rain of pine needles. "I'm afraid it's more complicated than that. Casey will still make his wish. But. The product of it will go to Joey."

"What does that even mean?" I asked. I was tired of this strange old man, tired of Joey's meanness, tired of these woods and all the dead deer. Anxious that he had somehow plucked our names out of our own mouths.

"If you wish for riches, Casey, Joey will be made rich."

Joey hooted in triumph, stirring birds from their forest perches.

"*However…*" The man pulled his stick free of the ground and moved toward me, wading through my puddle of sick with his bare, gnarled feet as if it were nothing, till he stopped inches from my face.

He smelled of sawdust and bird feathers, of mildew and lichen, of sugar sap and beetle pepper. His eyes narrowed at my face. His twisted hand rose and traced a dry finger over the crease between my eyebrows, the worry line that Emily said made me look old.

"Be careful, Joey," the old man said. "This child wishes for death. He wishes it every night. Sometimes because of you."

My heartrate stuttered. How could he know?

"And should he wish for death, really wish it, it will fall on you, Joey."

Joey dropped the flashlight and its beam landed right in my eyes.

"How will you know?" My voice was barely more than breath, but the forest had gone silent. "When I wish it, how will you know that it's the time I really mean it?" My eyes burned, maybe from the light, maybe from the secret laid bare, hanging in the rot-seasoned air between me and the old man.

The man reached for my hand, lifted it, and ran his thumb over the rough texture that scoured the back of it. He held it to the beam of light. The scar there shined, its collagen stretched thickly over my veins. Joey had done that. Pushed me off my scooter in the fifth grade, laughed as I slid down the street, abrading away in body and spirit. It had taken weeks to grow the skin back. My spirit stayed raw.

My hand burned again like it did that day. The scar stretched and twisted, bending itself into a vining branch with a knot like a heart at its center. A yelp of pain escaped my lips.

"Press here," the man said, "and make your wish. And I'll know that you mean it."

"How do I reach you? To tell you what I wish?"

"Press here," the man squeezed harder, his thumb shifting the narrow bones of my hand. "And you'll call me. When the mark is gone, you'll know your wish was delivered. Doesn't matter where I am. Doesn't matter where he is." He tilted his shaggy head toward Joey.

He let go, then, and turned to Joey. "It's a pity you've made him so miserable. But maybe it's not too late."

Joey's face had grown so pale that it shone with its own light, visible even over the beam that nearly blinded me. "That's not fair, little man." The edge of threat in his voice was new, even to me.

"I don't make up the rules, son. I must follow them myself." The man began walking away from us, into the shadow of the forest.

Joey turned to me, then. "Come on, Casey, wish for infinity gold and I'll give you half. Or make me king and you can be, like, co-king, or whatever."

"You tried to steal my wish. I should wish for, I don't know, like a hundred bees or something."

Joey flinched.

The old man laughed, this time like a raging crow.

"How long do I have to decide?" I asked the pale expanse of his disappearing back.

"As long as you like," he called back. "I can wait longer than you." He laughed again, the sound fading as the shadows of the forest closed over him.

Joey's face had gone from white to red. He bent and picked up the axe at his feet, choking his grip up close to the gore-flecked head.

I clamped my hand down over my scar.

Joey lowered the axe.

The old man's voice sounded from the dark thickness of trees. "I almost wish I could stay and watch this. Act wisely, fools."

"Where are you going?" I called after him. I didn't want to be alone in the forest with Joey, magic mark or no. I wasn't even sure I believed in it. And it was only a matter of time before Joey realized we'd had no proof that the wishes even worked. That we'd just met a mad old man hiding in a hollow tree and took him at his word.

"Home!" the old man called back. "My wife will be wondering where I've been these past four hundred years."

Joey looked from the darkness of the forest to the even steeper dark of the hollow in the tree. "Four hundred? How did you even get in there?"

"A much cleverer man than you wished me there. Good day, my lads. And thank you again for your service, even if it wasn't kindly meant."

Sound returned to the forest. Bird call and cricket, wind and straining boughs. I hadn't noticed their absence, and yet they all returned like a symphony at full strength.

And I was alone with Joey.

I squeezed my hand over my mark, not daring to let go, hoping that if I believed it long enough, or acted like I did, that he would, too.

I could see him weigh it, his face working. He calculated his odds and came up empty.

"You walk ahead of me. Where I can see you. Let's head back home," I said.

And so we marched out of the woods, away from the hollow tree—the prisoner in front, swinging an axe, and me—hands clasped almost like I was praying.

My mom scrubbed my hand, convinced the mark was dirt, though I told her over again that it was a scab on top of a scar, and that's why I hadn't finished my work in the barn yet. That she should go easy on me.

"Was it that boy again? Joey Spencer?" She shook her head, not waiting for an answer. "You need better friends."

She fell for my excuse, though she wouldn't have, normally. This time there was no lecture on pulling my weight, no implication that I was not part of the family unless I did my part for the family. I started to think maybe the mark was lucky.

Or not. Maybe it was just a scab on a scar, scratched raw by a hermit in the woods. My finger hovered over the knot on the twisted shape.

Do I mean it this time? Really?

I was forgiven for my undone chores. Joey had no such luck. Our adventure had made us late, and the missing truck was noted. He had a shiner to show for it, when he showed up at our farm the next day. I caught him staring at me through a gap in the barn clapboards.

"What are you staring at?" I asked as I hoisted a pitchfork, piling moldy hay into a cart.

Joey slipped around the side of the barn and came in through the wide door. He sat on the edge of the wagon and picked at the hay.

"Guess I can't be mad at you, can I?" he said.

I paused, pitchfork mid-swing. The hair on my neck bristled like a hay bale.

"Was your own doing," I said. "You should be apologizing. Was going to wish for a motorcycle. Would have let you have a go on it."

Joey stood. "Well, go on then, wish it. It's yours, we both know it. You take it and it'll be done. I won't even have a go—won't even touch it, swear. Let's get this over with and I'll leave you alone forever."

I leaned against the pitchfork and mopped my brow with a dusty glove. I peeled both gloves off. I didn't feel comfortable around him without access to the mark. His offer was tempting. But I didn't want to just be left alone. I wanted to be liked. But not by Joey, not anymore. "Figured you'd settle on that eventually."

"Yeah." Joey smiled and held out his hand for a handshake.

"Reckon I'm better off saving it, though."

Joey's smile melted. His fingers curled into his palms. "What do you mean to do, Casey?"

"It's like I've got a second life now, see. Like a cat, but two instead of nine. Seems wise to save it till I need it."

Joey sank back down to sitting. "But then I'd—" He couldn't even say it.

"Yep. It's what you get for stealing anyway, right? You stole my wish."

Joey sat and picked at the hay quietly while I continued to work. Then he jumped from the cart and grabbed the pitchfork from my hands.

I leapt back and grabbed at my mark.

"No! No," he said. "Not like that. Let me do this."

I stared at him, puzzled.

"See, you could get hurt. Way I figure, I can't let that happen. Ever. So. You're stuck with me. Forever. All day, every day, I'll be by your side, protecting you. To protect me. 'Least till you decide you'd rather have that motorcycle."

I don't know if dad ever noticed it wasn't me doing the chores. I sat and watched Joey work, sweat on his brow and blisters on his hands. Bruises on his arms when he didn't have enough time left to do his own work after.

I'd have pitied him. Almost did. But every now and then, if I dozed, I'd wake to catch him watching me—knuckles white around the pitchfork handle, weighing his options. Gauging the distance.

I wanted distance from him, but didn't want him out of my sight. And he neared fits every time he left me, spinning his head around, glancing back, eyes darting from my hands to my eyes.

I wondered how long we could both keep this up. Everything felt stretched tight, ready to snap.

Joey, who had been failing, studied like a fiend to stay in my class. He trained like a thing possessed to join my field team.

Everyone thought we were like brothers. Some even thought we were lovers.

He was in my life and in my face, always, and I hated him. Even when he took the bully's fist to the gut for me, I hated him. Even when he climbed the dead tree to get my model plane back, waded into the swift creek to get my shoe, picked up an angry snake and threw it near across the field, I hated him.

But not as much as he hated me.

We finished school hip-to-hip, him following too close on my heels across the stage to claim our achievement.

And then there would be six hours of every day away from him. Where he'd work his farm and I'd work mine, if I could remember how. If I could even still lift a bale. I'd wasted away under the years of him watching, lifting, doing. I'd grown thin—all sharp angles, like the rack of a prize buck.

"You got to be careful though, Case. You got to watch yourself when I can't." He spoke like he was choking.

I shrugged. "What will be, will be."

I suppose I wanted him worried. Didn't want him to forget his situation. Or why he was in it. His eyes were lit with anxiety. "Don't you want a castle? An island? A page 2 girl on your arm or on your... Don't you want out of here? Out of this town?"

I spun on him, face red, my neck pulsing. "I want you out of here."

He shook his head. "I can't. I have to watch you."

I placed my hand over my mark and he blanched, dropped to his knees, the corded muscles in his arms quaking.

"Get out of town, Joey. Get far away. The next time I see your face, I'll set coyotes to chew it off."

He stared at me, his mouth moving, knees grinding the dirt.

"Go!"

He jumped up and ran across the field toward the trees, head whipping back around, watching me, like always.

I should have known he wouldn't really go. That he would know every way into my house. Know the sound of every floorboard, which ones were silent, and which ones groaned like a felled tree.

It wasn't my life he wanted, not really. He just wanted his own. He wanted my wish. Always had. He had held it in his sights all these years.

He still had the axe, too.

The first blow woke me just in time to see the second coming.

I raised my hands to shield my face, but it wasn't my face he wanted.

My vision pooled black, dark as the forest at night, dark as the center of a tree, a prison where time means nothing.

WISH WASH

I woke in starched light, arms bandaged to the elbows.

My sister Emily sat at my bedside. Her nails were chewed raw with worry. She stood when she saw me stir.

"Casey. Can you hear me?"

I nodded. My ears were fine. But I stared at the bandages at my wrists, white gauze showing a hint of shadow below, of darkness soaking through.

Emily sniffed, her eyes going as red as her fingertips. "It was that creep Joey Spencer, wasn't it?"

I nodded, not trusting my voice.

"I'll be right back," she said, patting my bandages.

It didn't hurt. I felt nothing, except a nagging wish, the one I'd always had. An impotent wish. There was no way, now, to tie a knot, pull a trigger.

Emily stepped out of the room. A nurse took her place shortly after, fussing at dressings and tubes, thermometers and sphygmomanometers, tapping buttons to pump me full of numb.

But it was no use.

I wished for death, and I meant it. But there was no way to get it. No one to grant it.

The police caught up with Joey, holed up in a shack in the woods. When they cornered him, he raised not his hands, but mine, and wished aloud for Superman strength.

But either the wishes didn't work that way, or they didn't work at all. Superman can repel bullets, but Joey didn't.

When Emily told me, her raw hands cradling my bandage, my heart clenched.

Was that my wish? I'd meant it, that time. Did my one wish go to Joey, just like the old man said it would? Or with Joey dead, did my wish come back to me now?

"Are you okay?" Emily squeezed where my hand should be.

"I want to go for a walk in the woods."

Emily stopped our truck at the side of the road, where the faint game trail threaded off into the trees. "Here?" She looked at me, worry carved clear across her face. The line between her brows the twin of mine.

"Yeah."

"I think I should go with you."

"No. I'll be fine. It's not far. Just want to pay my respects."

She frowned, but didn't push the matter. Any accommodation, in the name of healing.

I hardly had to think or look to find my way back to the tree. It still lay, twisted and felled, across the clearing. Its hollow had become a den for countless forest life, nests and nuts and musk crowding the empty space where once a man had slept. For centuries, maybe, or maybe just after a day of hard drink.

I couldn't smell rot any longer. Just rich soil, as if all had recycled to new freshness.

"Did I make my wish?" I asked the tree. "I can't tell if the mark is gone or not…. Did Joey take my death from me, too? After everything else he's taken?" I choked, then, and wept. I poured out bile as I had on my last visit to the tree, the rot that set it off not so different than last time, though this time it was in my own hollow core and not the tree's.

I let it all out over the twisted roots, till I had nothing left.

"I just want my hands back," I whispered to the tree. "If I still have a wish, that's what I want."

I wanted to do the chores I hadn't done for a decade. I wanted to lift and toil, as Joey had done for me since we were fifteen and stupid. I wished I'd never told Joey about the tree, that none of this had ever happened.

I walked back to the truck lighter than I had been in weeks. The look of relief on Emily's face when she saw me exit the woods told me that my darkest wish was maybe not as secret as I'd always thought, that maybe she'd always known.

We made it halfway home before she spoke. "We've hired on help for the farm."

I didn't say anything. What was there to say? Of course they had. I wouldn't be much help, now. I never had been.

The house was quiet, empty, hollow as an old tree. Everyone was out in the fields, working.

"I'm going to lay down," I said.

Emily nodded. "Get some rest. Holler if you need anything."

My room smelled like rotten game, like old death caught in a tree, struggling in vain, wasted away, then split open.

I gagged and wretched. There was still blood on the floor, all over my bed, my sheets stiff with it, and my pillow... My hands lay there, nested in down. Their fingers twisted at angles, like a buck's prize rack. The skin of them greyed and set with putrefaction, but smooth. Scarless. Mark-less. Like I'd never fallen. Like I'd never been pushed.

Root Rot

They used to fear me.

They will fear me again.

The child sleeps, hand curled on her pillow like a soft shell, a pearl hidden inside. It's so much easier if they leave the tooth under the pillow. But they can't bear to be parted from it, knowing that someone is coming to take a piece of them away forever.

So they must make me palatable, for their own sake, deck me in ribbons and curls, delicate wings dusted in sparkle. My portrait hangs on the wall—a gleaming smile, hair as long as my body in broad curls, a star clutched in my hand. The sparkle of the painting refracts the dim nightlight from the hall behind the open door.

I clench my jaw and the forest of teeth inside my mouth shifts, sending a savory wave of hot blood over my tongue. There's space in my right cheek for one more.

I reach a long fingernail between the child's sweaty fingers and scoop the tooth out of the crease of her palm. It had settled there as if rooted in her lifeline. It is so small, so white, rootless, clean as a polished gem.

I push it past my raw lips and through the jumble of all the others, filling the last empty space in my mouth. My tongue presses to the back of my throat to keep them all from tumbling down my gullet. *Not yet.* It's been a long night, but there is work yet to do.

I pull a dried clover from my purse, spit gum socket blood on it, watch it turn to shimmer, to silver. I slip the coin into the child's grip, wipe the dampness of her touch on my dress, and I slide back through the crack in the mirror, into the night.

It is a long way home on the mirror roads and my lips are tired from holding in so many prizes.

I do not carry a wand; I don't need one. My hair is not yellow, save for where the grey has faded to white and aged to ivory. And it does not curl, save for where the fairy knots have creased it. My dress is not pink, except round the collar, where spittle and blood have dyed the flax the color of apple blossoms. I do not have wings; I have other ways to travel. I do not glitter, except for when I smile and the shine of a thousand teeth can be seen through the dark. None of them are mine. Mine wore away long ago, ground to nothing on millennia of gristle. Thistle Bristle Gristle is what I am called, where I am known. Humans long ago forgot my name, though they called me Tand Fae then, and were fickle with their offerings, keeping their cast-off teeth for themselves.

I am an ancient thing. And I'd have crumbled long ago if it wasn't for the precious kernels of youth nestled in the core of children's teeth.

Humans have trapped me in a pretty lie to soothe their young when a part of them suddenly falls away. The charming portrait strips me of my power, my ancient rite. They have turned my bristles to gossamer.

They used to fear me. They would fear me if they knew me. But they've cultivated my image as a benevolent blossom. I am loved. They look to my coming with sweet joy.

It's an impossible standard.

It ends now.

I lean over the copper pot, spread my split lips wide and pour forth my harvest. The sound of teeth falling and hitting the metal is like hailstones on a tin roof. The smell is like something long dead, lost and found again. I sweep my tongue round my mouth for the strays and spit and spit my rose water till the bright teeth are swimming. I strike a match and light the stove, revel in the ambient heat as the liquid starts to simmer.

That last tooth—the lifeline tooth—keeps bobbing and rolling into view, brighter than all the rest. As if it had never tasted candy or caramel, never bathed in cider or lemonade.

When the broth has thickened, reduced to a paste that clings to my wooden spoon, I move the pot off the flame. Steam clouds my vision as I lean over it, breathing deep, not wanting any morsel of nutrient to escape me.

The teeth have become fragile husks that shatter under the pressure of my spoon. I grind and stir and pop them all to dust that I mix to a steaming porridge.

It all slides down my throat in a thick, hot rush, rich with young life. I can taste the perfect tooth—that shining lifeline treasure. It adds vigor to the brew, but also a chemical aftertaste. Alcohol, fluoride, chlorine. Not the meaty taste of fresh pulp.

I feel the cells of my body spark. My skin tightens, firms, the sound of it like taut paper. My muscles lift and grow restless. My scalp prickles with new growth of supple locks, the dry, aged ones breaking free and falling away. The years fall away with them. I had held a few hundred teeth in my mouth, and each one dissolves a year, maybe two or even three years for the thickest molars.

I feel every fiber of cellulose spring into place, and I believe, for just a moment, that maybe I can be the pretty fairy in their storybooks. That I can be the portrait on the child's wall. That maybe, if I had enough teeth, enough porridge potion, I could sparkle.

But that cold taste of chlorine clings to the back of my tongue. Plants a throbbing ache in my head. Ties a knot in my gut that has me bent over the hedge before long, losing my precious potion, aging with every gargled heave as all my youth splatters into the grass and the shoots vanish into the dirt as seedlings unsprouted.

Whatever was done to that tooth, to make it so perfect, unmakes me.

I stagger to my bed, to rest. To try and regain a strength that only ever seems to be slipping away. To plan.

It's easy to find the house again. The scent of a fresh, empty socket lingers in the air, and that puff of chemical clean on a sleeping child's breath draws me back to that same bedside, that same child sleeping below my false countenance.

Again the child sleeps, a small spot tinged with pink staining the lace of her pillow, so like my dress. Golden curls darkened in sweat stick to her porcelain forehead. She looks more like me than I do.

I slip a careful finger into the child's mouth and press against her teeth. None move. She won't be summoning me again soon. Each tooth is perfect. Rich and unblemished. Save for some hidden toxicity, I know that this small mouthful would erase a century of my cares.

My hand, still wet from the child's mouth, moves reflexively to the sagging, sallow skin at my jowl. To the brittle hair cascading down my curtained neck.

"What have they given you that poisons the likes of me?" I whisper across her smooth cheek.

The sleeping parents' room is an opulent mess, strewn with fine things, a shrine of material wish-fulfillment. Their faces are slack and content, and their teeth perfect. Every flaw repaired, every surface scraped clean, and that same chemical breeze rolling off their tongues.

The bathroom spills their secret. Tucked away in a drawer is a set of tools, ones used by human dentists to clean mortal teeth. One of these humans is a dentist, and they have afflicted their practice on the others.

I smile and my empty mouth gapes back at me—black and red in the vanity mirror. These chemical treatments are temporary. The toxins can be washed away, leaving behind clean, perfect teeth. Teeth fit for an ambrosia of porridge that will vanish the years from my body.

All I need to do is get the teeth away from the dentist. Just for a while. Just long enough. Just till they ripen for harvest.

I cannot fit a whole child into my mouth, not even such a small one. So I empty my leather bag of dried clover and slip her inside. My leaves are strewn all across her bed. I spit and turn them to coin. It's more than the price for all her teeth, the price of a dozen children's teeth. More than fair.

The child is heavy in my satchel. The path behind the mirror is long, and by the time I reach my cottage, I have aged again. There are ice shards in my knees and my vision is fogged.

I drop my bag inside my threshold, and the child wakes with a muffled wail.

"There, there, little one, nothing to fear. Granny is here." I pull her upright and sit her on my bench. Her brown eyes rove over the inside of my cottage, to the clover hanging from the beams, to the tarnished copper pot, and my wall of tools suspended from hooks. Tools that no doubt look much like her parents', though mine are far more ancient and made of silver.

Her eyes widen at the blackened metal hooks and she begins to cry again, this time with the low moan of fear, her lips pressing and parting in a single syllable over and over "Mu-mu-mu-mu."

The child wants her mother. It's a feeling I remember, though I am too old to remember the being herself that was my mother.

I give the child warm goat's milk with honey and lavender and the ashes of a spell to cleanse the human toxins from her mouth. I wrap her in a warm blanket that I wove myself from black goat hair caught in night-blooming thistles. "Would you like Granny to sing you a song?"

She nods her golden head.

I sing her a half-remembered lullaby and watch as the firelight reflected in her eyes disappears behind heavy eyelids.

I rinse the goat's milk from her cup, and the thick poppy syrup that sticks to the bottom, and I select my tools. Lay them carefully on the table beside the copper pot.

I cannot risk waiting. Already my fingers fail to bend with the dexterity they had last night. I curse under my breath at the humans who have hoarded my offerings, kept them for themselves as mementos of their babe's early years, while my years slip further and further away. That poisoning has brought me nearly past the point of no return. I am nearly too weak to claim those offerings which might save me. Nearly.

I pray the spell works.

I kneel in front of the child and sniff the air by her lips. I taste the sour of the milk and the sweet of honey. I smell the oak that fueled the fire that burned the spell and the stream that fed its roots. It worked. She's clean.

It shocks me how hard the mouth holds onto its treasures. Or perhaps I have truly grown that weak. When the teeth come away, with much pulling and twisting, and a sound like the crackle of unseasoned firewood, they are barely enough to cross the palm of my hand, to trace the path of my long lifeline. It will not be enough to make even a spoonful of porridge. But perhaps it is enough to cure me of the previous night's poison. Enough to grant me the strength to walk the mirror road and back again.

I prepare my small meal, holding my breath lest I scatter a single grain of precious enamel dust. When it is brewed, it scents the air with vitality.

The flavor is like rich colostrum. I am new again. The change comes in a rush that burns not unpleasantly but intensely. My skin is smoothed in a way that makes me feel as if it will hold me together. My hair coils rich and brown. Not gold, but there is youth in it. I feel strength in its strands and in the strands of my muscles that move freely, feel capable.

The child's head has nodded forward, blood collecting in her lap as it drops from her empty mouth—a small, raw bow of red and black, framed in golden curls. She looks like me, transposed with the image of me that hangs on her wall.

I run my tongue over the worn flagstones of my teeth. Will any amount of porridge bring them back?

I am summoned. The tug. The call of bleeding sockets, the hopes of small children promised coin.

I leave the child to sleep in my own bed, and I fill my satchel with dried clover, freshly polished tools, and with a stoppered bottle of the milk and poppy spell. I cannot risk carrying her back with me—not yet, not while my strength sill wanes. But should my spell work again, I will soon harvest a copper pot full of the most potent of potions. I will return to the height of my strength, my youth, the return of Tand Fae, and all the humans shall know Thistle Bristle Gristle for the god that I am. They will not hoard their offerings but lay them out for me. Perhaps then, I shall trade my bristles for gossamer. Maybe then I will sparkle like their false icons.

Maybe then I will return the child.

Not all offerings are equal. They never have been, but I have never before had such a preference, been so particular. I refuse nothing, as I am in no place to do so. But I am on the hunt.

Some teeth are scarred, cracked, filled, stuck fast with growth. Some cling to the flavor of their last meal. Some cling to soft strands of flesh fresh pulled from tender mouths. I take them all, press them to my gums, fill my mouth till my smile reflects the night sky. I scatter silvered clover leaves, spreading my fey fortune.

But I cannot help, now, to tally the years I'm gathering. To keep score, and find it wanting. I want. I want dentist's teeth. It's no longer enough to smell and track the trace of blood on the air. Instead, I seek the scent of poisons. Toxins. I seek that chemical breath that promises death but for the spell in my bottle.

I catch my breath and chase it, knowing I flirt with my own end—and that prospect seems to give me yet more youth, as though the thought of the risk I take has granted me new life.

The very air burns my eyes. Three children, all breathing synchronous toxicity. Their mother, hands stained with the scent of latex, practically sleeps in her white coat. Her house is decorated with images of teeth, and of me. I stare back at myself from fridge magnets and tasseled pillows and posters. Bright smiles stretch in a continuous line across the mantelpiece. In one photograph, the woman herself wears wings, carries a star wand, wears a large plastic tooth around her neck on a string. My jaw tightens and the teeth cupped in my cheeks squeak against each other as they grind together.

I may not be what I once was. I may not reflect the image they expect of me. I am Thistle where they want Marigolds. Bristle where they want silk. Gristle where they want butter. I may never be the pretty pixie they imagine, but they will not dare to take my place. To wear my likeness. Especially not this poisoner of teeth.

My linen smock sticks damp to my back, coarse, where wings

should be. Did I ever have wings? Have these mortals passed down a memory I've long forgotten? Will enough teeth give me wings?

The three children each sleep in separate chambers. One has not yet lost her milk teeth. One has lost a few, though I was never summoned for them. Their usurper mother took them. They no doubt lie dry and wasted in a forgotten box. The third has lost all of hers, all replaced with deep-rooted elder teeth. The thought of those rich roots makes my stomach cramp with desire.

But the smell makes me cramp with warning. So much poison fogs their breath—far more than had been fed to the sweet child I left sleeping at my cottage. I hope I've brought enough of my spell milk. I hope my hands will be strong enough to pull out those deep roots.

I begin with the eldest, while I have my strength and to ensure I have enough spell milk for her and her bounty of teeth. There will be no placating a girl of her age with lullabies. I pray the poppies work fast, and pour. The milk is thick with honey and ash and opiate, and it moves slowly down her tongue into her throat. She coughs and sits up, choking, but swallows. Then she sees me, and she screams.

I panic. I rage. I bear my stolen teeth and I spit into her eyes, turning them to silver coins. Her hands flutter at her face, then grow weak as the poppy takes over. Her second scream is muffled by her own slacking lips as her body sinks into her bed.

My heart thunders. Face heats. Am I so terrible a sight, still, to illicit screams from children? Perhaps I am. I fold the blanket over her and step into the shadows of her closet, waiting to see if her scream has summoned the others. But the dentist, it seems, is too tired to be woken, too far away in this big house, too certain of her perfect world to sense danger.

When the silence is stretched thin and the air in the room turns sweet, I step out of the dark. The astringent scent is gone from her, replaced with the natural pulp of life.

I pull my silver grips from my satchel and set to work.

There is music in the snap of periodontal ligament. There is rhythm to the rocking of the grips. The grate of the silver on enamel like an ancient song.

I keep the perfect teeth separate from the rabble in my mouth. Twenty-eight I take from the eldest. Twenty-two from the middle child. Twenty from the youngest. There is enough milk for them all, and the younger two do not fight it, but slip sweetly into dreams. I turn them all on their sides so the blood will run free of their mouths, and I shower them with clover coins.

What will their mother do, without her garden of perfect teeth to tend? She will have to plant it anew, or make do as I have. If she wants to play at being Tand Fae, I will give her a taste of the game.

When I slip back through the mirror, I cannot help but glimpse its reflection. Like another picture on the wall. One that's not like the rest.

I hear the child long before the cottage comes into view. I hurry as fast as my tired legs will go. Her cries will draw darker things to my small hut. Things I've not the strength nor the time to contend with.

I burst through the door and I scream when I see the creature perched on my bed. Its eyes blaze, face gaping purple, neck soaked in blood. The teeth I held in my mouth scatter across the packed earth floor.

Then the wail comes again, a banshee screech. I clutch at the wet front of my dress to steady my heart. It is the child. Her face has swollen, jaw misaligned and bruised, contorted with agony and angry tissue. Her hair is soaked in blood and sweat, darkened, hanging limp around her stained gown. As if I face the mirror again.

I leave my satchel by the door, leave the common teeth in the dirt, and rush to the child's side.

"Shh, Liten Tand Fae, Granny is here." I sit beside her and wrap an arm around her small shoulders. She leans into me, and her wail lowers to a pained moan. "Lie down. Granny will make your medicine."

My hands shake. I want to be brewing my porridge. I want to pull the handkerchief of precious teeth from my pocket and wash away the weariness of this night. Instead, I mix more milk and honey and poppy. No spell needed this time, just sweetness and sleep. It is some time before she is settled. And though time has ceased to move for me the way it does for humans, that hour passes as a century does.

At last, with the babe asleep, I set my copper pot on the stove and empty my prizes into the bottom. I spit bloody water over them and let them boil. I am vigilant for any scent of poison, lest it ruin the batch. One tainted tooth and the porridge will end me rather than refresh me. And then what would become of the child?

But the batch is pure, unadulterated pulp, and it fills me with hope and purpose. A thousand years are ripped from me. A curtain of fog I hadn't even known was there is vanished from my thoughts. Colors I had forgotten burn bright in my retinas. Joints long frozen now flex with strength. My back has straightened, and I see, for the first time in centuries, the dust collected on the mantel shelf.

I stare at my reflection in the copper pot. I am still far from young, far from the pretty fairy in the pictures. But it is progress. This drug distilled from perfect baby faces works miracles.

The common teeth, filmed and yellow, crunch under my feet as

I cross the room again to check on the sleeping child. It's like we are trading places. Her twisted, gaping mouth was mine days ago. Now my jaw stands rigid, ready for more. But rest, first. Night will fall in a moment, and the work will begin again.

I drag a spare blanket to the floor in front of the fire and lie down. Only days ago, if I had done this, I would never stand again. Now I feel as though I could leap up, if needed. I curl up in the comfort of my own plush body and I rest.

The summons come, insistent, demanding. They have teeth for me, and a desire for coin. They place their small pearls under their pillows, sleep with one eye open, hoping to catch sight of the tiny, beautiful creature who will exchange it. We are both disappointed.

The energy I gain from harvesting common teeth is hardly worth the energy I spend. Not when I can wash away centuries with the takings from a single household. This is a new era of Tand Fae. One where I am called by my own desires, and not the desires of others.

I desire only flawless teeth. Ones preserved in poisons. I've become hungry for the toxin that once repelled me. And just as they perfect their teeth, their teeth perfect me.

Only by refining these poisons can I myself be perfect. Only with the purest powder can I be what they want me to be.

I ignore the call, the offerings, and follow instead the chemical tang of dentistry.

I will not ignore them forever. When I am young again, I will be strong enough to hold back the river of time with their meager offerings. It won't be long.

On a small stone road, in an apartment above a clinic, I find my next prize. A young boy, all milk teeth save for two ridged incisors, sleeps in a pile of small sewn bears. His arms are tangled in the toys and he sleeps with his mouth gaping, perfect teeth glowing in the dim light from the bathroom across the hall.

My sleeping nectar takes him quickly into dreams, and his pearls are in my pocket in minutes. But he is only one child, and I want more. The dentist's workroom is below, and I wonder if any teeth are saved there, still fresh inside, still worth the taking.

Again, I am faced with my likeness in pictures on the walls. But one catches my eye. Something about the figure's smile, the way she cups a tooth in her palm—she is more Fae than the rest. I pull the picture from the wall and place it in my bag.

I do not find any fresh teeth—only old ones, and poor replicas. I pick up the dentist's fine tools, precise hooks and drills. I smile into the tiny mouth mirror, and slip onto the roads inside.

I return to my cottage as dawn reaches the forest canopy, with enough fine teeth for a banquet.

The child does not wail but lies grey and damp-faced in my bed, breathing heavily through her twisted, meaty mouth. Her eyes are as fogged as beach marbles.

"Would you like some milk, Liten Tand Fae?"

She does not answer.

So I brew my porridge, instead. This time, my copper pot is half-filled with perfect teeth, all scented with spellwork and clear of the chemical wretchedness. I mix a potent, thick stew of it all, and eat my fill, till I feel the porridge backing up my throat, too much to fit in my hollow frame. There is still some left in the pot.

I carry it to the bedside. "Here, min elskling." I pry at her crooked jaw and insert the spoon. Her own mouth-blood thins the brew, and it goes down easy. Light returns to her eyes, and she pulls the spoon closer, taking it from my hand to scrape at the film in the bottom of the pot. I run my fingers through her damp hair and let her finish it all. I step back and watch her strength return.

I go to fetch my tools from my bag and find the portrait there. I hardly remember taking it from the dentist's wall, and its fey face stares out at me as if it were a mirror I could walk through. I hang her on my own wall, a reminder of my quest, my progress. A family portrait.

The child has licked the pot clean and has, at last, the strength to stand on her own.

"Are you still hungry, Liten Tand Fae?"

She smiles as well as her broken face allows and nods her head.

"Then let us go and get some more."

She slips her hand into mine, and I lift my bag to my shoulder. We will walk the mirror roads together till we both reclaim our smiles, our pasts. Till we are the perfect storybook fairies, as they have always wanted us to be. With enough of their drugs, enough of their sacrifices, we will make their tooth fairy dreams come true.

They used to fear me. They will love me, now.

INTO THE WOOD

I don't know whether it was Thea who changed the house or the house who changed Thea, but I noticed the house first. The way the woodgrain noticed us back—a thousand faces staring out from narrow panels that warped away from the cabin walls. And when the wind slammed the side of the house, the place would rock and rock and rock and boards would bob and nod. *Yes,* they said, *yes yes yes.* Though I hadn't been aware of asking any questions. Not at the time.

Thea stared, eyes wide as those wooden whorls, and nodded along. *Yes,* she nodded, "yes," she whispered. Her eyes as dead as the dark spots on the wood that looked more like faces to me than any face I'd ever seen. You wouldn't have blamed me for thinking it was all a game. She was an odd child. Not quite odd enough to put me off her daddy, but odd enough that plenty before me had been. Brian says it's my compassion that keeps me with them both, but he's never been on the streets. I can tolerate an odd teen. I can tolerate walls that stare back at me so long as those walls keep the warm in.

Desperation, I guess, looks a lot like compassion. Resignation looks like patience. You could say I gave an inch. Didn't know then how much a house could take. It's been too long since I've known a house at all.

There was a house. One that my mother ruled. My mother always loved birds best, which is why she called me after one, and why she kept me like one. My name is Cassidy Diana Dee. Cassi-dee-dee-dee, like the birds outside my window sang—the birds outside the cage.

Father flew when I was young, as soon as he knew that I would never know him, never see him for his face. He was always changing his coat, his beard—to me, he was never the same man twice. Always a stranger coming through the door, always a threat. I screamed every time I saw him, and eventually he stopped coming through the door altogether. Mama never forgave me. But mama always wore the same coat, and the same broken expression—the twist of her mouth so familiar, I could almost recognize her, almost.

I fell from that nest before I could fly—landed in the dirt with the worms. I don't like to be touched, but a girl can make a living on the phone. A bird in the dirt can glut herself on worms, if she digs. And in the forest of city buildings, every tree has an abandoned nest. Somewhere to roost, if you can stand the cold.

I can't remember faces, not even dangerous ones, not even my own. But I know voices. The way a bird can recognize signals in song. I can tell Landon from Justin on the phone, remember what they like—how to keep them on the line or get them off quick if another call is coming in.

INTO THE WOOD

I'd set up someplace warm, where I could take my calls in peace. Trevor's Tavern was best, where the man behind the bar was always Trevor, or at least always answered to the name. Where my face was as anonymous as everyone else's was to me. And when the phone was quiet, sometimes the drinks were free.

When I saw Brian come through the door of Trevor's, I knew he'd have a place, somewhere warm in the world. His coat was worn in a way that told me it was his only one; beard so long I knew he never trimmed it. I watched from the bar as I wrapped up my call, counting as the minutes on my burner phone ticked down. He sat, alone, in his coat with his keys in his hand, his hands as scruffed as old gloves. A big stack of keys. When he put that down coat around my shoulders at the end of the evening, I could feel their weight in the pocket against my hip, like a promise that there were sturdy doors to get behind. Heavy like an anchor, keeping me from flying away. It was his only coat, he said. I could always know him by it.

He told me about little Thea that night, before he even told me his whole name. The honest sort. I could probably have told him then that I had nowhere to go, but I didn't want to risk it. Nests with fledglings are often the most comfortable and I'd been sleeping rough for weeks.

So instead I danced—we danced. I tolerated the touch and I told him with my body that I wanted to go with him. We drove out of the city, into the woods, to his log cabin. His nest.

The cabin was a bramble of stacked trees, the bark still clinging in flyaway curls to the outside. Inside, a deep and dirty carpet grabbed at my feet. The walls were lined with thin pressboard panels that pulled away from their glue and tacks as the house shifted and aged. A threadbare velvet sofa sagged in front of a television, and on it perched a girl with braids in her hair, her hands over her face as she peered at cartoons through her fingers.

I suspected Thea had been a deal-breaker for him in the past—that her name became a filter I had slipped through. A test I had passed. By the end of the week, when he wondered where else I was supposed to be, he was more than happy with my answer, "right here." I've never had any experience running a home. No nest management. Never had any good examples, either, but I've seen them on TV.

The teens on TV want expensive phones, clothes. They want to stay out late, to fly solo. Thea wanted these things, too, but had to settle for less. Brian had gotten her the phone, scavenged the clothes, but friends to stay out with are harder to find, if you're odd. I've always been good at working with less. I could do that, be a companion for her. What I couldn't do was sit and watch her bob her head in time with the nodding walls, when the wind kicked up and the walls shifted and the boards danced. Or hold her gaze when she turned, and her eyes were as flat as wood, skin grained with whorls and knots. The curls that Brian would braid and re-braid hanging in a tangle like Spanish moss from a winter tree. I couldn't stop her from standing or hold her back from the door. I couldn't touch the dry roughness of her skin.

And I couldn't bring myself to follow her when she walked from the cabin, out into the bending and whipping trees, shaking their branches *no no no.*

I couldn't see her through the dark, through the storm. And I couldn't call Brian. The wind had knocked the trees into the lines. All was down and my burner phone had ticked all the way to empty. I could only wait in the dark and listen to the house. Learn its voice, learn its song. No light. No phones. Only the wind and me whispering "she's gone" and the house answering *yes yes yes.*

But I'm still here?
Yes yes yes.

Storms here seal you up against the edge of the wood and no light gets in. Not like the always-bright of the city. Brian came home early, but the dark made it seem late. It was too late, anyway.

"Thea! Thea! Thea!" He called all around the house, but the wind had blown over and the boards said nothing. Stillness. He found me staring out the back window, like an owl watching a bird feeder.

"Cass, where's Thea?"

"She went out."

"You let her go out in that storm? Where? Who with?"

He was mad. Was this our first fight? Our last? Would I sleep in the woods that night? Would Thea?

The boards were still.

"She just … left. I couldn't stop her."

"Who with?!"

"No one! She just walked out." *I think the walls told her to.* Maybe Thea had been the one asking questions all along.

He ran to the phone. Picked it up, slammed it down. It would be a while before the lines were repaired and before the lights came on. Nothing happens quickly in the woods.

"Which way did she walk?"

I pointed to the line of swaying trees.

He swore. I hadn't heard him do that before—that was a new note to his song, and he started for the trees.

"Stay here in case she comes back." He called back to me.

I nodded. *Yes yes yes,* and the house nodded with me.

I sat in the living room and met each pair of grainy eyes in the walls till I found her. Undeniably Thea. The curve of her face there in the grain. A burred rent for a mouth. A face I hadn't seen there before—a face I would not have recognized if I'd seen it a thousand times in the flesh—right there in the wall, nodding more softly than the others. A face I saw and knew, here in her home.

Brian carried Thea out of the woods in his arms, as he must have carried her as a child. Her head bobbed against the crook of his arm as he crossed the weedy patch of meadow behind the trailer. He laid her on the couch, not far from her face in the wall—and that panel seemed to twist, to crane—to see what had become of her.

Her skin was raked with rashes. Striped and whorled. Her fingers twisted into knots and unfurled like roots searching for soft earth. I brought her water and she drank, and even the water that she spilled seemed to soak in. Brian rushed between her and the bathroom where I could hear a tub filling. Could smell the clean steam. I wanted to crawl into that hot water and wash away the feeling of all those eyes on me, but it wasn't my bath. Not even my bathroom.

"Help me," Brian said.

We peeled off her damp clothes and clumps of soil fell to the carpet and disappeared into its pile. We carried her to the bathroom and placed her in that sudsy water. The rash had spread to the skin beneath her clothes. Her eyes were fixed wide, roving. Her skin hard and rough. She didn't even sigh when the warm water closed over her. She just lay in it. She said nothing. Brian whimpered.

The walls leaned in. The burred throat of Thea's wooden face twisted wider.

He took her to the hospital but left her face here in the wood with me.

I had the house to myself.

I took that bath. I took a nap. I took my time. I took and I took and it felt more like home by the hour.

I walked softly so the boards wouldn't sway. Only their eyes moved, tracing me into the lines of house.

I pinned a pillowcase over Thea's face. Didn't want to feel those eyes or see that twisting mouth. If I pressed my ear up against that sheet, to the place where the sharp edges of the wood split, I could hear her. Sigh or wind. Scream or gale. I never mistake a voice. But all she could say anymore was "yes" because that was how she was tacked down.

Tacked to the house like a specimen in a case. My heart pinched for her, then.

I took pliers from the case under the eaves. It was hard to find the small dark pins in that maze of woodgrain, but I found them and I pulled and pulled till the board came away. There was filthy paper and plaster and mildew behind where it had been pressed to the wall. Brown flecks of dried glue and the watermarks of the house's own perspiration. The fine sheet of veneer was adhered to a sheet of old vinyl as yellowed and brittle as old taffy.

I washed the board in the bath, cleaned away the dust and debris. Smoothed out the splinters. Let the dry panel soak lifegiving water deep into its processed pulp. I tucked the board into Thea's bed, but still the whorl eyes gaped.

I pulled the blanket over that wooden face and something heavy fell from the folds of the quilt. Her phone. Not like my burner, but bright, endless.

With the landlines down and my phone on empty, I couldn't work. No Landon or Justin—no income. My nest egg diminishing. But these expensive phones, they have ways of working when other things don't. I could work from anywhere, with this. Anytime. I navigated to my profile and updated the number to Thea's. And I was back to work in minutes, sighing, cooing, facsimile affection.

I wondered what the faces on the walls saw—the sounds of a show with no pictures, no images, just as they are only pictures that make no sound. The way I see faces, when they aren't the wooden kind.

The keys let someone in the door—it must be Brian—and I squeezed my eyes shut until he murmured for me, and I knew his voice.

I squeezed the button that sent Thea's phone to sleep, to silence, and its black screen gaped like the open wooden mouths.

He moved like a ghost through the house, pulling a bag from the closet and filling it with Thea's clothes. He didn't see the board tucked under the blanket, didn't see the face of his daughter frozen there in a silent scream. He didn't notice the one board missing from the peeling walls. The other faces nodded on and on as he walked back and forth, creating drafts, compressing the floor and letting it up again and setting all those loose faces in motion. I wondered if there were more faces beneath his feet. Under the carpet. Their open mouths pressed against our soles, trying to chew their way through.

He shook his stack of keys free from his pocket. He told me to make myself comfortable, to make myself at home. I promised I would. I said it standing in his kitchen, in his slippers, with the taste of his coffee coating my tongue. He asked me to watch the house. Though this house can watch itself.

He left again.

I made myself a meal, made a mess, made myself at home. Made myself *a* home. I watched the house and the house watched me.

Brian was back again in the night. I stirred from my nest of blankets on the couch. It was dark, the lights still off, but I knew him by his breathing, by the tension in his inhale.

"Cass?"

"I'm here."

"Help me with her. Help me get her into bed."

I raced to her room and slipped her face beneath her pillow, the thin wood fibers still soft with wet. I knew my running must have sent all those faces bobbing agreement, knew that they approved, but I couldn't see them in the dark. I hurried back, imagined another frantic wave of yesses, and I took some of the burden of Thea's body from Brian's arms. We folded the child into her bed, tucked the down around her, safe and warm.

Brian felt his way from furniture to furniture. Even he seemed to know not to run his fingers along the wall. He made his way to the kitchen, where he pulled a big flashlight down from the top of the fridge. I hadn't known one was there. Now I do. Soon I'll know the place for everything.

He checked the batteries and turned toward the back door. "The doctor wants me to look in the woods around where I found her. See if she might have eaten any toxic plants."

The wind had picked up again. In the light from the flashlight, I could see the walls nodding in agreement. *Yes yes yes go into the wood.*

"Will you keep an eye on Thea for me? Watch her till I get back?" I nodded, *yes yes yes.*

I perched, watching, at that same window as he disappeared, and then so did his light.

And his face watched me, over my shoulder, nodding and smiling himself away.

I lit one of the small candles on the mantle. I took another bath, another nap. Took the pliers and took Brian's face down from the wall. I bathed board Brian, his coy smile writ plain as day in the grain. I sat him in the chair by Thea's bed. He could watch her, now, always.

I pulled board Thea from beneath the pillow and I took the hammer from the case under the eaves. I gathered the old, dark pins from the corners of the carpet pile. I tacked her face back to where it should be. The pliable, wet wood shaped to her skull, to the curve of her nose and the hollow of her eyes, and the tacks held it in place. And for the first time in my life, I recognized a person there in front of me. It was her, and I'd know her when I saw her. I could see her even without her voice, written in the wood.

I stared, in awe of the convenience of recognition. And as the wood dried, it twisted, and her face twisted with it. Her, but warped. Her mouth too, too wide, her eyes not where they should be, but hers. And as he dried, board Brian curled and collapsed, with no skull to hold his shape, no body to hold him up. He twisted into a curl of himself, thin wood fibers bristling like pinfeathers.

They had no roots here, anymore, to hold them. You need to put down roots to build a home, and they had none—just drifting curls of wood silently screaming. I know that song.

I have a home now. A house. All you need to do to make a home is get inside the walls and stay out of the wood. Put down your roots. Keep the door locked and wake up to bird song, until it's time to fly again. Yes, *yes*, I'll fly again, when the nest gets brittle, as soon as I let go of this anchor of keys.

Pelts

My dread smells like sour ice and it is heavy under the scent of blood. I weave tracks through the trees as I run, snow packing the fur between my claws. The prey clutched in my teeth jerks and shakes, dropping precious mouthfuls in my wake. Scraps that will feed the black birds that are never far behind me. Scraps meant for my cubs, to fill their small, soft bellies. I drop the rabbit. Let the birds have it. Cold air rushes into my mouth and freezes my tongue as I pant. A deep whine grows in my chest and rattles my frame as it breaks into a bark, pitches to a high whine. I know this blood on the air. It is so, so sweet and it turns my stomach. And layered beneath the blood-pine and blood-ice rises the scent of an Unkind.

I am close. The trees thin as I near the clearing, where outcropped stones stand half as tall as the trees and have sheltered my Kind, my pack, since the first wolf cry cut the sky.

I howl and no voices answer. No chorus of excitement greets me as I bound up the hill to a sea of red snow. My meadow has been fouled, the snow-crust broken, plowed into desperate rifts. The pink and skinless bodies of my young pups are piled in a heap, the slick of their insides frosting over in the cold wind. They lie in a dark pool of packed snow, eyes still, wide, and golden. There is blood on their tiny teeth. Their bones are stripped of meat and gashed with the marks of an Unkind's blade.

I bellow, head tipped, so the faint trace of rabbit runs down my throat—the meal that should have fed my young, their meat now gone to feed another. Their pelts gone to warm another. My voice soaks into the pines. I pull hard on my lungs and howl again, sucking the wind from all directions, freezing the membranes of my throat. The trees bow over me, shaking loose their load of snow over the tall stones, casting the meadow in shadow. Wind whips, stirring the putrid tang of the invader, driving me into a frenzy.

I lick the blood from the corpses of my pups and then devour them. I taste their story. I see the Unkind's face in the flavor of their tender eyes. I smell him, taste him in the soft leather of their noses. His scent floods me. In the crunch of their fragile bones, I feel the vibration of the shots that dropped them. Their soft paws bleed the sharpness of the blade that scraped the skin from their sinew, rendering into offal what had once been young, predatory grace. I nourish my body with their knowledge, lick their blood from my nose, and I cry out again.

Trees bend back, branches cracking in a cold rush of pine sap. Timber falls away as if blown by a storm. The tall stones vibrate with a low tone that hums across the ground, sending flocks of black birds twisting into the sky.

The rage in my teeth aches for contact. My muscles shake, tightening, cramping into unnatural knots. I fall into the red snow and roll onto my back, twisting, grinding the frozen blood deep into the layers of my fur, rubbing it through to the skin where it melts against my heat and saturates my coat.

Sounds fade. Light dims. Even the smell of blood grows faint as it drips down my face. My bloodied fur smokes, curling away from my rage-hot skin. Clumps of it scatter, tumbling on the draft of my heaving breath.

My paws stretch, furless flesh pulling taut then splitting, dropping my claws into the snow.

My joints stiffen and crack as tendons pull from bone, whipping up my limbs. My spine and shoulders bend, thrown back as my hips pull straight, wrenching my legs. Cracks as sharp as the Unkind's gun echo through the clearing as my knees snap to bend the other way. My jaw pulls at my face, now full of rattling flat teeth. My snout crushes into itself and pours blood down the back of my throat. Cold penetrates my bones and I writhe as the last of my fur rubs away against the ice.

I squint through the dim daylight at the pink and wrinkled thing I have become—like a helpless pup, hairless and freezing. I pull my limbs toward me, fold them in, try to lift my awkward frame. I plant my hands in the snow and push, straightening my arms and legs. My joints shake, weak and aching in their new configuration. As I push my legs straight, my arms lift from the ground. I balance on two legs, lean my shoulders forward. I take a step and stumble on the bare and unarmed feet. Long footprints trail in my wake—ones like those surrounding my clearing, my den, the ground where my young fought their fate.

I place my footprints into the others, tracking them, following. Hunting the hunter, not to feed my body but to sate my rage.

I push forward through the snow, icy wind driving against me. I make my way down game paths where I and my pack have hunted deer and rabbits through the dark cover of trees. The freezing wet earth pulls my new flesh away from itself. It goes from pink to red, then white, and by the time the sun has set behind the tree line, my flesh is shadow-hued and hard.

The forest path spills onto empty ground, trees sparse and stunted. The deer path winds back around into the thick wood. The Unkind's trail diverges, stretching out into the openness. I step into his tracks, stalk his trail across open fields, toward a thin stream of grey smoke rising in the distance.

I stare at my blackened feet, at my own tracks, so like the Unkind Skinner's. I grunt in disgust, the sound flat and weak, swallowed by snowdrifts and pine needles. I try to howl but the wind will not carry my voice.

I lean into walking again, the scent of smoke bringing a promise of warmth, but this weak body fails me and I fall into the snow, the last of my heat bleeding into the earth.

I hear a cry across the drifts. Not a pack call that cuts through the sky, but the weak exclamation of an Unkind. I hear the crunch and scrape of movement. Two figures approach dragging a platform piled high with felled wood. They run to me and roll my frozen body onto their sled. The Unkind young smell of pine sap, raw hide, and wood smoke.

They pull me to their plank wood den. I see the glow of heat through the boards. The smell of fire and fur hang heavy on the air, masking all else from my enfeebled nose.

The door of the house opens, and a figure emerges, rushing toward me with the raw skin of my cub stretched between her hands. She throws the skin around my shoulders. I choke at the familiar smell, her blood and milk and breath diminished now by the scouring hands of the Skinners.

I shake, clawing at the musky pelt with frozen fingers that will not bend.

The Unkind lift me and carry me into their den.

My body bends, heaving, burning from my gut up my throat, though my mouth as I pour the sour flesh of my young across the threshold.

The Skinners lay me by the fire and I reach for the flickering shadow with dread and longing, resisting it till the heat soaks into me. I go rigid as life returns to my limbs on the points of a thousand needles, gnawing me as I thaw. I scream in a voice I do not recognize, ragged and hollow. I rake my fragile skin over the rough boards.

When my shaking muscles slacken and warmth softens my frost-stiff bones, I fade into sleep, wrapped in raw hide, breathing pine smoke deep and slow.

Hunger wakes me, and the smell of my cubs—a comfort grown rancid as my eyes shoot open. I strain through the flickering light of the fire. The Skinner's mate leans over her pot, silhouetted against the flames. Steam billows around her pinched face. In the corner, two cubs sit on a folded bear skin, peeling gnarled roots with small, hooked blades.

I clutch my cub's fur to my shoulders and push my chest off the floor. Folding my long legs beneath me, I sit, swaying.

They watch me, their eyebrows raised, furrowed, heads tilted like puzzled pups, unafraid. I stare back, twisting my body, feeling the flex of this strange form.

The female speaks to me, and gestures. I do not understand her. She bares her teeth, bobbing her head like a bird. She brings me a basin of hot water. I bury my face in it and drink. She brings a rough-woven cloth and dips it in the water, then touches it to my face. The coarse warm wetness reminds me of my mother's tongue, licking the blood from my lips after a kill.

I stare at the young ones while the woman bathes me. They peel their roots, looking up at me between swipes as they shake the rough skins from the tips of their iron claws. The woman finishes, rinses the cloth in the fouled basin, and walks into the shadows to a box built of rough pine branches. She bends over the contents, reaching in and shifting layers of skins. I see rabbit, elk, and deer. Bear, fox, and wolf. So many wolves. So many voices cut out of the sky and buried away to molder in a box. Some have spoiled, filling the air with the sweet smell of rot.

I rise slowly, legs trembling, and walk to the Unkind cubs. I take a blade and a root from the pile on the floor. The blade moves smoothly, separating the skin from the meat in a long curling strip. I use the tip of the blade to dig out tough knots of tangled tendrils. The hook slips over the round edge of the root and digs into the side of my fist. I pull it free and watch the red run down my arm.

The woman returns to the ring of firelight, holding clothes of rough wool patched with leather and furs. She holds them out to me, and I catch the faint, familiar scent of the Skinner clinging to them. The scent writ in fear inside my cubs' tender noses. The scent that hung like dread in my red clearing. I reach out and grab her arm.

In my rage, I forget the knife in my hand, and tear at her with my blunt teeth. She screams like a caught rabbit as I rip her flesh with claws rendered soft by my transformation—a disadvantaged parody of my former self. Her shrieks penetrate my dull ears and shock me wild, driving my desperation. I lift the curved blade and hook it through her throat, pressing my mouth to the flowing wound. The bloody meat no longer tastes of sustenance and life, not like the gamey tang of victory over prey. I choke, coughing her blood back into her face as her eyes dim. They are the color of mud, doe-eyes, prey-eyes.

The cubs tear at my legs, piercing me with their hooks, hollering. I lift them by the fine, limp hair of their heads and open their necks, letting the foul blood spill over the pine boards. They shake in the air, hanging from my fist, until they are still.

I bend to work, dragging the blade around the lines of their Unkind forms. I keep the pieces large, working with the natural weave as I pull apart the layers of skin and flesh and muscle and bone.

I remove my cub's pelt from my shoulders and replaced it with the skin of the Skinner's cubs. Their slick flesh warms mine, though it cools quickly. I tear the skins of my pups from the feet of the Unkind's pups and scrape away every strip of their hide, even the scraps between their tiny, blackened toes. I cover the entirety of myself in their pelts. The flesh sticks, their gore drying to a sap-like gum, bonded to me.

I leave the door open to the freezing wind. Drifts of snow whip over their wet, skinless bodies, soaking up the red of their blood, meat left to rot. The Skinner will return from his hunt, as I had done, to the desecration of his pack.

Their skin insulates me from the cold. The ice does not burn my feet through the tender meat with which I have wrapped them. The smell of blood, strong and musky now, even to my weak nose, comforts me and gives me strength. I turn toward the dark line of the forest on the horizon and follow my trail back into the woods.

The wind blows at my face, burning my eyes. Trees bow, pouring snow over the tracks on the deer-path. Shadows grow darker in my degraded sight, concealing the ways I had carved through the woods in pursuit of prey. I stumble over hidden roots. A harsh call, the diving swoop of a dark bird drives me deeper under the trees. I hear movement around me that I cannot see.

Clear notes carry on the wind, a piercing howl wrapping through the maze of trees. Answering calls echo off ice-encrusted walls of branches. I howl in reply, my flat voice hanging in the air, no longer the song of my once-kind. My hunger grows as the howling continues. I spin in place, ears perked for the call, awaiting my orders to flank, rush, take down prey. I hear the padding of paws on snow. I turn toward the pack and begin to run with them, to hunt with them. Their eyes reflect golden light from the shadows. They are everywhere, my Kind, my family. They growl and grunt, move into formation. Saliva hangs in ropes from their jaws. They smell blood.

I dig my hands into the snow, crouching, trying to run, stumbling on my long legs. I will my bones to shift, my fur to sprout, but nothing comes. I cannot twist myself back into the form of a wolf, cannot unbecome what I have willed myself to be.

I move to take my place in formation, but the circle moves with me. They come at my flanks, snarling, snapping, peeling strips of the Unkind skin away with their teeth. The circle closes in. I stand. My loping stride stretches to a sprint. My breath grows fast and ragged. White light floods my skull. Fangs graze my calf, tugging at the muscle fibers. I flee down the deer-path.

Black birds trail after the pack, screeching, diving down to collect the tattered bits of skin I leave in my wake, some of it mine, some the Unkind's, all of it the same.

Claws hook through the skins, pulling them away to tear at my flesh. I have no breath left to howl—my screams no longer a wolf-song. My naked feet slip in the icy snow, my tall, Unkind frame toppling to the ground. They leave no piece of me unwounded. My last cry a desperate curse falling helpless and echoing, tumbling through the cruel wild. The tall stones of the clearing are still, silent.

I hold them to me, my pack, my Kind, as my body fills their mouths, their throats, their stomachs, so soft and warm.

Bloody Bon Secours

I stood before the tall woman draped in black, Sister Mary Anthony, though we were to call her Mother Superior. The implication clear that we, "fallen women" as we were, were mother inferiors. And who was I to argue? There were more children here in her care at the Bon Secours Home than I had ever been charged with altogether, if you counted all the houses in which I'd worked. I'd nannied fifty children. None of them mine. And she, the superior of all mothers, had taken in thousands. And now she'd taken me in, as she would take in my child, when it was born—and I wondered if that would make her more its mother than I. The thought heated my face, squeezed my throat tight till I coughed.

The sound cut off Mother Superior's lecture. She'd been extolling on the gravity of my shortcomings, but the look on her face as I cleared my throat said more than all the words she'd thundered for the past ten minutes.

A cough at Bon Secours was the beginning of the end. If a girl had a cough, it was probably too late to save her, body or soul.

I wasn't ill. But it was definitely too late to save me.

Mother Superior nodded to the nun standing behind me, Sister Catherine Francis, who had led me from the taxi to this office in solemn silence. She led me down another arm of this H-block stone house, to a bathroom where my hair was shorn and I showered, then dressed in a different linen smock than the one I had arrived in.

I was put to work straight away in the nursery, where I'd earn my keep until my time came. They called it "my time" as if it belonged to me. The girls here say it often, "when my time comes," with a tone that makes it unclear whether they're speaking of birth or death. The boundary between the two is so thin, anyway.

"Your time isn't far off, Meredeth," they'd tell me, eyeing the growth round my middle.

I hadn't even known. Not until the day I couldn't fasten my dress, and I'd taken it to Mrs. Cranshaw to help me let it out. And instead she'd cast me out, all in a fury, me in tears, staring desperately down at my stomach. It should have been so obvious. Just as the worn patch of carpet in the corner of Mr. Cranshaw's library, where he'd made me kneel, should have been obvious.

"Do you think the father will change his mind and claim it?" Lucy asked. She was so sweet. Hopeful. Sang to her belly every night.

I shook my head. "No. He's married. Has a kid of his own."

Lucy paled, clearly scandalized but too sweet to say so. "So you weren't in love?"

Poor Lucy, it must have been so easy to break her heart. "No. But I loved his little one." Andrew Cranshaw. I missed his small hands and playful antics. I'd loved all my charges. I might not be any Mother Superior, but I had done my best.

Lucy had been right about one thing, though, and my time did come quickly. I had only been at Bon Secours a few weeks when "my time" ran in a rush down my legs and erupted in a crest of pain unlike anything I had ever known. Eventually that wave dragged me under and far away.

The next thing I remembered was waking, to silence, in a tangle of stiff linens. I drew my feet up, away from the tack of dried blood, and the blanket held the shape of my legs where it had molded to me in my sleep. Like a ghost of me lay in that bed.

"Meredeth." Sister Catherine Francis stepped up to the bedside. I turned my head toward her and my throat wrenched. My lips stuck fast when I tried to ask for water. She guessed my meaning and poured some from a pitcher on the bedside table.

"It's been three days," she said as she handed me the glass. My hand shook as I raised it to my mouth. "Mother Superior already read you the last rites."

Mother Superior. Mother?

I dropped the glass, the shock of cold water spreading across my lap. "My baby?"

"She prayed over him, too, though I'm afraid we didn't have time to baptize him."

The grip of pain ran deeper than all the aches and tears of my body. The whole world had split into a thousand shards and I had swallowed all of them dry.

"Do you think you can walk?" Sister Catherine asked.

I pushed myself to sit higher and shoved the filthy, glass-scattered blanket away. Scratches and bruises ran down my legs. My empty stomach still distorted from the life it had carried. I stood and advanced on the nun, drawing so close to her that my eyes were shaded under the awning of her wimple.

"Where is he?"

She met my countenance with a scowl of her own. "I see that

you can walk. Good. You leave first thing tomorrow morning." She turned away in a swirl of black and made for the door.

Shock overcame my rage. "Leave?"

Sister Catherine turned back to me, her hand on the door's latch. "This is a home for mothers and children. You are neither."

If comfort was a sin, as the sisters would have had us believe, then Mother Superior was damned long before I picked the lock on her chambers.

Her rooms were warm, heated by a humming radiator. Her blankets thick, her nightgown smooth. Free of a wimple, her hair hung in a long, brown braid that coiled across her pillow. It was long enough to circle her throat three times, and when I pulled hard enough, I could wrap it a fourth. Her face burned the purple of bishops, her eyes springing red poppies across the white. Her tongue dripped froth as it inched further down her spotted chin. Her arms flailed beneath the heavy blanket, trapped beneath the weight of all that wool, and me, sitting beside her and pinning the cloth to the mattress.

It took so long for her to be still. It was like waiting for a sermon to end, when your baby is kicking your bladder. Baby. The thought gave me strength. I wrapped the braid a fifth time, pulling till the roots sprang free from her scalp.

She had a fine carpet bag in the closet. Sturdy shoes close enough to my size. But her desk, in the adjacent room, where I'd so recently sat and was judged—that was my target.

My file was there. One of hundreds. Lucy's too. I recognized the address at the top of my first page—the Cranshaw's house in Galway.

There was information about my posting in the nursery. The storage box number where I would find my own dress. Another address, perhaps where they had intended for me to go in the morning. I would take that car, but it's that first address I'd be giving the driver.

Sister Catherine's yellow hair was shorn close to her skull, much like she had done to all of us. Perhaps the lice that plagued all the linens had found their way beneath her wimple. Her Bible, dutifully at her bedside, was heavy and bound in etched brass, the painted whore of Bibles, and it came down hard and fast against her pale temple. She did not even wake from the first blow to feel the second, or the fifth, and by then the pages were as red as communion wine, or birthing linens.

I retrieved my dress from storage, washed myself, changed, and made my way to the dormitory. The sound of soft breathing and the smell of sweet milk circled the room.

Lucy sat up when I gripped her shoulder.

"Oh, Meredeth." She gripped my hands in hers. "I'm so sorry."

My heart galloped. I breathed deep to hold my purpose. "I'm leaving in the morning, Lucy. Mother Superior's just told me. But she's ill and can't see me off. Neither can Sister Catherine. They both ate the same dinner and neither can so much as walk."

Lucy cooed sympathy.

I couldn't suppress a smile. "Too much rich food. Maybe they should stick to porridge like the rest of us."

Lucy smiled weakly and squeezed my hand. "Where are you going?"

"Back to Galway. I'll settle my business there, and then, who knows? Will you tell the others? About the Sisters, I mean. They'll have to get by without them tomorrow."

"Yes, we'll be fine." Lucy's eyes were already beginning to slide closed again. It was nearly dawn, and the Matin bells would be ringing soon.

Did the same fate I'd met await her? In all the weeks I'd worked in the nursery, not a single infant had come through the doors. Though plenty left, wrapped in grey sheets that reappeared after a haphazard laundering.

I sat against the wooden door and waited for the car. It was the same driver who came for me, his eyes cast down to the gravel as he placed my bag, Mother Superior's bag, on the floor of the backseat. It was stuffed full of files.

The drive seemed longer this time. As if I had come from so far away—another world, instead of the next town over.

"Why do you do all the driving for the home?" I asked the young man.

"Figure I owe it to 'em. Born and raised in those walls."

My heart went out to the boy. He could have been anyone's. He might as well have been mine.

"And was your mother like me?"

His complexion deepened and his knuckles whitened on the wheel.

"Wouldn't know," was all he said.

Of course she was, I wanted to say. We're all the same there. Mother inferiors.

The car pulled up in front of the familiar town house. Only two windows glowed: the library, at the top of the house, where Mr. Cranshaw would be taking his tea and paper. And the basement, where the kitchens would be hard at work. It was too early for anyone not driven by nuns or wages to be awake. Mrs. Cranshaw would still be sleeping. And small Andrew.

"Wait here," I told the driver. "I just need to pick something up. I won't be long."

I ascended the servant's stairs. All the way up, like I'd done countless times in the three years I'd worked here. I knew just where to step to be silent.

Mr. Cranshaw always faced the windows, with a view of the bay. His back to the room, to the hearth, which glowed amber in the reflection off his crusted old bayonet. It hung over the mantel like an eyebrow, placed there the same year Andrew was born, the same year Mr. Cranshaw had returned from the front to find his holiday leave that previous year had left his wife blessed.

Not cursed, like he'd left me.

The fire had warmed the bayonet till I could hardly feel it in my fingers. It matched my temperature perfectly, as if it were an extension of my arm. Or an extension of his throat, where I planted it deep.

The spray of blood dissolved the thin newsprint he gripped in front of him. It painted the bay window, its hue matching the glare from the rising sun on the water. It ran in waves like a tempest.

Mr. Cranshaw shook in his seat, rattling on the end of his own blade. And the more he shook, the more blood seemed to come out of him. An impossible amount, creeping across the carpet all the way to the corners, to the worn patches that likely held some of my own blood. Likely others' too. There does not seem to be a limit to the amount of blood a man will draw. Or bleed, when *his* time comes.

When the wet newspaper finally fell from his hands, I left. Back down the silent stairs to the floor below, a dainty trail of red behind me.

Small Andrew smiled when he woke to me standing over him, as he had so many mornings in his short life. His round arms lifted toward me and I bent to his embrace, scooping him up from the pile of tangled blankets.

"Meremere is here, my doll," I whispered into the damp curls at the back of his neck. His breathing eased as he settled back into sleep against my chest. I sifted through the blankets to find the balding blonde bear I knew would be there, and tucked it into my arm next to him.

Then back down the silent stairs again, to the waiting car.

The driver sweated, brow furrowed, as I settled Andrew in the seat, cradled against me. I fished a folded sheet of paper from my pocket. The page from my file. I handed it to him, pointed to the second address. I didn't want to speak. Didn't want to wake sleeping Andrew.

The driver shook his head. "I can't."

"That's where I'm going. Take me there. Now. It's my new post, isn't it?"

He looked at me though his mirror, eyes narrowed. "No. That's not... I'm not ever to go back there. Mother Superior said—"

"She isn't your mother. Never was. Drive."

Perhaps it was the blade forming in my voice, or maybe the blade in my pocket that I didn't think he even knew about, or maybe it was the red all over my shoes, but he drove.

The car slowed to a stop in a narrow lane flanked by rows of stout cottages. They did not look like the kinds of homes occupied by families that would employ a staff to manage their lives, their children. A thick coat of moss cushioned the edges of flint, and crumbs of slate littered the gutter where the roof tiles fell away.

I lowered Andrew carefully to the seat and stood from the car. The air was scented with damp fields and sour apples, wet stone and mildew.

Paint peeled away from the door where the house number had been carved into it. I knocked, and flakes of it tumbled to the worn threshold.

Inside, a baby began to scream. An ache blossomed in my chest. Not just in my heart, but my breasts burned. I felt the front of my dress dampen.

A woman opened the door, an infant curled in the curve of her arm.

"Yes? What can I do for you?" She struggled to fit a bottle to the baby's small mouth. It wrenched its head away and screamed louder.

"I'm from Bon Secours," I said. "Mother Superior sent me to help."

"Look, I took this one off her hands, and I'm not taking any more in just now."

The ache that started in my breasts spread throughout my body. I felt the pulse of my heart in every bruise.

"Miss, I'm just here for a short time. It looks like you could use a hand getting settled, that's all. Is… Is she yours?"

The woman looked too old to have born the babe herself, but perhaps life under these low cottage beams had worn her before her time.

"He. Of course not. Nuns brought him round to me after the last one didn't make it."

I could hardly hear her over the baby's cries, and the wet fabric at the front of my dress began to itch. I gestured for the woman to hand me the child. She did, and he immediately turned into my chest, rubbing his small face against my bosom, his cry becoming high and desperate.

"I'm a wet nurse," I said. "From the nursery. Let me see if I can get him settled for you. Is there someplace I can sit?"

Her eyes roved over me, but she stood back from the doorway and allowed me to pass through. I turned back to the car and motioned for the driver to wait. As if he could do anything else.

The scent of wet stone increased inside the cottage, mixed with old smoke and damp wool. I lowered myself onto a bench and began to unbutton the front of my dress. The small shell buttons were slick with milk, and when I pulled the fabric free, a fine spray crossed the poor baby's face. He stopped crying. I brought him to my breast and he latched instantly, both of us sighing with relief.

The woman returned with a kettle and cups.

"They never sent anyone round before. Just left us to it, babies wasting away by the day. Maybe this one will make it after all."

I could not tear my eyes from the baby's small mouth, from his delicate eyelashes, the tuft of brown hair that crested his soft head. The smell of him unlocked something primal in me.

"When exactly was he brought to you?"

"Three days ago. Hasn't had a drop since. Won't take the bottle. Thought he had no knack for living. Some of these whore babies, there's something not right with them. Like they weren't meant to live."

The baby eased back, stretching his soft arms. I moved him to the other side, and he fed ferociously again. "Perhaps he missed his mother," I whispered.

"Ah, well. From what I understand, she didn't make it. Probably just as well. A blessing. What kind of life could she have given him?"

My teeth ground like old mill stones.

When the baby had finished, he slept, milk pooling in the dimple on his chin.

"Let me put him down for you, and I'll be on my way, for now."

"And you'll be back? How soon? If he cries like that again, I may just leave him in the field. Or send him back, if Mother Superior will take him."

There was no cot for him, only a small wicker basket of soiled linen. I laid him down and turned back to the woman.

"How many children have you had from the home?"

"Had two of my own, raised up. After my husband passed, I thought I could take in others, raise 'em to help round the house. Keep me company. Three I've had, all dead before age four. The last one only lasted a week. Something not right about these babies."

"Sit yourself down," I said. "I'll stoke the fire and brew another kettle."

The woman nodded and smiled, as if she welcomed this role reversal. She liked to be mothered. Perhaps she would have done better to adopt one of those.

All the cottages in the row were adjoined, the little hamlet quiet and serene. Silence would be important.

I whipped the fire poker into her throat as I spun back to her, felt the give of her windpipe collapse. She strangled a whistling gasp that turned to a bubbling gargle as I poured the boiling kettle water into her mouth. Her legs jerked and she tumbled off the bench, convulsing on the floor as the hot liquid made its searing progress through her. Steam poured from her browning mouth. It smelled of rich soup, her evil words thick as bullion simmering in her soft membranes. Her tongue swelled, protruded like a belt of tough leather that twitched against the filthy flagstones long after the rest of her had stilled.

I used what was left in the cooling kettle to rinse my hands.

I searched the house for clean linens, but found only filth. Dirty diapers and dirty rags. I took them anyway, for washing, placed all in a canvas sack and then gently lifted the wicker basket, so as not to disturb my darling child.

He was mine, some part of me knew. And if I was wrong, so what? I'd love him as my own, as I had done for so many children. Would do for so many more.

I made my way back to the car and climbed in. Andrew had awoken, and sat nervously, relaxing as he saw my familiar face. I situated the basket between us, and watched warmth flood Andrew's face as he beheld the tiny, sleeping figure.

"Isn't he sweet? I remember when you were that small."

Andrew grinned and tucked his bear in beside the baby.

"Well? Where are you going? I want you out of my car." The driver's voice had grown hoarse, angry.

I reached for the carpet bag at my feet. So many files. So many names and addresses. Where to begin? I pulled one free at random. Sooner or later I'd get to them all. Every child deserves a mother. And we'll see, in the end, what makes a mother superior.

Diamond Saw

I don't know what the thing growing inside me is, but it speaks with Dad's voice.

I also don't know who put it there; which eager customer, or source of information, provided more than intel over the course of our illicit encounter. I had been careful. But careful isn't always enough, and now my dead dad is bossing me around again, speaking through his new pulse in the wormy clump of cells rooted to my middle.

There had been at least twenty men dad called his "right hand," but now I'm both his hands. And his feet, breath, blood, beating heart, eyes. And there is unfinished business to attend to.

Cancer had eaten the voice right out of his throat before the end, but he slipped me a note. Instructions: one more assignment. His way of saying goodbye.

I've always been in the family business. Useful by virtue of being nearly invisible. "The kid," even well into adulthood, and their eyes would travel up and down but dared not linger.

A boardroom ornament, just a pair of legs to deliver coffee and cocktails. No ears that hear, no brain to process what is heard, and no mouth to go telling tales, as far as any of them could see. Occasionally a bosom upon which to lay one's head, and sometimes, a bit of pussy. They tell me things. Sometimes the things they say are their last words.

Now Dad's gone, except for that nagging voice, and I've aged into my fake ID. One less lie to track, I suppose. They've been piling up for years. And as I blow chunks into this five-star toilet, I realize I've just replaced that lie with a dozen more.

My date, standing outside the bathroom door, isn't worrying about pregnancy or ghost fathers. Such concerns are beyond the realm of his understanding. He's worried I'll bail. Slip out through the lobby when he looks down at his phone. So, he lurks. And I take my time. Short leashes work both ways.

I reapply my lipstick. Suck a peppermint down to a splinter. He's wondering if he missed me, somehow, if the bathroom has a window...

What stupid game is this? You're going to lose him.

I'm not, though. He's getting anxious, turning desperate. Getting stupid.

Dad's getting mad. This isn't the hit he wanted, he's not even on the list, but he's a step closer. List-adjacent.

He's not happy when I come out. Frowning in his brown suit, thumbing his phone checking stocks like he does every ten minutes. He's selling, I see before he notices me standing at his elbow, and I wonder how long it's been since he updated his beneficiary list.

He spots me then, but his expression doesn't sweeten. I've got to turn that frown upside down; it's part of the plan. He's got to want to send me up the chain when we're done. Another step closer.

Do the thing you learned in Prague, Dad's voice urges.

I feel the ligaments deep in my pelvis stretch, ache. So, this Junior Partner guy's a bit of a freak? Easy enough.

Dad says I need more protein, more calcium, more iron. Folic acid. He always was a bossy bastard. It was bad enough when he was alive, always plugged in, just a call or text away, telling me where to be, what to do, how to dress, what to buy. "Bring my red Armani tie to the 3'o'clock at the Muriel suite" or "call Johnson and tell him I want my money or I'll bury him next to his missus." Now, it's "*Take your goddam folic acid and fish oil; you want me born an idiot?*"

I know there's no feet yet. Know it looks more like the shrimp cocktail on the table than the shriveled old man I burned three months ago, but I swear I feel a kick.

He was just a voice, at first. Like Obi-Wan at the end of *A New Hope*. Telling me what files to access, the safe combination, passwords. Promising I'd never sleep again if I didn't finish this last job. His unfinished work. He was just in my head, then, but now …

Junior Partner is still asleep—my pearls around his neck, each coated in lipstick and worse. There's gotta be blood on these sheets and I'm not going to be wanting my shoes back. But not much blood. He's more use alive, for now.

Take the pearls, they were expensive.

I bet the shoes were more.

Dad only ever gave me pearls—round and soft like breasts or doe-eyes.

I've only been awake for fifteen minutes and already I have to pee again.

I get clean, dressed, and order breakfast. Protein. I don't leave. These guys freak the fuck out if they wake up alone—check their wallets before they even wipe the drool from their cheeks. I'll leave once he's conscious and bill the breakfast to the room.

I'm going to get that recommendation. He'll at least pass along my card, maybe even send me as a gift— "to Patrick," he let slip, and now I have a name.

I'm going to get this done, get this whole ordeal over with. Finish Dad's business so his spirit can rest.

Little Dad stirs when I eat the bacon. He always loved bacon. I like it more now than I ever have.

Junior Partner's been smacking his lips in his sleep since room service tiptoed in with the tray. I ordered for him, too. But if he doesn't wake up soon, his bacon is forfeit.

He sits up in a rush and flinches. He'll be feeling me for days.

"Morning, sunshine," I say, before he freaks out.

Pleased, confused, embarrassed, shy, all dance across his face. He hasn't rehearsed *this* moment. There's no script for him to follow.

I've got one, though, because the lines are all mine. "Call if you need anything." I bite a corner off my business card and leave it by the orange juice.

The elevator smells like someone's secret cigarette, and it normally wouldn't bother me, but today ...

You've got him. We're going to take him out. I'm going to be born into a better world, without scum like the likes of him ...

"Tall and tan and young and lovely—" I sing along to the elevator music at the top of my voice till the door dings and slides open for an older couple and their wheeling chariots of luggage.

I search my brain for small talk, distraction. It's like I've forgotten how to talk to normal people. It's an awkward descent to the lobby.

Where I pee, again, because it's going to be a long cab ride back to the office, aka home.

It's not bad. There's a couch and a mini fridge and a water dispenser that does hot and cold. And the night security guy's like family. Back when Dad claimed to be a lawyer, and he'd bring me and my brother to his work on the weekends to do paperwork, Officer Mitch always gave us peppermints. He saved them from his lunches at the Chinese restaurant down the street. The wrapper was always a little bit sticky from the sweet-and-sour sauce. I used to lick the wrapper clean first—sweet, sour, and the inside of pockets. My life story.

My brother always saved his peppermints for later, stashed them in his own pockets till they were nearly powder inside the plastic.

I flop down on the office sofa (my bed) and peel off my emergency ballet flats. The elastic has dug into my swollen feet, leaving the ghostly outline of little shoes behind.

Water first, then rest, then egg rolls. Then more rest.

Turn on your phone. Make sure you keep it on. And no egg rolls, no cabbage. What if he calls tonight?

You'd think that, being in my head, or my wherever, he'd feel that first trimester exhaustion. That bone-tired weariness that only comes from building intricate life structures. But he's too in awe of his own development. I can hear him count the jelly-like stubs that will be his fingers. He coos, proud of himself.

I flick my phone off silent.

No calls, but I've been Googled twice. It won't be long.

A full day spent soaking in the sink and my pearls still aren't clean. It's that goddamn long-lasting lipstick. I scrub them with toothpaste (old family secret) and they're mostly white again. Mostly ready, before the call comes.

Baby Dad is anxious, my insides like a hornet's nest.

Calm down, I think. *I can't do this if I'm sick. Not unless he's into that.*

Did he say who you're meeting? Who is it?

An important guest. That's all he said.

There's no one more important. More important more important no one no one...

He's shouted out. Turning flips, burning too many calories. I'll be starving soon.

But I'm going to the DeLion Plaza. Can't think of a better place to eat for two.

The green dress hugs my figure. It's not a belly—not yet. *I* can tell, now, but I can pass for soft, maybe voluptuous. It's a girl-next-door pooch. I can make it work.

But I'm running out of time. A few more weeks and this gig is up.

The very important guest is not *the important one.*

Baby Dad is losing his shit, throwing me off my game.

But it isn't taking much game. Important Guest has starlight in his eyes. He's older than Junior Partner, but I don't think he's slipped a ring into his pocket. He's got the schoolboy glow that tells me it's been too long. Good. I could use an early night.

Junior Partner excuses himself after coffee. Important Guest tells him to say hi to Caitlin. He darts a glance my way and I make sure he sees me wink.

Junior Partner can still blush. He won't last long in this business. Important Guest slides his hand across the starched tablecloth and wraps his fingers around mine. The starlight in his eyes has gone a bit manic. This might actually wind up sucking.

The coffee has set Baby Dad spinning like a gyroscope in my gut, his thoughts a stream of anxiety. Important Guest doesn't notice. He's playing with my fingers.

He pays the check, hits a button on his phone, and his car is waiting when we exit.

I'm not surprised to get out of the car at the Montesartre Grand. It's the dormer of choice for Very Important Guests with busy evening schedules. I'd be afraid of being recognized if it wasn't for the fact that the staff turns over every few weeks. And they clearly don't give a shit.

He's in the big suite: six bedrooms shared between business partners, joined by a communal living and working space. A productivity retreat.

I eye the other bedroom doors. Partners?

He might be here he might he might one of those others he could be here.

I nod toward the doors. "Will your partners be joining us?"

"What? Oh. No. No, no." His manic smile wilts a little. "They won't get in till late. It's just us."

He grabs me then and clamps his mouth over mine. It's horrific, and I'm trying to make this sexy, but there's just too much saliva to work with. He's feeling me up over my dress like we're two kids at the drive-in. So, he wants a girlfriend experience.

Then he's lifting me, carrying me, mouth still over mine, and we're in his room. He sets me down and turns to lock the door.

Something about him is setting me off, not in a good way, and I've got red flags waving me down till red is about all I can see.

There's a dress laid across the bed. Beaded white satin, and a set of black velvet jewelry boxes.

He pulls me up against him. "These are for you. Go ahead and get dressed. I'll watch."

He doesn't sit. He stands too close and doesn't help with the zip. His eyes trace over my arms as they twist around, contorting behind me, fingers scrambling for purchase.

When I open the jewelry boxes, I know I'm in deep shit. A rope of diamonds, stud earrings, and a ring with a rock the size of a beetle.

"They're yours," he says, finally reaching up to help fasten on the necklace clasp.

I can only assume he plans to kill me. Or he plans to try to. It's not going to fucking work, of course, but I need information, first.

I run my fingers over the diamonds. They're cut smooth, but I can feel the edge on them. "Do your partners know you dropped this much on a naughty girl?"

"You look sweet as honey to me." He kisses my forehead and traces his fingers over the beads on the dress.

It's disturbingly bridal. Shit. He's not the first to make me dress up, but he's the first to make me think it's for my funeral.

The door to the suite slams hard enough to rattle the ornate handle of Important Guest's bedroom. He nearly jumps out of his trouser socks and his face twists into a snarl.

There are two voices in the suite common room, and one of them shouts, "Jones, goddammit!"

The wild look in his eyes has turned from lust into rage. For a moment I'm glad I'm not Door Slammer or Shouty Face, then I remember I'm on the menu, too.

He cups my face in his hands and kisses me on the nose. "Excuse me, darling. I'll just be a moment." He gestures for me to sit on the bed and turns to the door. His hands have started to shake.

I wait till he's mostly through the door, then I slip silently up behind him and peek through the crack in the door as it closes. All I can see is the back of his shirt and the shoulder of a black suit jacket.

"What do you want? I'm busy with a guest," he says before the door latches and the voices grow muffled.

It's him it's him I know it I know it.

We've got bigger problems right now. This guy is dangerous.

Of course. They all are. So are we.

I can hear angry voices, but not their words. They've moved out of range.

Search the room. Find a weapon.

I've got mace in my bag, of course, and a decent knife. I slip them out of my purse and go to put them in the nightstand drawer, but there's already one there. Bigger than mine. I put mine in the other nightstand. I'm sweating, now. Going to ruin this dress. But as it heats up, I can smell history in the fabric. I'm not the first to sweat through it.

There's nothing else here but decorative pillows and satin curtains. Everything else is bolted down. Even the remote is wired to the lamp base. There isn't even a phone, though there's a dark spot on the desk where one used to be. Also not a good sign.

I think, for just a moment, about getting my cell and calling the police. If I call now, there's a good chance they'd get here in time. But that would be it; game over. Unfinished business left unfinished and Baby Dad probably stuck in my head forever, even if I can get him out of my …

Footsteps outside the door interrupt my dangerous train of thought. Mustn't think it too loudly.

I drop onto the foot of the bed and play with the diamond on my finger, pretend like I've been happily hypnotized by its glitter this whole time.

"Sorry, darling. Business." He undoes his cufflinks and tie.

I pat the bed. "Come here and let me rub your shoulders, honey." Turn your back to me. Just for a minute.

"Oh no," he says. "I have better things in mind for those little fingers." He raises my hand to his mouth and nibbles at the skin on my knuckles.

I can blush on command, but I'm losing focus in a fog of anxiety and irritation.

This isn't what I signed on for, not in the beginning. It's a far cry from typing meeting notes, even questionably legal ones, and if I didn't need to quiet an unwelcome spirit, I'd have been perfectly content to leave the past undone.

He's down to his undershirt and boxers, socks and bracers. He's still after me with his saliva and I wonder if he plans to digest me this way—slowly, death by enzymes.

"I know a secret," he says, wrapping long fingers around my wrists, pressing them into the comforter above my head as he climbs atop me.

I know I'm not hiding my fear so well this time. My mask is slipping and he's loving it. The tighter my chest gets, the harder his cock.

Baby Dad's shouts have devolved into a white noise of anxiety.

"You've been up to no good, princess." Now he's sweating and it's dripping in my face.

"What did I do wrong?" I'm trying to play coy, but I can't act anymore, and he loves that I'm still trying.

He grinds against me and fills my ear with spit before whispering, "You're not 25." He practically comes when he says it.

He doesn't really know doesn't know doesn't know doesn't know.

I can't tell if the relief is me or Baby Dad.

Play along, delay, get the knife.

His eyes dart to the nightstand, so I'm ready when he twists away to reach for the drawer. I slide out from under him, the satin slick against the sheets, and I grab my knife and mace from the other drawer.

I can tell, from the way he screams, that it's his first time being maced. He's a charmer. Used to getting his way. Used to getting the girl—having his cake and eating it, too.

I need him to shut up, so I go for the artery behind the collarbone. He's gone, or good as, before Door Slammer and Shouty Face are even at the door.

Shouty Face is screaming for Jones and the door is rattling on its hinges.

There's no point in trying to hide what I've done. The pretty satin frock is ruined.

I've got to open the door. It's coming down, eventually, anyway.

Important Guest still has the knife in his hand. And these guys were mad at him earlier.

I take a deep breath, find my calm ...

Open the door open it open it end this.

... and scream as loud as I can.

The shaking door stills.

I scream again and then I throw open the door and run into the arms of the men on the other side.

It's not hard to cry. It's more hard not to, most days. But I don't mean to puke, though, with as quick as they let go of me, then, I wish I'd thought of it earlier.

It *is* him. Baby Dad feels like he's swelling, like an angry frog. My hips strain against the pressure. I can barely hear the men over the shrieking spirit in every cell of me—like I've turned into the ampoule of his voice. As I suppose I always was, always have been.

They've seen inside the room and they're assessing and grabbing their hair. Door Slammer has a gun in his hand.

"He tried to ki—tried to kill me," I sob.

They don't even question me; they know him better than I do.

They're looking from me to each other, to the mess that was Important Guest, and I can hear what they're thinking almost as clearly as I hear Baby Dad.

Shouty Face pulls his gun, too. Shit.

"We can't let her leave," Shouty says.

Door Slammer, also known as Original Primary Target, shakes his head. "Naw, fuck him. She did us a favor."

It's been so long since I've seen him, since I've heard his voice, I'd forgotten the way he always sounds like he's smiling. How much that always pissed off Dad.

My muscles are twitching, jumping with spasms as I feel Baby Dad reaching for puppet strings that should be out of his reach. The scent of his target has made him wild. His spirit is getting stronger, outgrowing the gummy cluster of cells where he'd rooted. He's going to get us killed.

"A favor, yeah?" Shouty is pissed. "Why don't we just give her his cut, then? She's made a lot of work for us, is what she's done."

"So? Extra work, extra money. That's how the world fuckin' works, right, sweetie?" He turns to me and grins. "Ain't that hard to hide a body."

But as he looks at me his grin slips. His head tilts. Some recognition stirs in his eyes.

"Just as easy to hide two bodies," Shouty says, and he levels his gun at me.

Primary Target turns and fires first.

Shouty drops and his late shot goes askew into a wall.

My hands are at my neck before I can think, pulling, and I whip my rope of diamonds across Target's throat and lean. Pull. I saw at the tender flesh of his neck, feel the ragged cut of stones bite into his skin, and I drag, feel the lubricant of blood course from the jagged wound.

He's making sounds like a drain as he sinks to his knees. Maybe he'll wash this little ghost down, too.

But Baby Dad is swelling like a supernova and this dress already feels tighter.

Target's face is in the carpet as he shakes. His throat tries to pulse itself clear.

I roll him onto his back. Red foams from his mouth and neck.

His eyes look as sad as they ever were, since mom left.

"Had to," I say. "Because of Dad."

There's hurt in his eyes, but knowledge, too. Acceptance. He knows what he did. He knew this was coming. He stops shaking, then. He's limp, done, bright gems buried in the gore of his throat.

Search him.

He's got nothing in his pockets but two crushed, linty peppermints. I take them both. I'm eating for two, after all. At least until tomorrow.

Baby Dad's voice isn't little anymore, but deep, ragged with cancer, like it was in life. The ghosts of his tumors back to mulch his words into broken growls.

I yank the necklace out of the meat in Target's throat.

Dad only ever gave me pearls. Men like a lady's pearls around their throat, teasingly tight. Soft, like our hands. Give a woman diamonds and you make her into a saw blade.

I take the necklace to the sink and start to wash it. Pull the strings of skin from the gold prongs, rinse the gelled blood from behind the settings.

I squeeze a little hotel toothpaste into my palm, scrub with it, and everything starts to shine again.

Toothpaste—that's the family secret.

Well, one of them.

When Auntie's Due

The museum is chaos. It always is. If you can even call it a museum—there are no dusty exhibits here. Everything here is sticky, interactive. And the children are everywhere, interacting. My two-year-old niece, Cora, spins a crank that dumps a bucket of plastic balls down a chute. She stomps her feet and shrieks with glee, the sound weaving through the other children's shrieks, the wails that spill from strollers, the shushing of mothers. I bring my niece here every week, to give Caitlin a break. She's home with her latest addition, my new nephew Paul, round and perfect.

"It's good practice," she always says, "for when you have your own." She says it like she's not six years younger than me, like she doesn't know I want kids more than anything. Like I haven't sunk my last dollar at the clinic, over and over again. She knows. "First you need to get a man," she says.

"You don't need a man to have a baby," I say.

"If you've been trying without one, it explains why it hasn't worked yet."

I ignore the knife she's twisted in my heart. "You don't need a man to have a baby, you just need a man to get pregnant."

"I just said you needed to find one, I didn't say you needed to keep him. Good riddance to them all," she says. And then she laughs, forgets she was picking a fight, but the knife still twists, will keep on twisting till I'm distracted enough to ignore it.

My niece is distracting. So is the cacophony of the museum, but it's hard being around so many babies, so many moms. So many moms who don't even look like they want to be there, don't even look like they want to be moms. Moms who yell and scold and snap. I watch from the bench along the wall as they supervise their phones, ignore their kids, only lifting their gaze to shout, redirect, threaten to leave but never do, because at least here their kids stay busy. Entertained in a place where Mom doesn't have to be the entertainment, waiter, and main course all in one. I get it. Caitlin thinks I don't, but I do. She probably doesn't even think about all the times I had to take care of her, entertain her, so our own mom didn't have to.

I watch, and I rub the bump on my midsection, tight against the waist of my pants. I rub it and adjust it, so it sits the way it should. Looks the way it should. So the straps holding it in place don't chafe against my hips.

Then Cora's small fingers close over mine. "Come, An-tee Soapy," she says, pulling on my arm.

I'm Soapy, because Sophie is hard to say. Caitlin thinks it's hilarious. I think it's the best name I've ever had. This girl has my whole heart.

I stand and stretch my back. A mom nearby glances my way, sees the bump, and offers a sympathetic smile, one that says, "It's so hard, isn't it?"

It is. She has no idea.

WHEN AUNTIE'S DUE

"You won't even tell me his name? Wait ... do you even know his name?" Caitlin bounces in the deep knee-bend-rock that keeps the baby asleep while Cora squeezes a pouch of apple mush onto the table.

"He doesn't want to be involved," I say. "And frankly, I don't care."

"Don't be ridiculous, of course you do," she says. She says it like she wants it to be true, like she wants me to feel abandoned instead of elated.

I go with it, because elation is harder to fake.

"Whatever. It's not up to me. He made his choice, I made mine." I rub the bump again, but back away when Caitlin reaches for it.

"What, it's not like I'm some stranger at the grocery store!" She laughs and reaches again, and I dodge, and Cora, that angel, chooses that moment to spill her juice and her shriek wakes the baby, and in the chaos, the bump is safe.

While Caitlin is distracted, I pull on the straps, line everything up. It looks good. But it doesn't feel right. It's a good thing Caitlin has her hands full.

An-tee Soapy's bump makes her feel sick, I've explained to Cora, to buy some time off Auntie duty, to hide from Caitlin, to switch to the bigger bump. She misses her weekly museum, but I've promised, soon, we'll go back. And we will, when I'm ready.

And when the air turns cold, and I can finally pull a thick sweater over the swell of my stomach and the weight of the bump makes me ache and waddle, I go back to Caitlin's to get Cora.

"Don't you know you're supposed to glow?" Caitlin says.

"Eat shit," I say.

Cora laughs.

"Sophie!" Caitlin cups a hand over my girl's ear.

"Soapy!" Cora reaches up for me, but I take her hands in mine and give them a squeeze.

"An-tee Soapy can't lift you right now, baby girl. My back is killing me."

Caitlin nods and starts to walk us toward the door, anxious for her break. "It won't be much longer." Her tone is chipper, but with the weight of *I know I'm about to lose my babysitter* behind it.

Cora is wilder than usual on the drive to the museum, all her pent-up excitement after time apart coming to a head as we park, and I shut off the engine. She's pulling at the straps of her car seat, ready to hulk her way to freedom.

"Hold on, baby girl, An-tee Soapy needs to get ready." I reach behind my back and squeeze the clip, release the heaviness from my front. I pull the pillowed rubber out from under my sweater and tuck it under one of Cora's old blankets on the passenger seat. The skin of my stomach feels wrong, cold without its comforting layer. Empty.

I pull a bag out of my backpack and put on my kit, watch myself transform in the rear-view mirror.

"You look like Elsa!" Cora squeals.

I don't, but I could pull off blond, I suppose.

"Mama's Elsa," Cora coos, proudly.

"You bet she is. The ice queen, herself."

We go in, and the noise hasn't changed, like it's just kept on going the whole time we were away.

The staff have changed, though, and I was counting on it. A

fresh batch of high school students watching the desk, the turnover like clockwork every semester. We disappear into the crowd.

The families have changed, too, but haven't. They're different, but all the same–exhausted, letting their kids burn themselves out, praying for a good nap later, watching their phones, not watching their kids.

I count the strollers, but it's hard. They all look alike, which is good. I note the wails coming from each, pinpoint which have the right sound to them. New, but not too new.

That one.

The woman's hair is half up in a sloppy bun, half spilling over her ear in greasy tangles. She's leaning against the railing of the toddler area as if it's the only thing holding her up. The four kids rattling around inside the arena are hers, all boys under six, all wearing each other's misfitting clothes. And the stroller by her hip, which was wailing till a moment ago, now silent after she wheeled it back and forth and back and forth.

Now one of the boys is wailing–the smallest, at the top of the slide, too scared to go down, but with all his brothers jammed into the tunnel behind him, pushing.

The slide is shaped like a green bean, the tunnel a vine, the only way in is up a climbing wall of tomatoes and carrots and berries–a food pyramid to fun. Or torture, if you have three brothers. It would be worse to have four.

The boy is crying, his brothers shouting, and mom has to lift herself from the railing. It looks like it takes her last ounce of strength, and what she hasn't realized yet is that she's going to have to climb that pyramid, work her way through the tunnel, past the blockage of brothers, to even get to her crying child. It's going to take minutes. It's going to take all her focus.

"Cora, honey. Come on, let's go get some ice cream and play dolls."

She abandons the clay table at speed. I know what my girl likes. I'm fast, but not too fast.

The stroller handles are still warm. One wheel drags–it's been through four kids already–so I have to lean it to the left to make it go straight.

Straight onto the elevator, where I risk a peek under the blanket. Round and perfect. Straight to the coat check, where I lift the baby out, tuck him into another parked stroller.

"Is you doll?" Cora asks.

"It is!" I say. "And if you're a good girl, it will be your doll when we get home."

Cora squeals and jumps, clapping. The sound of her squeal masks, for a second, the sound from two floors above.

"Hurry up, baby girl."

Sleepy mom was faster than I thought. There will be at least a minute where they all assume some innocent mistake. Mistakes, at least, are thinkable.

In that minute, we're at the car. I put the stroller, and the *doll*, in the trunk. Give him a little more than a dose of something sleepy, the pink allergy goo from Cora's diaper bag.

"I hold the doll, An-tee Soapy?"

"When we get home. If you're good."

I buckle Cora in, then bend down in the front of the car, and stuff my wig into the storm drain.

Cora is too excited to notice I'm no longer Elsa. She sings an ice cream song while I pull my bump back under my sweater, buckle it in place.

We're far enough away, at the ice cream shop, when the perimeter closes like a cage, when all the phones in line blare the alert and we all look at our screens and look around, into the faces of strangers. None match the description.

Caitlin meets us in the yard, her face pale, her phone in her hand, Paul on her hip. Cora runs up to her, a new doll clutched in her sweet arms.

"Look what An-tee Soapy give me!"

I smile, tight-lipped, at Caitlin.

"I saw the alert, were you—"

"Don't worry. We were already at the ice cream shop by then."

Caitlin's shoulders visibly drop in relief. But not all the way. She's lost the "it can't happen here" innocence that all mothers lose, sooner or later.

At least I'll never have that moment. I already know.

"We're okay. Why don't you go take a nap. You probably didn't rest at all, and I promised Cora we'd play with her new doll." I reach for Paul, and Caitlin hands him to me, her eyes already glazing with early surrender to sleep.

Paul has enough clothes for two babies, which is my fault. I can't resist the tiny outfits. He's never worn most of them. I fill my backpack with diapers and onesies. I play dress-up with Paul while Cora dresses her doll.

"Okay, sweetie, it's time for you and our dollies to take a nap." She tucks in her doll, and I tuck in Paul, then Cora, and hum a lullaby.

Cora's out fast, after the museum and sugar crash. Paul isn't—he never sleeps—but he will, with a little over a dose of the pink goo.

I carry him out to the car, open the trunk.

The round, perfect baby is sleeping like an angel. I lay Paul down, dose him, and tuck him in, then lift the sleeping baby and carry him inside, change his limp body into Paul's clothes, not a perfect fit, but so close, and tuck him in to Paul's crib.

I give Cora a light forehead kiss, and I'm gone.

I don't dare stop, not even to take the screaming baby out of the trunk, in case someone sees me taking a baby out of a trunk. The pink goo did not work on Paul, and I wonder if Caitlin's been using it, too, desperate. If he's built up a resistance.

Not till I'm in my garage, the door closed, do I open the hatch and see that angry pink face, mouth stretched in demand, tiny hands clawed at the air.

He's hot from screaming as I lift him, hold him to my shoulder, shush him and start those deep knee bends.

I carry him inside, where I have everything ready.

He's changed and fed, still whimpering, but soon he cries himself to sleep and I lay him in the fresh crib on the fresh sheet.

I watch him for a while. His soft puffs of breath, milk-scented. Milk-based formula-scented. I told Caitlin she should breastfeed, but she told me to mind my own business. I'm glad she didn't, now.

I reach under my shirt and unhook the bump, let it fall away, rubber sliding to the floor leaving a slick of sweat behind, my back lashed with the strap marks that have been there for months now, that feel like they might never go away. I feel transformed. It's something like a birth.

Report: The suspect is on camera, on six cameras, including the elevator, where we get the best look at her face. As much of it as we can see, as she only ever looks down, to the stolen stroller and the bouncing child with her.

She's on camera in the entryway, with a different stroller than the one she had in the elevator.

She's on camera as she came in, an hour before that, with the same bouncing child but no stroller. She paid cash.

We don't have a name, and we barely have a face.

At least, not her face.

The bouncing child, though–the smiling little girl is always grinning upward, and she's our only lead. But we don't even know if she belongs to the blond woman, or if she herself went missing from somewhere, sometime.

Video from a bus stop security camera shows the blond woman and the child, and the stolen stroller with the stolen baby in it, walking into a parking lot. There are only six cars in that parking lot.

I call Caitlin as soon as I can, when I know the kids will still be asleep. From the sound of her voice, she was still asleep, too.

"Sorry I had to bail. The kids were down for their nap, so I figured it would be okay." I give her a minute to catch up to where she is, that I'm not in her house anymore.

"Oh, right. Yeah, fine. Thanks for getting them down. I don't even know how you got Paul to sleep."

"I think we wore him out playing dress-up. Look, the reason I had to go … The dad called. He changed his mind. He wants to try and be involved."

"What the fuck do you mean *he's changed his mind*?" Caitlin spits over the phone, now wide awake.

"He wants us to give things a try. Talk about us. Maybe we have a future after all, I dunno."

"I don't like this, Sophie. Your one-night-stand sperm donor wants to meet up, right before you're due, to talk, and he makes you come to him? How do you know he's not a murderer? How do you know this isn't some ambush to avoid child support?"

"You really need to stop listening to all those murder podcasts." *Especially in front of my girl*, I want to add.

"I'm actually being literally serious here. I'm worried about you. And you're due any second, you shouldn't even be on the road."

"You're not worried about me, you're worried about your babysitter." My throat feels tight. It feels wrong to match her cruelty, especially when she's not showing it, for once. She doesn't answer. "I'll check in, okay? I'll send you reassuring texts. Pictures of me, holding the day's newspaper, okay?"

"Give me his address. What's his name?"

"His name is Craig, and he lives in Portland. And I don't have his address because I'm not actually dumb enough to go to his house. We're meeting at the art museum."

"Sophie, that's a long drive. What if you pop?"

"Then my poor kid gets a Maine birth certificate."

Caitlin takes a moment. "You'd better text me every day. Every hour."

"I'm not going to text you while I'm driving. But I promise I'll check in every day. Several times." It's actually sweet, if she cares, and it tugs at my heart a little. She'd make a nice auntie.

It's been three hours since we left the museum. Longer than I wanted. I need to move fast. I load Paul into the car seat, latched in place and perfectly buckled. Trunk packed with baby essentials.

He screams for miles, for hours, then finally passes back out as we hit the highway through Syracuse, heading south.

We're almost to the Pennsylvania border. Then the next part of the plan.

Report: The suspect's car is a white Honda Civic. The footage is too grainy to get a license plate and the car too common to get an ID, but it's a lead. There were no clues found in the parking lot. There might be a thousand white Honda Civics in town, but how many are driven by white women in their thirties who are blond? The list is getting shorter.

We enter the empty no-man's-land of farms and buggies, where the fields are shorn short and ready for a long winter. The roads go on for miles without a sign or streetlight, and the only sign of traffic is the horse shit piled along the median line.

We enter Millersville from the west, and find a bed-and-breakfast, the kind that caters to the looky-loos who want a taste of local culture, but not too much. Every fucking surface is quilted. It's like a padded cell.

"These are lovely," I tell the old woman who runs the place, as I run my hands over the quilts folded on the chair backs. "I've always wanted an Amish quilt, but they don't sell them in Arizona." Or Upstate New York, but I'm sure they don't sell them in Arizona, either.

"Oh, they're all over the shops downtown," she says, dropping a room key in my hand. "You can have your pick of a hundred. I know I can't resist them; I'd buy them all if I could."

"Are you sure you didn't?" I ask, and fortunately she takes it in good humor, laughing as she totters back down the stairs to the reception hall.

My skin is crawling, but I don't think we'll have to stay here long.

Report: The suspect was found at home at six p.m. The child seen in surveillance footage was with her and was taken immediately into protective custody. The body of the abducted child was also recovered. He had been placed, deceased, into the crib of the suspect's infant son, whose whereabouts are currently unknown. The suspect was combative, accruing additional charges of resisting arrest and assaulting an officer.

Attempts are being made to contact the suspect's sister.

When my phone rings, I have to run, out of my quilted room, down the stairs, out of the house. As far away from the crying baby as I can, so they won't hear him.

"Hello? ... Yes ... Oh, my god ... I'm out of town, visiting my boyfriend, but ... I'll be there soon. I'll start back right away. Tell her Auntie Soapy is coming."

I can hear her in the background, wailing. "Aunty Soapy! Mommy! The lady hit Mommy and she's gone!"

"I'm coming, baby girl."

WHEN AUNTIE'S DUE

Back down the long road, the countryside unlit, the view a patchwork of fields in varying shades of dark. I drive till we're far enough away from any buildings, the only farms set back against a distant line of trees.

It's cold. Maybe too cold. Paul's naked, no modern clothes or diapers, but the quilt is thick. Heavy cotton layered in patches over lofty batting, trapping all the heat of his endless tantrum.

I swaddle him tight, so he won't fight his way out of the warm, and I lay him by a spindly sapling on the roadside.

This road will be full of buggies in the morning, those buggies full of families in their Sunday best. The bright quilt colors will catch their eyes. They'll see him, or hear him, probably in time. And if what I've read is true, they'll keep the secret in their community. An abandoned Amish baby is none of the modern world's business.

I get back in the car, but I don't drive, not right away. It feels wrong, to let go of something I've wanted for so long. I can still hear him through the window glass, and the sound keeps shredding at raw nerves. My head is spinning, like it's been flushed down a funnel of noise. Just before I clap my hands over my ears, I hear another noise. A horse? It's gruff, a nickering—maybe in one of the fields.

But if it's on the road, if someone's coming ...

I get out of the car and go to Paul, lift him from the cradle of tree roots and hold him close, shushing, cooing, stifling his screams against my chest, pulling his face to my breast as if to nurse him, but pressing him deep into the flesh there to dampen the sound. I listen. I hear the horse again, but the wind moves the sound so I can't tell where it's coming from.

Paul is writhing against my chest, his small arms pinned by the quilt, his small face buried against me, my heartbeat now as loud for him as his cries were for me, all-consuming, and as I wait and listen, he quiets. He stills.

The whole night silences. Not even the crickets want to wake the sleeping baby.

I wait a few more pounding heartbeats, a few more slow breaths, and I pull him away from my chest. All the red of his face has collected in his eyes, his cheeks now the color of stone. His lips, a tiny bow relaxed for the first time in days.

I lay him back in the tree's cradle.

My head is still spinning, now from silence. My arms feel empty. My chest aches.

I climb into the car and start the engine, its roar a comfort, proof that I have not stopped hearing altogether. I pull my belly out of the bag beside me, struggle it back into place. The rubber is cold until it warms against my skin, and already I feel less empty. Full and heavy. And my foot is heavy on the gas as I pull away, back home, back to my girl.

"Your sister says you were the one at the museum," the detective says.

I sip the small paper cup of water that he brought me a moment ago. "I usually take her. But I haven't been up to it lately." I rub the bump. It's big, now, as big as it gets.

He nods and makes a note. "But you drive her car."

"She lets me borrow it. She has a nicer one she uses more."

He writes again, but not much. They lost interest in me when they saw the bump.

"And do you know where your nephew Paul might be?"

My eyes well up. I'm not pretending; I'm exhausted. I shake my head.

"Did she ever say anything that makes you think she might hurt the baby?"

My voice is thick with everything I've felt these past months; giving up on the clinic, seeing Paul born, finding the bump set in a thrift shop, the hordes of unwanted children at the museum. Paul, screaming through two states. "All she ever really said was that he wouldn't sleep. I tried to help her out, I came over as often as I could to give her a break, but ... " I let my voice break off. "I think ... I think she was getting pretty desperate."

The detective flips his notebook closed. "We may need to talk to you again."

I nod.

"Your sister would like to see you."

My face hardens, like cold rubber strapped to the front of my skull. "Tell her she can see me, and Cora, when she tells us where Paul is."

He leads me to the advocate's office, and Cora runs, wailing, into my arms.

"It's okay, honey. It's going to be okay. Auntie's here."

The advocate hands me a suitcase of Cora's things, but the detective steps in and takes it for me. He carries it to the car and puts it into the empty, clean trunk while I strap Cora into her seat.

He's back inside the station when I slide into the front seat.

"Let's go, baby girl. Let's get some ice cream and a new doll."

I'm going to need a new doll. Soon. I'm due.

SEEING STONES

The Death of Madam Doris
Sunday, April 12th

I've had a hundred men pissed at me. At least, at me as Madam Doris. So I wasn't scared, at first, when an angry man in a pressed polo shirt came storming up to my table like a force of nature.

I shuffled my deck while the usual question danced on my tongue. *Did I tell your wife about your side chick?* It's why my business card says, "Don't shoot the messenger."

Until Mr. Polo came along, no one has really tried.

As far as farmers' market violence goes, it's usually over baked goods. Religious disputes are between chickpeas and quinoa, which is why I have my table here instead of at the flea market.

But it's been a while since I took the time to read the cards for myself, and it shows. Not that it would have changed the outcome to know, but I could have been more prepared. Had a few more of my affairs in order. Picked my funeral dress so Caroline wouldn't bury me in blue.

And I could have left a note to warn my niece, Helen.

Because Mr. Polo wasn't mad at me. He was mad at all of us. And his anger was the kind they write psalms about.

Shannon
Wednesday, April 22nd

Detective Kurella glowers at me from across the morgue. He isn't angry, though. We've worked together often enough that I know what he's thinking. He is, as he explains it, afflicted with a serious face. The medical examiner beside him has no such excuse. I've worked with him, before, too. He knows what I'm about to do, and I can't help glancing his way before I do it. I reach out a bare, ungloved, finger and gently run it along the tendril of hair that trails from under the white sheet.

The dead woman's hair feels like wet silk between my fingers.

Your hair is just like silk

Save for where it has been shorn, where it spikes like duck down.

I will take this from you, you Delilah

A white sheet covers the woman from her forehead down. It always amuses me that the medical examiner seems to want to protect me from *seeing*.

In my other hand, I clutch the ME's report to my chest, the file too thick to be contained by the plain cardstock folder. I haven't read it, yet. It would help, if I had—more information is always better—but the expectation of psychic investigators is that we must first prove ourselves by telling men in suits what they already know. And if we can tell them enough things that they already know, maybe they'll believe us when we tell them things they don't already know. It's an inefficient process.

Don't drop the folder this time. I pick up the fine strands of hair again and run my thumb along them.

There is water, and the water is moving, but hands are holding her still. The hands push her under deeper, and pull her up, over and over, until she struggles in a ring of foam. His voice roars over the river, chanting something she can't understand. Hot metal is pressed to her chest and the slickness there turns to steam and her scream punches a hole through the vapor, a tunnel, and she can almost, almost see his face ... Her mouth is heavy, throat heavy, chest heavy, stomach heavy. Teeth like powder.

"You must be clean before I can touch you. You must be reborn before you die."

I let the hair slip from my fingers.

"He burned something into her chest," I say, reaching a hesitant hand for the edge of the sheet.

The ME and Detective Kurella exchanged a glance.

While his gaze is averted, I grip the sheet and pull it back. The cloth itself has many stories, all trying to fight their way through my skin. I peel it down past the wound in her chest. The flesh there decomposed more quickly, the wound a doorway for nature's psychopomps. At the center, though, where the burn hardened her flesh into a scab like a shield, is the shape of a cross. Below the cross, her skin lies tattered in rotten gashes. I reach out a fingertip and gently brush a jagged edge of flesh. It has hardened, thin like parchment where it curled away from the wound.

A word. Cut into her skin while she was still living. I hear her scream. I hear him chanting again, spitting the word over and over as he cuts.

"Adulteress," I say aloud, and pull my hand back, willing the vision to fade.

Detective Kurella makes a note in his book.

"That would fit with those markings we could identify, yes," The ME says. He sighs, a sound almost obscene in a morgue.

"A married woman, then? Could be the work of a jealous husband." Kurella makes more notes.

"No. He didn't really know her." I pull the sheet further to see her hands, but her arms end in severed stumps, bone shorn sharply. Her stomach bulges at odd angles. Jagged cuts cross it where the ME explored the strange protuberances. I touch her again and feel the heaviness in my gut again, a weight like an anchor. The heaviness that scrapes all along her throat, starts at the mouth. I open my eyes to see I've traced the path to her lips, which I've parted. There is gravel in her cheeks. Her teeth are gone.

So much of her is gone. Physically. Spiritually. This body is now just a container for the incident—her violent end absorbed into it so deeply that it erased all trace of the woman she was before. I hope wherever her spirit has moved to, it left these memories behind.

All I can do is gather what impressions remain. I lay my fingertips across her cold forehead.

Detective Kurella drives like detectives do in the movies—too fast, and looking at me as much as he does the road. As if his sixth sense is vehicular. He often asks me if I can tell what he's thinking. I tell him yes, but not because I'm psychic. He hates that answer.

"Could still be a jilted lover of some kind. Maybe some random from a club that she doesn't even remember rejecting."

"No. I just don't get that feeling. This isn't like other cases. There's no desire—not even for control, or power, or revenge. This freaks me out. There's something ... ritual. Religious. This was a spiritual experience for him."

"Like, satanic?"

"No. The feeling in his actions isn't evil. At least, not to him." As they say, the villain always thinks he's the good guy.

"Yeah, I think Jane Doe would disagree."

"He felt righteous."

"That's not good." Kurella slows to stop at a red light and picks nervously at the steering wheel threads as he waits for it to change.

"No. It really isn't. He was proud of his work."

"So, some kind of religious nut kills a woman he doesn't even know, for reasons he's made up ... "

"She was unclean to him. A sinner. He wanted to save her—and then destroy her before she sinned again." We always do this. He asks questions, helps steer me to solidify the ephemeral impressions that otherwise dance out of reach.

"Exactly, for made-up reasons—and then he's proud of it. You know what that means?"

"That Christianity and misogyny are bedfellows of the worst kind." Also the most common kind, but that's not a button I want to push today.

"Well. That's a broader philosophical take. But what I'm saying is that it means he's going to do it again." Kurella's shoulders visibly relax as he accelerates.

"Unless we catch him first."

"I'm willing to bet you it's already too late."

The Fall of Lady Helen
Thursday, May 6th

When they told me Aunt Doris was dead, it was like I forgot her name. Or never knew it. Just for a moment. My mind buying me time—*Who?*—before I crossed the threshold into a world irretrievably changed.

The worst part was knowing that the world had changed, and I didn't notice. That I had been living for hours in a different place, as if everything was okay—as it never would be again.

The cards confirm what the police said. I sweep the offending deck off the table. They scatter, flutter, land, and once again confirm it. Fate isn't swayed by gravity.

"Killed by one of her clients last Sunday. We're sorry to notify you so late, but it took some time to identify ... "

The body. She'd been ruined. Mutilated. She'd never worried overmuch about "the corporeal" as she'd called it, but it enrages me to know her end was painful.

A client. Abducted her from her table at the farmers' market—stolen like a honey bun from the bakery stall.

And no one to bury her but my mother, Caroline, who rants at me on the phone, who *"always knew those witchy games would lead her to a bad end."* As if the statement itself wasn't prophecy. The "I told you so" starts before the grief has even materialized. For my benefit, of course—to dissuade me from walking that same path.

A knock at the door saves me before the passive-aggressive turns aggressive.

"I have to go, Mom. Someone's at the door. Might be the detective." I hang up with her voice still ringing through the receiver.

The man at the door looks more like an accountant than a

detective. "Helen Barths?" He pulls a small notebook with a pen clipped to its cover from his pocket.

The press? Oh, fuck no. I stare at the logo embroidered on his polo shirt, so I know where to direct my angry letter, and maybe a hex, but the logo isn't a news source, it's a cross with a sunset behind it.

Shannon
Friday, May 7th

"The scene goes from this line of gravestones all the way to the river, then up onto the bank in that path of trees—"

Detective Kurella keeps talking, says something about where different clues had been recovered, but I can barely hear him. Cemeteries are loud. Not with the dead, surprisingly, but with the echoes of thousands of mourners. Grief lingers like nothing else.

The hard part is not letting each wail set its hook in my heart. I do my best to filter. Not grief, terror. Not the eternity of death, but the moment of it.

Kurella is still talking—something about tire tracks.

"They walked here barefoot." I know it as I say it. "Both of them. From over … " My face turns as if of its own accord. " … that way." I feel the pull toward the trees that line a steep embankment that cascades down from the road above. That road frames clusters of shops and restaurants with vast parking lots and anonymous crowds. "They came down the hill. To the riverbank first. He … cleansed her in the river, like the last one, then dragged her … there, to that grave. He cut her, killed her right there. Filled her with river rocks."

Kurella, silent, pulls out his book to write down my thoughts, his eyes following my finger as it traces the path of Jane Doe #2's end. Though Jane #1 isn't Jane anymore, she's Doris.

I step as close to the headstone as I dare. This is the oldest section of the cemetery, the markers long ignored, erased by lichen. But the face of this one has been rubbed clean.

"He with whom the lord is angry will fall." Kurella reads aloud.

Rebecca Burgess belonged to this grave, born in 1908, died in 1932. "Not, 'Beloved Mother,' then." Kurella pulls out his phone and taps away.

The proximity to Jane 2's last living place makes me lightheaded. Makes it more difficult to focus on a single event. I sit in the grass and drop my forehead into my palms, and the vision fills me completely. The hard pack of dirt against his knees as he knelt over her. The faces hidden in the woodgrain of the knife handle. The way her hair caught in its teeth. The weight of all those stones. She could hardly move by the time she lay here—arms shaking with fatigue if she tried to raise them. Eyes dark with river water.

The man with the knife spoke, and Kurella speaks in unison.

"The mouth of an adulteress is a deep pit; he with whom the Lord is angry will fall into it. Proverbs 22:4."

Shannon
Monday, May 10th

Another detective identified the body of Jane 2 as Helen, the woman he had just spoken to a few days previously about the murder of her aunt, Doris.

"I know you feel otherwise, but this is clearly a family matter." Kurella always uses the word "feel" instead of "see" when he's dismissing my visions.

"It's not. He didn't know either of these women." And they didn't know him. The taste of their confusion still burns the back of my throat.

"You think it's a coincidence that the same killer targets two women who just happen to be related?"

"Not at all. He went after them both with intent—but not because they're related. He just found Helen because of Doris. Remember, I said this was ritual. Spiritual. They were both working psychics. He saw Doris working at the market, targeted her, and in stalking her learned about Helen." I've been telling Kurella things he already knows for almost a decade, and sometimes that's still not enough.

"He referred to them both as 'adulteress,' which implies some kind of relationship."

"It's just a fancy word for 'slut.' It doesn't mean anything. It's the church's favorite word for 'woman I'd like to get rid of' now that 'witch' has gone out of fashion."

"It's far more likely to be an estranged relative acting out some sick revenge for some transgression, real or imagined. That's what it almost always is."

I shake my head, but he's gone stubborn. I don't blame him. Ninety-nine times out of a hundred, he'd be right. He's only got my word that this time is the exception, and in the end it's never enough.

Shannon
Tuesday, May 11th

The graveyard is even louder at night, perhaps because the traffic from the road above isn't there to drown out the mourner's echoes. Mothers, themselves long-dead, keening over the graves of their children. There is no unity beyond the grave. I once saw two spirits searching for each other in the same room, each in a separate time, parallel, but eternally a hair's breadth apart.

It's true your loved ones wait for you on the other side. And they always will.

The river runs lower, now, without a fresh rainfall to feed it. I step down the bank and out onto a mudflat, and I find a smooth, round stone. *This one would go down easy.*

I find Rebecca Burgess's grave in the dark by following the sound of Helen's weak, last shout.

I place my business card, *Shannon Dale, Psychic Detective*, at the base of the headstone and cover it with the river rock. It has my address on it.

If this man is hunting witches, it's time to bait the trap.

The End of Caroline
Friday, May 14th

I told them. I warned them. I didn't see this coming, not exactly, but I saw something. And I see them, now—both of them, Doris and Helen, their mouths full of stones. And I see him. Not his face, but his hands, and he's bleeding from two large wounds in his palms as he reaches for me. He's coming.

Doris and Helen—they had to ply their trade, turn their cards, turn their visions for profit. It took them down, and they've taken me down with them, even though I've kept quiet. Laid low. I've been caught in their fallout. I blame them, but they were innocent. Our visions shouldn't be dangerous, but they are. The man with the bleeding hands knows it.

My house smells like casserole and lilies. There are fresh lilies to hide the wilted ones. Fresh casseroles stacked atop dry ones. I have two new dark dresses, each that I could never bear to wear again. I won't need to. Instead, I choose the yellow one. It complements the blue I chose for Doris and the white I picked for Helen. The three of us will look ready for a garden party, if we can ever find each other again.

I lay out the dress and my pearls and I add my diamond, because there's no one to leave it to, now. My heart twists. My Helen, my baby girl. I will find her. I leave a small note, "Lay me to rest in this," and I put on my white nightgown.

I don't know how one is supposed to dress for one's own murder, but a white nightgown seems like a good fit. I unlock the door. There's no need to break in—best to leave it all undamaged. Enough damage is done already. I lay down on the couch, pull Doris's old granny square blanket over my bare legs and wait for the sound of his toes in the grass.

Shannon
Sunday, May 16th

Kurella takes the death of the third Barths woman, who was not a practicing psychic, as proof that the crimes are family business and not a witch-hunting serial killer. My argument that just because she wasn't practicing doesn't mean she wasn't psychic does not get me far—it doesn't even get me to the crime scene, this time. He doesn't say it, but he doesn't have to—I know what he's thinking. I'm off the case.

This woman's body wasn't found on Rebecca's grave, but a different one. Another sinner's stone, carved with warning psalms of retribution. Kurella didn't mention my card, which means it wasn't there. He'd have said something, and I'm certain they checked the old grave, too, for any new clues.

There's no groundskeeper for that part of the cemetery. If my card is gone, that means *he* took it. He took the bait. I've already begun to prepare. I don't know how soon he'll be here.

Kurella
Monday, May 17th

All of the Barths are dead. It's tragic, but it's also a problem, because I still think this is a family affair. There are no more living relatives, by blood or marriage—the line is dead.

I want to call Shannon. I want to tell her that I'm stuck—that I'm off somehow, and there must be something I'm missing, but I already know what she'll say. It's not impossible that she's right, it's just so extremely unlikely.

The files on my desk loom, judging me as the dead have been judged.

My last hope is that the lab will come back with another lead, that something scraped from those poor women's bodies will send up a flare that leads me to the man who did this. Who is doing this.

If all the Barths are dead, does that mean it stops? Is he done?

Not if Shannon is right.

I don't think she is. Still. I'll stand guard at the cemetery, just in case.

Shannon
Tuesday, May 18*th*

A man with too many psalms in his head and too much hate in his heart wants to hunt witches? Let him come. I am ready.

The deer's bones are rough and cold against my skin. The narrow floorboards of my front room shift and bend beneath my feet as I rock from foot to foot, swaying to the tumble of my heartbeat as I radiate waves of energy across the city. They meet him and we tangle, and I feel him draw closer. I feel the cold pavement beneath his bare feet, the heavy blade against his thigh, the hot ache in the center of his hands where they bleed a trail from the cathedral to my home.

Let him come. I am ready.

The cloth across my eyes glows in the light from a hundred candles. The warm wax pillars heat the room and a trail of sweat runs down my bare backbone.

The tangled rage of his energy pushes close, a pressure against my stomach.

The wave of my light eddies around him, like he is a stone in my river.

A stone in my mouth.

And then he is at my door. The panel falls into a pile of damp sawdust, splinter and rot.

The cloth across my eyes darkens with the admittance of night, and the man, and I cannot see but I can feel the slick grain of the knife handle in his hand, the way it fits so perfectly into his wound. The air is cold where he stands.

I feed the small flames from my own fire and the room brightens, warms.

"Seek and you shall find. Knock and the door will be open to you."

I smile and feel my lips stick to the violet that coats my long teeth. "You found me."

His rage cools the room again, and I feel a few candles wink out, the light darkening against my blindfold. I push heat again and the candles reignite.

I hear the creak of the floor as he takes a step back.

"You hunt witches for your God, but never thought you'd find one? What will you do now?" I can feel him gathering himself, fighting his own energy and mine, summoning his righteous rage.

His voice is quiet for all the buzz and sting of his anger. "A man or woman who acts as a medium or fortune teller shall be put to death by stoning; they have no one but themselves to blame for their death. Leviticus 20:27."

I laugh and the candles melt by inches.

He is a shadow silhouette against my blindfold, a cold spot in the ocean of my heat. My warmth brings the scent out of the bones that cage me, out of the old wood of the walls, from the shadows beneath my breasts and arms, between my legs.

The cold man in the doorway gags. He fights his gut, and straightens, clenches his blade tighter. "I can still save you." He lifts the blade toward me. "We're going to the river. You will be baptized, and silenced."

"Come for me, then."

The antlers at my brow smoke, the air acrid with burnt bone and hair. His feet echo like thunder on the floorboards.

I feel the knife like ice slash at my chest, and I feel the ember of his brand as it draws close, a cross on a torch. I feel the metal press against my skin and melt, molten in my heat, running back down his fingers, dripping from his elbow as he shrieks.

The knife drops from his other hand and he rakes at my face, his fingers hooking my blindfold and pulling it away.

It is too much seeing. My sight and my *sight* overlapping, overwhelming.

His face and the dark shadow of his righteous rage twist together. He grabs the antler at my left brow and drags me to the floor where he retrieves the knife.

But my rage is as dark as his. And the rage of my lost sisters even more so.

The floorboards are gone, and our knees hit the hard-packed dirt of a fresh grave. We kneel, facing each other, our eyes locked, his face latticed in the shadows cast by my horns. Fabric swishes around us—blue and white and yellow—skirts swirling like the river, voices heavy with stone, singing.

The man severs our gaze and squeezes his eyes shut. His collar is torn and his face is sallow, the shadow of his rage flickering as fear overcomes him. "But the cowardly, the unbelieving, the vile, the murderers, the sexually immoral, those who practice magic arts, the idolaters and all liars—they will be consigned to the fiery lake of burning sulfur. This is the second death," he mutters and clasps his hands in front of him. The wounds in his hands are cauterized, burnt black by the heat of my body where he grabbed me.

The earth beneath my knees thaws. The light returns though the candles are far away.

The man on his knees in front of me prays, and I embrace him. I wrap him in fire. His God does not save him because his God is a child, and children do as their mothers tell them.

The man's flesh melts into the grave dirt. His bones smoke into ash and mix with the mud.

The spinning skirts of the spirits around us stir his greasy smoke into the wind.

Shannon
Thursday, May 20th

The floors of my front room are freshly waxed, and my new red door welcomes Kurella as he brings me the news that the case is closed. Some of the blood on Helen's mouth had belonged to the killer—a man named Joseph Pillar, a pastor with mommy issues. He'd been in the news before for his nut-job literal takes on scripture.

"Apparently he set himself on fire on top of one of his victim's graves. A priest found his body, or what was left of it."

I nod, waiting for what I know Kurella will say next.

"At least he can't kill again. That's the important thing."

I smile. "And the important thing is that I was right."

Kurella picks at the corner of his notebook, scattering a few motes of paper dust to my clean floors. "You were. I'm sorry. I'm just glad this nut didn't come after you."

My smile twitches a little. "The thing about witch hunters, detective, is that they don't believe in witches. They just hate women. They wouldn't know what to do with a witch if they really found one."

Kurella just stares at me and blinks.

I laugh, and a small pebble tumbles from my lips.

Death Plate Seating for 1,000

The house would never fall. That's what the seller's listing promised. But the listing of ancient beams promised otherwise, as did the eroded cliffside that weathered closer to its doorstop with every storm.

"That's just the soft rock," said the seller, an old man with a face as eroded as the cliff. "The bedrock is stronger stuff. Hasn't gone anywhere for two-hundred million years; isn't going anywhere anytime soon."

Dad believed him. Mom didn't. But she wasn't moving with us, anyway.

The house was ten times bigger than her city apartment and cost ten times less. Fixing it up would narrow the gap, but Dad didn't want to fix it *too* much.

"Just think of everyone who has ever lived here," he said, running his hand along the shaking banister where countless hands had worn away the stain and polished the wood to a natural shine. Polishing, I thought, is just another kind of erosion. Less violent than a cliff face. Or a crumbling marriage.

But the house's dark past was exactly why Dad had bought it. "Smuggler's Cove," it was called, the seaside destination for Jacobean criminals.

"Maybe we'll find their cache of treasure," Dad said.

I nodded. They had mostly smuggled priests and potatoes. Discovering a cache of four-hundred-year-old potatoes did not seem unlikely.

I got the master bedroom—a trade for losing everything else. I had my own hearth and a bathroom with a clawfoot tub, an enormous closet, and a bay window with a seat that overlooked the sea. And the cliff, which had crept so close to the foundation that I had to press my face against the glass to see any land at all. But from there, nose and brow held against the cold windowpane, I could see sideways along the edge of land. That was how I saw the stairs. They had been cut into the rock itself, steps worn low and smooth at the center, some crumbled away altogether, tracing a sloping line down the seven-hundred-foot precipice. Iron spikes for handholds protruded along the steep path, weeping rust stains down the rock face.

Our first meal in the new/old house was cheese and crackers, the cheese not cold enough because all the ice in the cooler had melted and the fridge, of course, did not work.

"Go check the fuse box in the basement. I'll tell you if anything comes on." Dad brushed cracker crumbs from his lap and stood, handing me the small flashlight from his pocket. It was uncomfortably warm.

An earlier trip to the basement revealed that the network of pipes that crisscrossed the low space created a kind of maze that was impossible for a grown man to cross. A scrawny sixteen-year-old girl like myself could squeeze through, if I waved a stick ahead of me to gather all the webs that filled the space like insulation. I made my way through the tangle of old pipes, some rattling, some warm, some coated in oily deposits.

The basement spanned the whole width of the house, irregularly shaped with an odd number of dark corners that swallowed the flashlight's glow. Only the cliffside wall ran straight.

An orange glow caught my eye. It came from the wall—a flash that disappeared when I moved my head and suddenly sparkled back into view.

As I got closer, the light grew in intensity—neon orange, then magenta. It poured through a crack in the damp stones of the basement wall—the setting sun beaming through the cracks in the old stone foundation, the only skin between our basement and the open air of the cliff face. Irregular rocks piled against the wind, moss and lichen for mortar. The stones were oddly patterned, writhing lines and sunburst sprays etched into the surface of each, and the shifting light cast the shapes into motion.

I pressed my eye to the hole and felt a breeze against my lashes. The view of the sea through the cracks seemed distant, but the percussion of the waves at the foot of the cliff below felt near enough that my toes curled as if to avoid the splash. It shook my heart free of frozen dread and I backed away from the wall, pressing against the sticky, web-covered pipes.

"Dad!" I called across the dark basement. He didn't answer. I turned and scrambled across the floor, web stick left behind, fuse box forgotten. I wanted to get out from under the house, out from the crushing weight I could feel pressing down on me, as the foundation groaned under the lash of the sea. I crawled out of the basement and didn't stop, running hard for the front door.

"Callie!" Dad called after me.

"Get out!" I shouted back over my shoulder.

He followed, more concerned for me than alarmed by my words, I was sure, but relief washed over me as soon as we were both clear of the porch.

I stumbled to a stop in the weeds of the overgrown lawn.

"Callie, what's wrong?" Dad grabbed my shoulder, pulling me to face him. I gasped to catch my breath, wiped web and dust from my face, the grit of the basement floor rough on my fingers.

"That house is coming down," I said. "Any second. The basement wall isn't even there anymore. It's open to the air."

"Callie, the house isn't going anywhere. I'm sure it needs patches, yes, but it's not at risk of coming down. I did have that checked, you know."

"I promise you, the foundation is broken. It's not stable. None of this is safe."

Dad let go of my shoulder, his hand dropping limply to his side. I thought for a moment that he was finally listening. "Did your mother put this idea in your head?"

My breath left again in a rush. "No! I saw it myself—the wall has crumbled away and there are holes in the stone big enough to look through."

The sun had set further, dipping into the waves, and the house's shadow fell across us.

"I'll take a look at it myself," Dad said.

"I don't even think you should go in there. You can't fit through the basement, anyway."

"Then will you come and show me? Here," he held out his cell phone. "Take a picture of the wall. Show me what's got you so upset."

DEATH PLATE SEATING FOR 1,000

My knees felt weak at the idea of going back under the house, back to the broken wall.

"It's going to be fine, Callie. I promise."

I took the phone from him and gripped it tight.

The basement was darker without the orange glow of sunset. It would be hard to even see the cracks in the dark. Would they show up in the picture?

"Flip the fuse while you're down there, please." Dad's voice chased me through the dark maze of pipes.

I made it to the wall, hands shaking. I could still feel the crash of the waves below, and the soft fall of old stone turned to sand. I set the flash on the camera and snapped a few shots, inspecting the photos after. The holes were just black spots on the grainy wall, their nothingness appearing as solid black—solid, though they were anything but.

I switched the camera over to video and filmed my own hand receding into one of the spaces. I pressed a finger against a small stone and filmed it falling away into the dark, the hole it left behind now wide enough to reach through.

A shaky sob caught in my throat as I pulled my trembling hand back through.

"See?" I whispered to the camera, as if it alone might believe me. "There's nothing here."

I stood another moment, listening to the wind pass through the holey wall. What if Dad didn't believe me? Would anyone? I switched off the camera and emailed myself the video, just in case.

I made my way to the fuse box, my path lit by the phone's flash, and pried open the rusty door. The inside was all web and corrosion. There were no visible labels and no switches, just old glass plug fuses that looked like they might crumble if I touched them. Just like the wall. I snapped a picture of them, too.

I turned and made my way back, trying not to panic, trying not to rush. Dad was waiting at the basement door.

"None of those fuses do anything," I said, and handed him his phone. I moved toward the front door.

"Where are you going?"

I turned back to him. "We can't stay here. Look at the pictures, the video. No one should stay here."

He thumbed his screen to life and swiped through the photos. The static rush of the wind filled the house as he played the video. I heard my own frantic voice: *"See? There's nothing here."* I heard the wind howl through the open spaces like a rough voice, *"I'm here."*

Dad's head snapped up to look at me. My heart stuttered.

"Is this a joke?" Dad asked.

"I didn't say that! I didn't even hear it!"

He shook his head. I reached for the phone, but he slipped it into his pocket.

"I'll ask the contractor about the wall. But I'm done talking about it tonight. Now, get inside." He turned away and walked deeper into the house.

I stood in the doorway, half in and half out. *I'm here.* Just the wind.

The wind blew through the cracks in my bedroom window as it had in the basement, eroding the face of the house as the waves eroded the cliff below. I opened my laptop on the dusty desk. There was a red sliver of battery left, despite the fact that I had left it plugged in. Whatever fuse supplied this room was as dead as the one in the kitchen. I opened my email and clicked the message from my father's phone. The computer screen dimmed to conserve power, but it seemed bright in the dark room as the video played. So many dust particles flashed across the screen, blowing every time I exhaled, that it was hard to see past them. The camera's focus slipped in and out as my hand disappeared into darkness, reappeared pale and shaking.

See? There's nothing here.

I'm here.

Wind buffeted my window so hard that the curtains swayed in the draft. The computer screen went black, the red glow of the power light fading, then winking out.

I switched on the camping lantern on the dresser and eyed the corners of the room, every shadow unfamiliar and stark. The draft's subtle movements made the LED seem like flickering candlelight. I carried the lantern into my closet, changed out of my clothes covered in basement filth, and put on my robe. The thick fabric had trapped the smells of home, releasing them as I pulled it close, my eyes stinging with tears that had stayed hidden until now. I crawled under the blanket, flinching as the bed groaned, and I pressed my head into the pillow, trying to block out the wind's rough voice.

I'm here.

The wind both pushed and pulled, knocking me back, then tugging at my jacket, unsure if it wanted to drive me away from the cliff or drag me over. I had to stand close to the edge to see the stairs. The top few had eroded away so that it was a drop of two feet, at least, to the next intact stair. The iron handholds were long railroad nails, jutting out, rusted to sharp points. But the stairs were broader than they had appeared from my window, carved deeper into the rock so that they didn't seem quite so treacherous as I had first thought. They cut back and forth across the cliff at a steady decline, disappearing from view below a scrub-covered outcrop.

I sat in the tall grass so I could scoot closer, hanging my feet out into the air, lowering them over the edge so that I sat with my feet on the first solid stair. I looked back to the house.

Dad had begun to demolish the kitchen, fuses be damned, tearing into the old cabinets and plaster walls—a force of erosion himself at high-speed, wearing it all away from the inside out. My gut fluttered. One heavy drop of his hammer and the whole house might come down.

Would it come flying past me on the stairs? Would we wave to each other in midair?

I pressed away from the reeds and stood. The stair felt solid beneath me, more so than the house did. Perhaps the wind would pluck me off the cliff face and I would disappear, tossed to the sea.

I wrapped a cold hand around the first iron spike and took a step. The open air to my right felt like a gnawing threat and I pressed myself close to the rock face. Here, too, it was patterned like the stones of the foundation. I traced the shapes with my eyes as I walked down, clinging to the vining impressions of some long-lost life in stone. The turn when the stairs switched back was almost enough to send me scrambling back up the cliff face, but I spun, faced the wind and the sea. At the next switch I was low enough that the spray of a wave hit my face.

And then I came to the scrubbed outcrop, the protrusion of stone to which desperate, stunted trees clung and somehow lived. Their branches were stripped by wind, beaten by the constant force, and where they crooked, sea birds had built nests. They all stood empty, now. I hadn't seen or heard any birds since we'd arrived. That seaside sound had been absent. It would have felt more like a holiday with reeling gulls.

I edged below the outcrop, gripping the iron spikes as the stairs stopped in the shelter below the overhang, the tree's roots forming a curtain along its edge. I took a deep breath and looked down. Only waves and foam below, reaching up for me, and where the rock wall had been, gaping between the hanging tree roots, an opening. A cave.

I turned myself toward that darkness and stepped inside. The wind was instantly silenced. My ears rang in its absence, their numbness fading to a sting in the cold stillness.

The cave was not natural. It had been carved out of the cliff face; the scars of old tools marred its surface. Fragments of broken crates and glass lay scattered across the entrance. It tunneled far into the darkness, an unknown depth. As far back as the light hit the walls, I could see the now-familiar markings, depressed shapes crossing the stone surface, and here, away from the wind and waves, they were bolder. The crisp outlines of fish, and twisted plants, and curling, thick tentacles. Some even looked like bones—an eye socket, a joint. And wings. So many birds. They grew larger and clearer the deeper into the cave I walked. I wished I'd brought my lantern.

I pressed my hand against the stone, tracing the curve of a feather. Stone crunched under my toes. I bent down and ran my hands over the cave floor and picked up a slab of stone as broad as my palm. A fossil. I traced the surface along a stem or twisting spine. I tucked it into the pocket of my jacket, intending to come back with the lantern, maybe with Dad, to show him this strange wonder. The smugglers had only left garbage, but the real treasure had always been here.

I hesitated at the mouth of the cave. The stone felt so strong, secure. Safe compared to the flimsy house, safe out of the whispering wind.

Climbing up the stairs was harder than descending had been, and by the time I reached the dry grass of the cliffside meadow, my legs trembled both from exhaustion and strain. I wrapped my fingers around the fossil in my pocket and made my way back to the house.

The seller's blue truck stood parked in front. He crouched on the porch, peering through a front window.

"Hello," I called out. He started and turned to me.

"Oh, there you are. How you settling in?"

I frowned. Politeness and honesty warred in my mouth. I shrugged, not trusting myself to speak.

He laughed. "I'm sure it's not much of a fun project for a young woman like you."

I didn't like his smile. His comment decided the outcome of the war on my tongue. "You really shouldn't sell people houses that aren't safe."

He shoved his hands into his pockets and I pulled my hands out of mine, the stone gripped tight under white knuckles.

"Now, don't worry hun. Like I said before, nothing ever leaves these cliffs. What's here has always been here."

I'm here.

His eyes lowered to my hands. "See there for yourself." He pointed to the rock in my hand. "Two-hundred million years and it's still here, intact, undisturbed—until you picked it up." He raised his eyebrows.

DEATH PLATE SEATING FOR 1,000

I lifted the fossil and looked at it again. Outside of the shadow of the cave I could see it was speckled with hundreds of small fossils—a matrix of stone shapes.

"It's called a death plate. Stone that once was seabed. Everything that died settled on the seabed, layered over, fossils on fossils, all the way through."

I turned the rock over. All sides were covered in shapes, in death.

"Nothing ever leaves this cliff. Even in death." His lurid smile had fallen away, but his slack intensity was even worse. A strange light shone in his eyes, like the light shining through the cracks of the foundation. "The house is part of the cliff. It always will be."

I wanted to throw the rock, to hit him in the face and make those strange lights go out. I resisted. I wanted to show the rock to Dad more.

As if he heard my thoughts, the man smiled again. "When your dad gets back, have him give me a call. He said he had a question about fuses."

I nodded and backed further into the weeds as the man passed me on his way to his truck. I watched the truck disappear across the field before I turned my back to it and headed inside.

"Dad," I called. There was no answer.

When your dad gets back, the man had said. Had he gone somewhere? Perhaps he'd gone in search of tools, hopefully for some food. I rubbed a spot clear on the dining room window and peered through. The tail of the car poked out of the shed. He hadn't gone anywhere, unless he'd walked. It was twenty miles to town.

"Dad!" I called again. Silence, not even wind. Anxiety gnawed at me. What if he was hurt? I raced into the kitchen, empty, up the stairs to his room, the bathroom, all empty. Might he have tried to get in the basement? Cold sweat sprung up on my face as I raced back down the main stairs to the basement door.

161

"Dad?" My feet felt heavy on the steps, this enclosed stairwell somehow more terrifying than those on the cliff face. The basement was dark save for the swords of sunlight cutting through the walls, crisscrossing the maze of pipes and web. My eyes followed the sunbeams, tracing their paths over the stones of the foundation to a place where one disappeared into shadow. In the dark of a corner, a shaft of sunlight was swallowed. I climbed over pipes and under wires to that corner, to the mouth of a tunnel in the rock. Another room? Another level of basement? The smuggler's storage?

I breathed into the space and the sound echoed back, hollow.

"Dad?" It echoed.

I'm here, the wind whistled through the stones. It froze the cold sweat on my lip, my brow. Was this a part of the cave? The end of the cliffside tunnel?

I'm here, louder this time, less wind and more voice. Was he lost, trapped? How stable was the rock of the tunnel?

My heart raced. "Stay there, I'm coming!" I shouted into the echoing darkness and the stone shouted back.

I stepped into the narrow space, remembered the darkness at the back of the cave, the way the stone shapes seemed to move, and I pulled my foot back. I turned instead and raced for the stairs, up through the house and up again to my room, my legs straining, my lungs aching for air, choked on the dust and damp of the house. I grabbed my lantern and swung back toward the stairs, thundering down over the wooden treads that screamed in protest, my footfalls enough to bring the whole house down. With Dad beneath it. I slowed my pace, tried to step softly, but still swiftly, willing myself to fly.

The basement felt darker, the sun, having arced high, no longer shot its beams through the wall; instead light fell in weak streams to

DEATH PLATE SEATING FOR 1,000

the floor. I clicked on the lantern. It glowed dimly, exhausted from a long night of keeping the shadows of this house at bay.

I made my way into the tunnel. The stone walls were narrow here, more roughly cut, as if fresh, and the patterned facets of stone felt like eyes tracing my progress into the heart of the cliff.

"Dad! I'm here!" I followed the tunnel farther back, the weak light of the lantern reaching only as far as my own outstretched hand. Grit on the floor of the tunnel rolled roughly underfoot. Stones scattered against my toes as I pushed ahead. Still, I felt wind on my face, like the whisper of a stranger standing too close.

I do not know how far I had gone before the rock ceiling grazed the crown of my head, stone scraping and tumbling away from my shoulders as the passage shrunk around me. The walls seemed to constrict and relax with the rhythm of my breath, as if I were an obstruction in some stone creature's throat.

As the light grew dimmer, the patterns in the rock grew larger, teeth as big as my palm, eye sockets that could have swallowed my arm. Plant fronds like sails, tentacles like grasping ropes. I tried to shrink myself to fit the space, to peel away from ancient stone faces.

"Dad," I whispered.

I'm here.

The stone breathed against me. I knew, then, that he would not have come here. Would not have gone this far into the dark, into the close, heavy stone inside the ancient cliff.

The space was too tight for me to turn around, my shoulders wedged as I tried, abraded by ancient corals, stuck fast against calcite bones.

I wrenched myself loose and stepped backward, toe to heel, eyes stuck on the dark beyond the lantern's reach. I slipped on a loose stone under my heel, feet sliding out from under me, and instinctively I

163

grabbed for the walls, hands raking across the stone surface, palms tearing on sharp rock. The lantern fell, blinking, and rolled away down the slope, farther into the tunnel.

I sat, panting through the sting in my hands, watching the light recede. My own breath became the wind in the tunnel, swirling off the walls and back at me. The orb of light grew smaller as it rolled away, disappearing to a pinprick then winking out.

The dark pressed in like a thick blanket against my skin. I gripped the walls and tried to pull myself to stand, and my fingers slipped in the wetness of my own blood. I struggled to my feet, pulled my arms in close, and held my hands protectively under my chin. A shaking sob escaped my chest, echoing off the stone.

"Callie?" a voice came from down the tunnel.

My voice caught in the pain that choked my throat. "I'm here," I struggled to whisper.

A spot of light appeared far down the tunnel. I squeezed my eyes shut, convinced it was an illusion, firing neurons or a specter born of pain. When I opened my eyes, the light had grown. A soft crunch of stone approached.

"Dad!?"

"I'm here!"

I moved forward toward the light as it advanced. I pressed past the tightness of the stone, beyond the hollow eyes that once again grew visible as the light approached. I stooped, crouched, then crawled as the tunnel tightened, so low my head scraped the ceiling, my shoulders pressed between its walls. I folded myself into the tight throat and knelt in the crumble of loose rock that littered the ground, all death plates patterned with a thousand lost lives.

The lantern rolled to a stop in the dust against my knees. It flickered. Its glow did not reach even as far as my breath as another sob escaped me. Faces peered out of the stone. The curve of a brow, grinning rows of teeth, the shape of human hands gripping at my hips and shoulders. My father's face, wrought in stone, poised as if to kiss my bleeding forehead.

"Dad?"

The stone around me groaned.

I screamed, the sound tearing through me like a knife as the rock walls screamed back at me in violent echoes.

I writhed backward, setting the lantern rolling away again, its light disappearing almost instantly, the faces winking out in darkness. I pushed against the stone with my torn hands, leaving pieces of myself behind, another fine layer in the cliffside, another death on its plate.

The flesh of my arms became the mortar between the ribs of trilobites, the skin of my knees cement to build a stronger foundation. As the tunnel constricted around me, the howling breath of wind narrowing to a whistle that piped through my ears like a million screams, I stopped pushing and lay in my stone bed.

And I knew then that I would be here forever, one among thousands, holding the cliff in place. Holding the house up.

The house will never fall. Because I'm here.

Inn of the Fates

New York is far behind me. I step through trees as straight and pale as marble columns, and for the first time, I stop to breathe. The Lieutenant has not followed, not this far. He has not come after his coat, which I pull close across my chest, nor his cap, which hides the fullness of my hair, nor the document pressed against my skin, beneath my stays. I lost my pursuers on Wooster Street, near Washington Square. Before me is a ribbon of road leading into Avonshire.

My feet should hurt after a night of running, but they don't, and I set my feet, in the officer's heavy boots, onto the pebbled path that starts at the edge of the woods. The meadow that slopes into the Avonshire valley is studded with white birds—swans strutting in the dawn, and large grey geese roosting in grassy nests. White sparrows circle above, their bright feathers catching the secret, high rays of light that have not yet arced to earth.

As I make my way toward the leaning structures of Avonshire, I see that the grey geese are not birds but stones, graves settled into the meadow. They dot the grass at intervals, growing thicker as I near the town, till what I took for a slate-paved plaza reveals itself to be a thicket of headstones each leaning into the next. The white sparrows settle on them and watch me pass.

The stones crowd right up to the bronze gate, which gapes open as if left by a forgetful hand or nudged by a gust of wind. The gate is unguarded by anyone save for a white cat that yowls as I press my fingertips against the panel and push, the hinges yowling in return. Sunlight flashes through the tarnish as I push the gate open and step into Avonshire.

The cat runs ahead through the empty street, and I follow. Buildings crowd the lane, leaning across the gap of road, sagging into a low canopy. It is much darker beneath them than it was in the meadow and I pull the Lieutenant's coat closer and bury my hands in the pockets. My fingers flinch away from the folded knife there. They clutch, instead, at the silver case full of coins. My stomach yowls like the cat, and the gate, and I train my eyes along the eaves of the buildings, searching for any sign of an inn.

The white cat scratches at a door below a placard with three dancing maidens on a field of green. "Auberge des Destins" is painted in fading silver.

I pull my hand from the pocket and squeeze the door latch. It's unlocked and lets me in to a warm hall. A fresh fire crackles in the hearth, a kettle suspended over it on a metal hook. The scents of bread and tea fold into me. I push the door shut and wait for my eyes to adjust to the gathered shadows.

"Can I help you?" A woman's voice, low and angry, booms from behind a short counter in the corner. Her words are strangely formed, the sounds bent, like music.

I spin to face her. Her brows are thick, black, and lowered over dark eyes. Her jaw is set in rigid confrontation. She takes me in, from the lumpy cap, to the oversized, decorated coat and the muddy boots. Her brow relaxes, only slightly. "Can I help you, Lieutenant?" she asks again, this time without the rage, but with the vowels held too long. *She knows.*

"Are you serving breakfast?" I ask in the lowest timbre I can manage. I wonder how long it will be before word reaches Avonshire of the naked lieutenant found in an alley. Of his missing clothes, and the stolen plans—orders meant for the *Sea Fox.*

"For those with coin." The woman pulls a towel from her apron pocket and stuffs it into a horn cup.

I dig in the pocket, past the knife, to the coin case. I fumble with its latch, but finally pull a silver dollar from its sleeve and place it on the counter. I retreat quickly, but she is squinting through the dark, examining me, the corner of her mouth rising.

"Are you traveling alone?" she asks.

"Yes."

She nods. "Most do who come here. I have bread and butter, eggs and cheese, tea and coffee."

"Yes, please. All of that." I turn away and hurry to the back corner of the room, farthest from the fire, though its heat tempts me. I can't risk the light.

The woman cranes her neck and shouts down a hall behind the counter, "Phillipe! Pierre! Bring a full tray at once for the Lieutenant!"

Two boys, with identical dark eyes wide with curiosity and skin as dark and glowing as the polished wood of the Lieutenant's pistol grip, appear behind the counter, arms laden with food that they tumble onto the tray the woman holds for them.

"Now go and dress the sow for supper," she says, waving them back toward the hallway. They vanish, after taking another pointed look through the room toward me.

The woman sets the tray before me. Steam rises from the fresh cut in the bread and wisps around the tea and coffee. I reach for the cup first, warming my hands on its sides.

To my horror, the woman sits. I struggle to control my features, to disguise my alarm and desire to shrink away.

"My name is Maria," she says.

I nod and bring the cup to my face, hoping to bury my identity in its fog.

"And you are?" she asks.

I drink, to buy myself time to think. The coffee scalds my tongue, but I draw it slowly, letting it burn its way down my throat.

"Lieutenant Jones, of the *Sea Fox*. Hudson Pier." It is almost truth. Though I do not know the name of the man I lured away from his squadron, into the shadows between the white granite barracks.

"You know, Lieutenant Jones, most service men remove their caps in my presence." Her smile grows. Her teeth are not so white as New York women's, nor as straight. They twist, like her vowels.

She stares at me, and I stare back. Is there any point to continuing my charade when she clearly has seen through it already?

I reach up and pull the ill-fitted cap from my head. My hair falls, all snarled curls matted with sweat from my run through the back streets to Washington Square.

Small gasps sound from behind the bar.

The woman and I both turn to see the two boys duck quickly from sight.

"Phillipe! Pierre! Faire du travail!" Maria shouts.

They vanish again and she turns back to me. "My sons," she says.

"Twins?" I ask.

INN OF THE FATES

"Yes." Her smile broadens.

"I hardly hear of women surviving the birth of twins."

"No," her smile saddens. "We don't."

I fill my mouth with egg, hiding behind the curtain of my hair.

"If I had thought you were really a lieutenant, I would have thrown you out," she says. "You don't have to hide from me. You are hiding *with* me."

I raise my eyes to her face and search it for reasons to trust her.

"You don't have to tell me how you came by that coat, or what you did that made you run here, of all places."

"They didn't follow me here. I checked."

Maria laughs, a deep sound that warms me as much as the coffee does. "No. No, they would not have followed where you've come."

She watches me as I tear into the warm bread. Butter runs down my chin, and I wipe it away with the satin brocade on the coat sleeve.

"What is your name, truly, child?"

"Why must you know?" I ask between mouthfuls. My burnt tongue hardly tastes the food.

"For your stone, my dear." Her smile is gone, the lines of her mouth set deep with concern, instead.

The bread, eggs, and coffee are gone, and now I have nothing to hide behind but the tea. It has cooled too much and clings to the burnt skin inside my mouth as I force it down. "I do not have a stone, nor do I need one."

"They say all who come here carry their stone with them. If you're here, a stone stands for you on the hillside."

I set my empty cup on the tray and brush my hair out of my eyes.

Maria takes the tray and stands. "You look tired. There is a room upstairs where you can rest. Come down when you're ready and we'll talk more."

I shake myself from the fog of sleep brought on by the warm bread. "Do you know where I can find the Marquis of Avonshire?"

Maria nearly drops the tray, and the horn cup goes tumbling, rattling to the floor and rolling to the hearth where it taps the grey stones piled there.

I stand and go to retrieve it for her, and she tightens her grip on the tray.

"Why are you looking for him, child?"

"I have something for him. I'm sorry, I must take it directly to him. I cannot show you, despite your kindness. For which I thank you."

I hand her the cup and she takes it with a wavering hand. "He isn't here. Not anymore."

My heart falters. "Where has he gone? I must find him. Soon. It is a matter of great importance. If I don't deliver this—"

She holds up a hand to silence me before I reveal too much. "He left, long ago. He is the only one to ever depart Avonshire. He said he was going to New York. If he is not there, then I can only assume his departure did not succeed. Perhaps his stone stands lost in the woods."

We both stand distraught, each of us clutching the tray to keep the other from shaking it.

"Maria, how do I get back to New York?"

She sets the tray back on the table and places her hands on the sides of my face, as I had long imagined a mother doing, her fingers pressing through the tangle of my hair. "My child, the gate only opens one way. You are here, now. The worries of the world are behind you. Go upstairs and rest. When you wake, we will find your stone." She kisses my forehead, and it sends a shock to my heart, this compassion, this rare expression. To be cared for. I feel my mission falter.

I pull away from her. "The bronze gate?"

"Yes, child, that one."

"I did not close it behind me. I left it how I found it. Open."

The daytime streets of Avonshire are no less quiet than the dawn streets. Nothing stirs save the angry white cat who dogs my heels and runs ahead, hiding in side alleys only to dart out and nip at my ankles as I pass. But the gutters run with fresh offal, and I hear the splashes falling from windows even if the residents remain hidden. Shutters creak in front of invisible faces. An imperfect silence. Watching me. I pass through town to the bronze gate where I entered.

The white cat sits high upon it, in defiance of gravity, glaring down at me as I approach. It is still open, as I left it.

As I reach the tarnished bronze, Maria steps out from behind the broad panel. She grasps my arm.

"Do you see the white stone, there—high on the hill by the tree line?"

I do.

"That one is yours." She moves her grip from my arm to my shoulder and pulls me close. "Adelyn. That is your name. It's beautiful."

My face heats, eyes sting as I lean into her embrace.

"Come. There is more bread, and honey. The room upstairs is yours for as long as you desire it."

My mouth waters, but the dead skin of my tongue feels alien to me, the taste of bread no different than sand.

"Maria, if I don't deliver my message, many will die."

"Many have died. Many will. The meadows of Avonshire welcome them all, as we have welcomed you."

I twist to look into her eyes, and she releases her grip to return my gaze, and as I feel her fingers relax, I pull away and run.

I feel her tear at my curls as I dart through the gates. The cat's claws rip at my back as the officer's long boots pound past the tall grey teeth of stones crowding the mouth of Avonshire. The ribbons of the Lieutenant's coat trail behind me as I race toward the woods.

The croon of white swans marks my passing through the meadow, white sparrows circling my progress, till I pass the white stone bearing my name. Under a noon sun, it casts no shadow. It is straight and clean, like the teeth of New York. Like the birch forest beyond it—trees tall and straight as ionic columns.

I do not stop to pay reverence to an empty stone. I keep running, into the woods and beyond, my curls in chaos, my stolen coat in ribbons, my stolen boots hammering a trail that runs in a single current like a river, back toward Avonshire. I run upstream, the paper against my chest soaks up my effort, absorbing my desperation.

Cannon fire and bugles and dimming light. The crass call of an amorous peacock. The scent of horses and flowers and industry. New York. I peel my eyes open and they are met with thorns and white roses—a canopy of florals against a white marble wall. My body is numb with cold and I am missing one boot, my stolen coat in rags beneath me. I struggle to rise, my limbs a riot of pinpricks as movement wakes them.

I shrug out of the broken coat, peel the orphaned boot from my foot. I pillage the coat pockets and slip the knife into my stays, the coins into my stockings. The ice of the air, the cold against my simple shift feels natural to me. I push through the thorns that hold me to the wall and tear my way into the open lawns of Washington Park. I stand in the shadow of the death house.

Here a painless death awaits him who can no longer bear the sorrows of this life. If death is welcome, let him seek it here.

The columns around the bronze door stand as straight and tall as a forest of birch.

My own blood burns me as tea scalds a tongue, but I force myself to walk. I smell the air and follow the scent of the river. The papers against my skin itch with dried salt, their edges grown stiff as razors against my ribs.

It is dangerous to carry these papers through the city.

Are they still looking for me? How long has it been since I passed through the bronze gate?

I make my way through the streets till I hear the lapping of water against the stones of the riverbank. The river spans before me in the fading light, shadows lengthening across its vast expanse, the ghosts of submarines casting stillness on the surface.

I run my hand over the front of my dress, the fabric grown delicate with abuse, the paper beneath it falling into lint. The paper may be lost, but the message stays with me. I will memorize it and then destroy it. The paper may never reach the Marquis, but the message may yet, through me. It will never reach the *Sea Fox*. I will drown it. *They will send another.* But not today. I unfold the papers, stiffened with my sweat as if they had been borne by seawater. The excretions of my body have carried the ink away. My stomach runs sepia with the ghost of the ink laid down by the pen of the commander, would-be-destroyer. All that remains is an inkblot of my efforts, a shapeless sign where the ink gathered round the creases of my body. A sigil, hooked and curved, alarming yet familiar, as if I had seen it once in bronze. A sign, in the yellow of washed-out iron gall.

I hold the paper before me, rising moonlight carrying the sigil to my eyes, through me, searing it upon my soul.

A voice shakes me from my study, punctuated by the tap of a cane against the planks of the boardwalk.

"So, you're the one who bears the message," the man says, lifting his chin, showing his face to the moonlight.

I crush the paper in my hands and toss it into the river. The current carries it like a small boat, and we both watch it navigate its channel to the sea.

"They're looking for you, you know," he says.

"I know."

"*Most Wanted*, they say."

I swallow. The dead skin of my mouth makes it feel like someone else's, forced into my face. I choke.

"Quite a reputation for a young lady such as yourself." The man taps his cane again. He wears a tarnished crown low around his brow, brass like the doors to the forest, to Avonshire. He turns to me and smiles. "I know someone who can help you with that."

"The only person who can help me now is the Marquis of Avonshire."

"How fortunate," he says. "They happen to share an accommodation." He hooks my arm over his and leads me away from the water. "My god, you are as cold as ice, child."

"You know where I can find the Marquis?"

"My dear, he is an old friend. And I believe he has been waiting for you."

"Are you from Avonshire?"

"We all are, my dear, and to Avonshire we will return."

"Yes. Yes, I would like to go back, once my message is delivered."

"You shall, my dear. You shall. I will see to it myself.

The knife sits hard against my breastbone, slick with purpose. I shall see my mission through. And I will return to Avonshire. Bread and honey and a white stone await.

Trouble with Fate

Ill-wishing always leaves me fuzzy-brained. Like I'm trying to think through pudding. I like to think I'd've seen trouble coming, elsewise—but there are no portents to be seen in the glow of a washcloth draped over one's own face.

I've been told the headache is my punishment—a part of it. Small part, really. That there's more to come. But that's from folks who may not understand just what heaps of adrenaline and intense focus can do. I may have earned this pain, but not for moral reasons. I'd argue that's arbitrary.

But just the same, punishment or not, Trouble found me.

Trouble had a voice like gravel slung in a silk hanky.

"Maybelle wants to see you." He smiled his troublesome smile.

"Of course she does. How long did it take you to find me this time?"

"Eight years."

It had been a good eight years. No Trouble. Far from my sisters.

"You're getting better." I pulled the cloth from my face and sat up, the pain in my head beating fresh as I shifted.

"You're getting sloppy."

It was the ill-wish. I was sure. You don't send something like that out into the universe without leaving a trail. I'd sent up a cosmic flair for Trouble to follow.

"Yeah, sure. Where are we going this time?" She's always sending Trouble for me. And Trouble always finds me, sooner or later.

"Edinburgh."

"Ugh. And when?"

"1512."

"Jesus."

He held out his hand for me. His nails looked like wasp wings left on the windowsill too long.

I grabbed my bag—mostly for the hand sanitizer (Trouble's hands are in everything), and took his hand. We took two steps back, and I turned around to see Maybelle standing in front of a polished silver dish, a servant behind her brushing her black hair all the way to her heels. She was naked except for a rope of beads that crisscrossed her body, tangling in her flowing hair. Her skin was tiger striped with soft scarring; her stomach draped in loose crepe ripples across her front.

"Adrenaline. Sister, it's good to see you," she said.

My name sounds prettier the way we say it. But it's appropriate enough, the way it's used nowadays.

"Why must we always meet where there are no engines?" The room smelled of hot lard candles and wood smoke. Slow burns.

"Because you'd drive off." She waved her hand and the servant backed out of the room. Trouble settled himself in a corner. He's never far from Maybelle. "Adrenaline, come back to us. We have work to do—Father's work—and we need our third to get it done."

"I'm not interested in Father's work."

"That doesn't matter. He left it to us." The beads chimed as she spun to me. Her eyes were as black as her hair, no sclera—just pits of night in her face. She could drive a mortal off a cliff with a look. Had done. She could make a fortune in my line of work, but she preferred prophecy. Or, writing books that few would read and fewer understand, and fewer still believe. She insisted that it was not a waste of time—that humans would see, in the end.

Yeah, the end. As in, too late. She might not even have time for an "I told you so."

"It's your unfinished work, now."

"So? I have unfinished work back home, too. Unfinished work everywhere. I like to stay busy."

Trouble nodded his agreement from the corner.

"You don't want to die with unfinished work on your conscience."

Somehow I knew she was looking deep into me. As if the blackness of her eyes was making itself at home in my heart.

"Die?" It was the strangest thing she'd ever said. "We don't die."

She turned to Trouble. "Perhaps you'd like to explain this one."

He leapt from the corner stool, ever eager, and sauntered over, began gathering Maybelle's hair into a plait. Most would have lost their arms for touching her, but Trouble always could get away with more.

"You can. You might. All of you. She's seen it."

Mention of her gift usually brought a smile to Maybelle's lips, but instead they seemed paler.

"And what should be the cause of our downfall? What power is there to snuff the three weird sisters? Who besides Father ever commanded such destruction?"

She held out her bare ivory hands, fingers overlong and beckoning for mine.

I rubbed the engine grease from my palms onto my jeans and took her hands.

"Sister. Daughter. You do."

AllysaAndrina's tongue had grown so dry in her papery mouth that we had to push the bone paste down her throat with our own fingers.

"We need you, sister," Maybelle said. She cleaned her fingers with her hair.

I reached into the crisp pit of Ally's nose and grasped a silver hair, jerked it free.

The ropes that suspended her over her pedestal snapped and her narrow, knotted fingers circled my throat.

"Oh good, you're awake," I choked through her bone grip.

"I was busy." She breathed dust across my face and I felt it settle on my eyes, against my teeth.

Maybelle's pale fingers caressed her grip and the dark stars dispersed from my vision.

"Allysa, there has been a prophecy."

"I know."

"About Adrenaline."

"About us all."

"You've seen it?" Maybelle's brow drew down. She did not like to share her gift.

Allysa turned her empty eyes toward Maybelle and grasped her hair. She brought the plaited tresses to her mouth and licked the bone paste residue, her tongue like a long-dead mouse.

"I wrote it," she said. "Of course, then, it was about me. But now

I am this." She turned to me again. I flinched as she raised her hands, but this time it was my breasts she grabbed. "I remember these, oh yes. Now these are yours, and so is the prophecy."

"What do we do? We must stop it?" Maybelle's face had flushed and it occurred to me—for the first time in millennia—that she did in fact care for me. That I was hers, once. That she probably still thought so. And I felt, for a moment, the first stirring of worry for myself—her worry. And I felt safer, knowing this harridan fought on my side.

"You don't need me sisters, daughters. Not yet. Not anymore. I'll be there at my time. At the end." As she spoke, she slid effortlessly back onto her pedestal. She dragged strands of Maybelle's hair with her and used them to affix herself in place.

"Surely we can change this course. We are fate! We decide all paths." Maybelle grasped at AllysaAndrina's rags.

"And we did. I did. This is the path I set long ago. Now follow it, sister-daughters, and I will meet you at the end."

Some absent light left her eyes and she returned to her rest—or to her work—whichever task diverted her ancient mind.

Maybelle paced, Trouble at her heels, matching her step-for-step over the uneven stones of the floor.

"I need to see more. I need more detail about what's coming so we can try to stop it."

"It doesn't sound like we can stop it." I was experiencing the unique relief of powerlessness—of letting go and floating with the current, whether it carried me to a calm lagoon or over the edge. I suppose there's always an edge, eventually, beyond the lagoon.

"Trouble, bring me a mirror, some ice—a pound of it—and some hemlock tea."

Trouble's smile unnerved me. "I'll make your tea," I said. "I don't think you want Trouble brewing your toxic tea."

I suppose, of all the advances in building and architecture, the kitchen is the least changed over time. And the kettle unchanged at all. I brewed the tea to a concentration just shy of deadly and scowled at a cup of water till it froze. Slower than a man's heart.

Maybelle assembled her kit and began sipping her tea. "Now leave me. I need quiet for this."

I left the old stone house and set off on a path across the field. The sky of the past always felt more open than my own sky—as if the airplanes and satellites weighed down my shoulders, somehow. As if the sky here was aware of its wilderness.

I picked my way over broad rocks speckled with small yellow flowers and around bristled shrubs. Trouble followed.

A cluster of thorn trees had colonized a hollow in the stony landscape. They grew up and over an ancient stone circle that had fallen out of alignment. Its broken barrier rang like a bell in my ears, but I climbed atop one anyway and sat, staring into the shadows beneath the wind-stunted trees.

Trouble was still somewhere close, but our paths had diverged. Doubtless he was off laming a horse or setting a rockslide.

The trees at the center of the broken circle stirred and two hands emerged. "I'm sorry," a voice followed. A tattered head followed the voice. The nest of hair was as brambled as the thorn trees and the lichen-colored eyes were barely visible through the mess.

"You're sorry?"

The man still held his hands aloft. "I didn't want to scare you," he said.

"I'm not scared of you."

"Oh." He lowered his hands and began climbing out of the thorns. They plucked at the dark kilt that was all he wore. "Good." He scaled the rock that was next to mine.

He was younger than he had first appeared. What I had taken for age lines were simply streaks of mud.

"You picked a strange place to rest, thorn-hollow-man."

He nodded, his wild hair and beard accentuating the movement. "And yet, you rest here, too."

"And the noise doesn't bother you?"

"Noise?"

He couldn't hear the scream of the broken circle. Just a mortal, then. A simple madman.

"The wind, howling like it does?"

"Oh, that—no. Good as music, to me."

Definitely mad. But well-formed, I noted, his wanderings having carved him into a roughness that appealed to the ancient in me. "Have you been here long?"

He pulled at his beard, smoothing the hairs down into something more civilized. "I suppose I have." He looked down at the nest of hair in his hand. "Don't remember having this."

Not just a madman, but a cursed one. A young, chiseled Lear.

I reached into my jacket pocket and handed him a plastic comb.

"What's this, then?"

Ah. I had forgotten we'd left my time. It's impossible to tell on the moor, where change is measured geologically.

"Here. Let me help." I leaned across the space between our stones and began pulling the comb through his wild hair, removing thorns and leaves and even small rocks. Patches of lichen that had rooted to his scalp. He smelled like the stones and the small purple flowers that blanket them in spring.

"That's kind of you, miss."

It was more selfish of me. He was well enough without, but I wanted to see more of him. Find out how he came to be spell-trapped in a broken stone circle.

I pulled him down from the stone and rubbed the dirt from his skin with a fistful of dry grass, cleaned the clay from his nails with tree thorns. I cleared the sleep from his eyes with caresses. I cleared the spell from his mind with a wild romp in the bracken that shook the grouse and plover from their nests for miles.

I left him sleeping there in the circle, the spell once again taking hold, wilderness growing over him like a warm blanket.

Trouble joined me outside the circle and I realized he'd been there all along. His grin was over-wide and his teeth overlong and twisted like the broken stone circle.

We walked in silence and returned to find Maybelle asleep on the cold stone floor in front of her mirror. Trouble woke her.

"Adrenaline? Daughter, where are you?"

"Here," I said, and touched her wrist. I had never seen her so tired. Never seen the lines in her face hold onto their shadows the way they did now.

She lifted herself on her soft arms. "We need to get you out of this time and away from here."

"Damn straight."

"No—this is where it happens. The act that unmakes us." Her hands climbed me, making their way to my face. She pressed them to my cheeks. Even her stone-chilled palms felt warm against my wind-

186

kissed skin. "Where have you been? What have you done?" Her voice was crumbling, the lines around her pit-eyes arching and twisting.

"It is done," Trouble said.

Maybelle looked as if she might scream, but instead she folded, her hands slipping from my face. "It is done," she repeated.

"Done? What is?" My confusion was creeping into alarm. "If we need to go, let's go!"

"There's no point in going, now. It is as AllysaAndrina said. The path is set. We must walk it. And meet our sister-mother at the end."

I stared into Maybelle's mirror, searching for my own face in the mess of shadows flitting by. "I didn't know that could even happen." I ran my fingers over the front of my shirt, as if there was any chance I might already feel the quickening there.

"The Maiden never does. Never thinks it will." Maybelle lay back against a velvet pillow and closed her eyes, her face now crossed with lines like the thorn bracken on the moor.

"Do you remember your first?"

"We were all my first. I was always this … I think. I don't remember a time when my arms were empty or my breasts dry."

"We must have begun somehow."

"Allysa seems to know something of it. At least in riddles."

"She's not being super helpful."

"She exists to be served now, not to serve."

"She barely exists at all."

"Soon, none of us will."

The sudden sour heat in my throat might have been fear, or regret, or the thing inside me. "I'm sorry … "

"It's not your fault. You couldn't have known. We couldn't have predicted this."

"Allysa could, apparently."

"Yes. Well. As you said … not 'super helpful'" She cast aside her ropes of beads and pulled a soft robe over her sagging belly.

"Does it hurt?"

"What, dying? How should I know?"

"No, this thing." I turned sideways. Was my stomach bigger? Would it sag like Maybelle's?

"Yes. It does."

I wanted to scream and curse and rage, but for the first time in my long stretch of existence, I felt impotent. Like I could raise the sea or turn the sun to stone and it would mean nothing. A pointless fraction of what I felt. I wanted to ride. I needed speed—to outrun this path laid at my feet or ride it over the edge at my own pace.

"I still want to go back to my time. My place. I want to die at home."

"I don't think that's a good idea," Maybelle said.

"Why the fuck not?" I might raise fire, instead. Vent the raging mantle of the earth.

"Because this has happened here and now. In your time—it may already be over. Your time might not even be there, now."

A hammer isn't a wrench, but it was all I had. The wrench wouldn't be invented for 200 years. Or maybe not at all.

The banded wagon wheels weren't perfectly round, nor the roads smooth. I had nothing to construct gears or brakes, but I could push with my feet, and—just for a moment—feel speed on my face.

"Should you be doing that?" Trouble asked. Just as he spoke, the wheel hit a rut and I toppled to the side into a patch of gorse.

"Why should it matter? Doesn't seem to matter what I do or don't decide."

Trouble smiled and helped me to my feet. "If the baby comes ahead of time, so does the end."

Something about his words struck me. Something about new life and the end of things. I walked my bicycle home, Trouble ten steps behind me.

I had felt pain before. I was no stranger to it. But this was enormous. This pain felt universal, sentient. As though I had been unmade and remade.

My back arched and ground against the slick stone floor. The flood from between my legs rushed between the stones, soaking my hair. My screams echoed through the dark passages.

AllysaAndrina stared down at me from the pedestal, choking and chanting. Maybelle knelt at my head, holding my hands, sobbing. Trouble crouched between my knees, grinning as he pulled something wet and dark from my center.

He placed the creature in my arms. Her skin and eyes were blue, but then her tiny lips parted—her complexion brightened as a wail to rival my own split the air.

"Here is your tiny maiden, mother. And here is the daughter of your daughter."

AllysaAndrina's chanting stopped and the stones in the walls fractured, raining sand and dust that stuck to the slick, wet skin of the mewling baby.

My breasts began to tingle and burn. Golden milk flowed in rivulets. The tiny maiden's screams grew more insistent and I scooped her up and held her to my flowing breast. She took the nipple in her mouth and began to drink. Trouble took the other side.

AllysaAndrina's figure—stone, now, on the plinth—gazed down on us. The mother, maiden, and crone, remade for a new age, and nursing Trouble.

The Terror Bay Resort Experience

I chewed the end of the old burr pipe, sipping on smoke as I watched the boat pull into Terror Bay. Arctic palms swayed outside the library window, the breeze kicking up a surf that licked the beach and sent the antique ferry shuddering along the dock bumpers. The tourists on deck clung to the railings, swaying like the palms.

I tapped the warm window glass with a fingertip and the view switched back to a windswept blizzard plain, with boulders of ice under chill blue light. I wiped the pipe's mouthpiece on the knee of my gown and slid down from the windowsill, then placed the pipe back on its brass display. "Sir John Franklin's Pipe" was etched into the plate, though its provenance was suspect. It was one of Corram's "close enough" artifacts. I tiptoed out of the room, replacing the velvet corded stanchions behind me.

"I smell his tobacco!" one of the tourists would probably say later.

Or, "Look! Footprints in the carpet!" I couldn't help but smile. Corram, my boss, was onto me, but the rumors of ghosts didn't hurt business. It helped. So he'd never given me more than a scowl over it.

I straightened my shawl and smoothed the hair slipping out of my elaborate coif, which was as much wig as it was my own. The lace at my cuff was discolored where I'd accidentally dipped it in ketchup at lunch. No one would notice. They wouldn't be looking at me. Their eyes would dart a hundred places, soaking in the artifacts pulled from the sea floor—the seven-hundred-year-old remnants of the Franklin Expedition, *Erebus* and *Terror* and their crews, all lost in the ice. Back when there was ice, back when the Arctic was cold.

I was already too hot under the layers of dress, and sweat dampened my collar as I hurried through the maze of resort corridors toward the King William's Visitor Center, where the Saturday boatload of tourists would soon arrive for their introduction, wind-tossed and rattled from their ride on the antique boat. It wasn't a boat from Franklin's time—not even from the same century—but Corram brushed off my suggestion that he learn to sail a tall ship. It served the purpose, at least, of indicating to the guests that they had left the 26th century. That they'd been brought back to a time when the world looked very different. I'd lead a tour through the dozen halls of displays, then serve lunch, then Corram would take them on their Neotropical Arctic Excursion to visit the cairns of the lost crews and to frolic in the surf, before returning for dinner and their night at the Terror Bay Resort. Then, on Sunday, another tour, afternoon tea, and the ride back to the mainland. Every weekend a new cohort arrived, and every weekend we replayed the same scenario, as if we were frozen in time. Like a boat frozen in the sea.

Sweat trickled under my corset as I ran. I'd stayed too long in the library. I always did. I'd even read all the books, or what I could of them, their language antiquated and almost indecipherable. They'd given me ideas for my performance, both as Lady Franklin and as the maid, Lucy, whom I'd need to transform into before lunch. I preferred playing the lady to the maid, but at least the maid's costume was simpler, and cooler. At least I didn't have to play a sailor, wrapped in furs as if lost on the ice, baking under the 20-hour sun. Every guide we'd ever hired to play a sailor had quit in their first summer. Corram had long since replaced them all with biomatronics. Corram and I were the only tour guides left, costumed, scripted. I was sure that as soon as he could find biomatronics who could change bedding and cook meals, that the rest of the staff would be gone, too. And he only kept me on because, as he said, "having a young lady around kept the place from getting creepy." So I assumed my position was limited to my fleeting youth. Eventually he'd be alone with his bots.

I stared at the pictures on the walls to cool myself. Blue ice crusted over buildings and ships, frozen waves like razor mountains; men in wool clotted with snow, their mustaches like icicles over peeling lips. I shivered. Nunavut hadn't seen snow in over a century, and that had been an anomaly. The locals still talked about it, relaying their grandparents' memories. It didn't look like it had been an easy place to live. Still, the people in the pictures were smiling. And some of them, dark eyes peering out from deep fur hoods, looked as if they had ice for bones.

Moving from the long, narrow corridors to the open circular room of the visitor's center always made me dizzy. It was like stepping through a portal from the past to the present. The frameless glass cupola above let in the bright summer sunlight that glittered off the gift shop wares welcoming visitors to the resort. It was the only window that wasn't programmed to show the Arctic as an ancient ice world. The only dark spot in the room was at the very center, behind the round service desk, where there stood a mound of carefully stacked stones. Rumor had it that the hotel had been built over a burial site, and that this cairn covered the bones of dead sailors. Human bones that bore butcher marks.

We didn't talk much about that part of the lost Franklin Expedition—about how desperate men get when everything is ice and the food runs out. Not in front of the tourists.

I assumed the cairn was a replica. Most of the land where there had been burials was now below water—graves flooded when the seas rose. The beaches that the tourists spread their towels on, sipping fruity drinks, were not the beaches where Franklin's men had scrounged for sustenance and failed. Most of them never even made it that far inland. Still, the cold stone always felt heavy at my back as I took my place at the service desk. Today I welcomed its cool presence. I pressed a handkerchief to my nose to dry the sweat beading there and tapped the com bell that would signify to all the staff throughout the center that a cohort was incoming, and I reset the carefully timed performances of the elaborate biomatronics.

Places, everyone.

The bright voices of visitors always carried far ahead of them, signaling their imminent approach. This weekend's reservation was for a women's retirement group. I recognized the name—The Past Perfects. They were former teachers, touring historical sites across the globe, moving from century to century, like time travelers. They came every year. Most of them were pleasant enough.

I ran my fingers over the map set into the desktop, waking up the lights and holograms in the attractions, starting the sound displays and bringing the past to life in the exhibits. I always felt, in that moment, as if some sort of magic happened. As if I were sailing our entire island into the past, or pulling history into the present. I could feel the whole building hum with it.

I took a deep breath, smoothed my skirt and hair, and took on the persona of Lady Jane Franklin. Grieving, but determined. Her husband lost to sea and ice and time.

But not to memory.

I brushed ash from my white apron, watching it fall to the dark grass like snowflakes. I'd stepped out for a break after the lunch rush to have a smoke and watch the sea. It was hard to imagine the lush island coated in sheets of ice and frozen rock. I wondered what cold truly felt like. I'd been chilled before, but had never experienced cold that could kill you—cold that could stop ships and drive men mad. The ash had left a dark streak on my linen. Both my costumes were in need of cleaning, but I'd have to convince Corram to give me a lift on the ferry to the mainland to take them to the specialty cleaner. I hated asking him for favors. The cost was always an extra chore or errand, like I didn't already devote my life to his employ.

As if summoned by the scent of insubordination, Corram kicked away the stone I'd wedged in the back door and peered around the panel to my not-so-hidden hiding spot.

"Smoke break is over, Marta. I need you to—" He paused and looked me up and down. "You're a mess."

"I know. I need a trip to the mainland. Are you going Monday?"

He sighed dramatically. *The setup.* "Well, I wasn't planning to, but I guess I am now." He pulled at his untrimmed beard. He always did that when he was thinking. I could practically see the blood flow to his brain as he thought of some way to make me pay for the inconvenience.

I stubbed out my cigarette and dropped the butt in the can by the door. Corram's face twisted in disgust.

"While you're in town, you can pick up our fish order." *And there it is.* The grossest errand. Picking up the pallets of frozen fish that once would have been native to these seas, for next week's menu. They'd be half-thawed and reeking by the time we got them back to the island.

"If you're driving the boat, then technically you'll be in town, too. Why don't you pick up the fish while I go to the cleaners, and we'll be done in half the time." I smiled my most annoying smile. He tugged on his beard again.

"What did you come out here for?" I interrupted his sputtering cerebral engine before he could escalate his plan and make me suffer even more.

"Right. I need you to go clean the dust out of the fans on Crozier's bot. He's overheating and keeps shorting out. Last group said they couldn't understand what he was saying."

Corram always gave me cleaning tasks when I was dressed as Lucy, as if the maid's uniform somehow transformed my job description as well. As if he was as fooled by the act like the tourists were. I'd spent six years on my degree in tourism, when all I really needed was one lesson on how to do everything your boss tells you. Never did master that skill.

He shook his head at my messy dress again and disappeared back behind the door.

THE TERROR BAY RESORT EXPERIENCE

I hauled a hand-vacuum, a rag, and a bucket of water down the long corridor to the replica of the officer's cabins. Crozier's bot stood there, bent over a table of charts lit by hologram candles, his silicone face molded with worry, knuckles white as they gripped the edge of the table. A porthole to his right showed a swirling blizzard, the landscape tilted as if the ship were frozen at an angle. I always felt myself leaning into that tilt unconsciously, my brain fooled by the illusion. The improper gravity made me unsteady.

I hauled at the Crozier bot's waistcoat, pulling his shirt up to his shoulders so I could access the panel in his back that concealed his hardware. "Where's the ship's surgeon when you need him, right?"

The surgeon's display was the hardest to view in the whole resort. I avoided that entire hall when I could help it. We don't even take children's groups past it. The medical procedures now accomplished with micromuscular threading were once done with a thick, rusty saw. The bot on the surgeon's rough plank table had a face twisted in agony. He screamed and writhed as the doctor sawed away at his mangled leg. I had turned the volume down on that display so it couldn't be heard from other hallways.

Bots were harder to cure than humans, now. I didn't really know what all the bits and wires did or went to, but dust was dust, and that I could handle.

The latch of the panel was stiff, stuck. I pulled my pocketknife from my apron and pried at it till it sprung open with a crack. A shock of cold moisture hit my face. I wiped the sting from my eyes and stared at the motherboard—as green as the resort lawn, speckled with a white dusting of ash.

No, not ash. Snow.

I reached out a finger and brushed at the white powder coating Crozier's components. It hurt. Cold that sent an ache through my joints like a bolt of arthritis. I watched the white powder melt to water against my skin.

"How the hell did you get like this, Francis?" I lifted my rag to the panel and swept away more of the white powder. I jumped as Crozier's voice, garbled and fraught with static, croaked as if in reply.

"We'll get you fixed up." When I'd brushed away all the snow, I used the tip of my knife to chisel at the ice that had stopped the fan, frozen it in place like a ship's rudder trapped in an ancient Arctic. "How did all this moisture even get in here?"

Crozier barked out another unintelligible reply. His voice sounded like the groan of frozen metal.

As soon as the fan was free, it began to spin again.

"I'm going to leave you open to let you dry out. And I'll talk to Corram about what's gone wrong with your guts."

Crozier's biomatronic arm lifted to clutch at his furrowed brow, his head moving, nodding in hopelessness. "We are lost," his deep voice replied, low with heartache.

Corram stood at the service counter, ringing up a stack of t-shirts for a smiling older woman. The woman wore last year's tour shirt, and I searched my memory for her name. I tried to remember the regulars. I never could, and Corram berated me for it. I supposed my brain was too full of Franklin trivia to take on any more.

"There you go, Mrs. Heathrow. Enjoy." Corram handed the woman a bulging shopping bag. Some of the tourists spent more on souvenirs than I made in a whole month.

I waited for the smiling woman to leave, then cleared my throat for Corram's attention.

THE TERROR BAY RESORT EXPERIENCE

"Got Crozier sorted out?" he asked.

"I tried. He wasn't full of dust, he was full of ice. I got as much of it as I could, and left him open to dry, but you might want to take a look at it."

"Marta, that's ridiculous. He doesn't even take a coolant."

I shrugged. Corram sighed and grabbed the rag and hand-vac from me. "Mind the counter for me." I watched him disappear down the hallway, his dark waistcoat and wool trousers blending in with the wood panels.

I checked the clock. Nearly dinnertime. I was meant to be preparing the dining room, helping the kitchen staff prep for the rush of thirty-two orders all coming in at once.

When Corram hadn't returned in fifteen minutes, I set the "closed" sign on the counter and made my way to the dining room. We might lose a postcard sale or two, but I wasn't going to send a boatload of guests to bed hungry.

I grabbed a stack of saucers from the cabinet and carried them to the long trestle table Corram had built from scavenged wood. I set them down and realized my hands were covered in grit. I looked from my palms to the stack of dishes. All were coated in sediment. Sand and crushed shell, small stones all dried together in a fragile matrix that crumbled as I brushed at it. "What the hell?"

I grabbed a tray from the cabinet. It, too, was filthy. I piled the dirty dishes on it anyway, and carried it all to the kitchen, dumping the whole load in the sink. I scraped at the sand on the porcelain, but it was fused there, as if glued. They looked like the plates from the wreckage—artifacts salvaged from the centuries-sunken *Terror*, now in a lit case down the hall. Anxiety gnawed at my gut. The china was made to look exactly like those used on board the ships. Someone must have taken this set to the beach for a picnic and not bothered to wash them.

I scrubbed my hands and filled a cart with fresh china from the dishwasher, and with all the accoutrements needed for dinner service. I could ask Corram about the dishes later. If a customer had borrowed them without permission, he may want to bill them for the hours of extra washing, especially since the kitchen staff always left after dinner. It would be me elbows-deep in this mess all evening. I cursed under my breath. Sometimes the hospitality industry felt more like running a daycare.

I forgot my troubles in a room full of happy visitors. Tourists always loved Lucy, and I thrived on their affection, even if it was just for a character, and not for me. It was as good as I could get. No one enjoyed my company as much as tourists enjoyed Lucy. I'd been taught young that people only loved me when I was helping them. It's why I went into tourism.

They finished their meal and made their way through the visitor's center to the guest wing. Their rooms were all replica ship's cabins, some with bunks and some with hammocks, depending on how much they'd paid.

I let my shoulders drop, my posture easing as much as my corset would allow. There were still dishes to do, and closing duties. But if I was going to have to act like a maid, I at least didn't have to dress like one anymore. The show was over for the night.

I stepped behind the counter and tapped at the control panel, putting the bots to sleep and dimming the lights in all the displays. Undoing the magic. I'd do it all again in the morning, and again, after that. Over and over, history in replay.

THE TERROR BAY RESORT EXPERIENCE

I was Lady Franklin again before the guests awoke—mourning in the morning, my black shawl held close over my broken heart.

The group was only twenty-nine people, several short. It's not unusual for a few guests to skip the early morning tour, especially if they overindulged the first day. But several women kept peering over their shoulders as we made our way through the halls, their brows furrowed and their attention far from the glowing cases of artifacts we passed by.

They forgot their absent friends as we rounded a corner and screams echoed down the hall.

The women gasped and clutched at their throats.

I frowned. Then I gathered my tour guide wits. "That will be the surgeon's galley. Poor James has gone under the knife after an accident on the ice." I must have accidentally turned the volume up as I set all the displays that morning. It had been so long since I'd heard those echoing screams that I hardly recognized them. But my assertion was confirmed when the recording looped, and the screams started again in the exact same pattern.

The women smiled nervously and dropped their hands from their necks, though their brows stayed furrowed. That's why I skip that display. That's why I turn it down. There are some parts of history best left in the past.

At lunch, the guest count had dropped to twenty-seven, and even Lucy's cheerful banter couldn't lighten the mood in the room. It didn't help that the kitchen was short two staff and every course ran late, orders akimbo and underprepared.

No one seemed to know where the five women had gone, but attendance wasn't mandatory. Guests often opted for more beach time instead of more history lessons. But that explanation didn't satisfy the Past Perfects, and their worry was as catching as a plague.

I'd never been so relieved to wrap a cohort, to dismiss them from the dining room and call an end to the act. They were Corram's now—their bags all packed and loaded, ready for the boat ride to the mainland and back to their own time.

I washed up, pulled off my frilled cap, and made my way to the library for a smoke and a rest before the long list of end-of-weekend duties began. The halls stirred and echoed, blizzard wind whistling past round windows. I'd forgotten to turn off the displays and effects. The library, at least, was minimally animated, with just a flickering hologram lantern and the blowing snow in the window.

The tables there were strewn with maps, books cast about, open to pages of ancient Arctic fauna, essays on Inuit hunting techniques. I gasped, then felt my throat clamp down on the breath to stifle the scream that wanted out. These artifacts weren't meant to be touched, not by anyone save for the archivist who only visited once a year, in the off season. *And me, sometimes.* Someone had ransacked the place, treating it as a browsing room instead of a private collection. They'd tossed the artifacts around with a disrespect that made my face heat. The velvet cords meant to keep people out lay in a tangle in the corner, the brass posts that suspended them dented, bent.

I stooped to pick up a book from the floor; my eyes prickled with frustration. I wondered if this was where the five missing women had been, and if they were the same inconsiderate people who had left their dirty dishes in the cabinet. Corram could review the cameras and find out. They wouldn't just be billed for this, though; they'd be banned, possibly even prosecuted, if anything was damaged. I decided to leave the mess as it was, as evidence, in case such measures needed to be taken. *They'll be lucky if I don't catch up with them and take the damages out of their backsides.*

THE TERROR BAY RESORT EXPERIENCE

I pulled the broken stanchions from the corner, though, and spread them across the entrance as best I could.

I rushed through the halls, wondering if I could catch Corram before he launched, before the culprit disappeared into the anonymity of the mainland harbor.

"Excuse me, miss?"

I stumbled to a stop and blinked at the older woman before me. It was the one from the shop, in last year's t-shirt. She should be at the docks. "Yes? Can I help you, Mrs. ... Mrs. Heathrow? We need to get you to your boat before it leaves."

"That's why I've come to find you, dear. We were supposed to leave already, but our boat man hasn't come. Could you let him know we're waiting?"

"He's not at the dock? Or in the visitor's center?"

She smiled at me, as if I were simple for suggesting the obvious. "No, dear, we haven't seen him since yesterday's excursion."

I tried to gather my roving thoughts. Life on the island was routine, predictable, and today had thrown me off at every step. I realized I hadn't seen him, either. I struggled to find my stride. "I'm so sorry. Yes, I'll find him. You'd better get back, in case he gets there first."

The woman nodded and headed back toward the visitor's center.

I stood and thought. Might he be in the staff room, napping? It wouldn't be like him. Could he be ill? Still in his room? I decided to check there first, and headed down the hall in the opposite direction from Mrs. Heathrow.

The screaming from the surgeon's display came into hearing again as I made my way through the corridors. I realized I'd be forced to walk past it this time. All the sweat on my body felt suddenly cold.

I had to cup my hands over my ears as I passed it, even my eyes narrowing involuntarily, as if I could shut out more of the noise that way.

The sailor on the table shuddered and flailed as the ship's surgeon wrenched the saw deep in the meat of the sailor's leg. Other bots grasped at his limbs, trying to hold him still. Their faces were creased with terror. Blood pooled around the table's legs. That was a new effect. I didn't care for it. The last thing this display needed was to be more disturbing. I did a double glance at one of the bots by the injured sailor's doomed leg. It was Crozier. What was he doing outside of his own display? His face did not hold terror, but the same expression of grief that he'd had bending over his maps and charts.

This must have been where Corram had been spending his time. Altering displays. Maybe he couldn't fix Crozier, and had decided to place him here until bot repair could come out.

Crozier raised his hand to his brow. "We're lost," he said, voice choked with hopelessness. Then he reached out and set his hand gently on the sailor's bloody leg.

Corram was not in his room. I figured my best chance of finding him was to use the coms. I retraced my path down the long corridors, and tried to rush past the surgeon's display, but it drew my gaze. It had changed again. Crozier was gone, and so was the sailor's leg. Corram must have come up the hall behind me and slipped away before I'd turned back. He couldn't be far. I rushed down the hallway.

The visitor's center was empty when I arrived. I stepped behind the counter to send a broadcast through the building for Corram. The floor crunched under my feet. I looked down. More sand, scattered across the tile all over the floor. And stones, large ones, grey

THE TERROR BAY RESORT EXPERIENCE

and rough. I raised my eyes to the cairn and saw that it had been torn down on one side.

Fury rose in my throat. Who would do something so disrespectful? The dishes were just replica dishes, and the books, while valuable antiquities, were just books. But to desecrate a grave?

I stared into the hollow at its center. I could see now that it was, indeed, real. Bones lay stacked at its center like grim firewood. And it smelled. I raised my apron to my nose and leaned closer to see what caused the noxious odor.

The bones on top of the pile shined, wet. Red. The grooves cut in them left splintered, jagged edges from which spilled dark gobbets.

I vomited into my apron, then pulled it from my neck and tossed in the trashcan beneath the desk.

I leaned against the counter to catch my breath. My hand swept its surface, lighting up every hall and cycling every display, till I found the com button. "Corram," I croaked into the speaker. "You're needed at the service counter immediately."

I stepped out from behind the counter, staggering toward the main door. I needed air. I wanted cold air, but instead I was met with the humid furnace of the Arctic summer heat. Palm trees whipped overhead in a hot wind.

I held the door open and stood in the entryway, leaning my forehead against the cool inside of the glass.

The crunch of footsteps in sand sounded from the room behind me.

"Corram?" I lifted my head and turned.

It was not Corram behind me. And it was not the crunch of footsteps, but the crunch of teeth on bone.

Crozier stood by the counter, his lively glass bot eyes wreathed in frost, his mech arms digging through the neck hole of Mrs.

Heathrow's teal t-shirt and pulling free another rib with a snap that straightened my spine. Acid rose in my throat again.

I stepped slowly outside and let the door swing shut between me and Crozier. My eyes locked on the bot as it chewed, then placed the old woman's bones inside the cairn.

Sandy steps sounded behind me again, and I spun in panic, but it was more guests, concern writ deep across their faces.

"Isn't that man coming to take us to the harbor? Some of us have planes to catch, you know."

I took three deep breaths to steady my voice. They couldn't see behind me, through the sunlit window, to where the creature bent low behind the counter. "He's ill. I'm afraid he can't take you today. But I'm going to call a sonicopter from the mainland to come and get us all." I tried to smile, but knew I'd failed, by the lowered brows on the faces before me. I needed to be Lucy now, not Marta, to keep them happy.

"Well, maybe we could wait inside, then. We'll have some calls of our own to make, of course." They made to move past me.

"No!" I pressed my back to the door. I fumbled for the keys that dangled at my waist and slipped the lock on the door. "I'm afraid we're closed now. Come to the docks. We'll wait there together."

"Well, we're not leaving without Susan and Angelina."

"Who?"

"Susan Miller and Angelina Heathrow. They came back here to find our boat man."

"Mrs. Heathrow?"

"Are you okay, dear? You seem a little unwell yourself."

"I am. And we need to get off of this island now."

"But the driver—"

"I'll drive." I had never driven the boat—Corram had never let me—but I'd watched him do it hundreds of times.

206

Corram. Were those his bones in the cairn?

I took three shaky steps down the lane before I stopped. I still clutched my keys, sharp in my hands. *Keys.* Corram kept the boat key on his own keyring, clipped to his belt loop. That was, presumably, somewhere inside. Wherever the Crozier bot had left that piece of him.

I turned to the small crowd of guests. "Go back to the dock house. Lock the door and wait for me. I'm going to get the keys from … from Corram. I'll look for your friends. There's a phone there behind the desk; you can make your calls."

The group murmured discontentedly as they made their way down the path.

I turned back toward the resort, keys cold in my hand despite the summer heat.

I pressed my face to the glass. There was no sign of Crozier, nor the tattered remains of Mrs. Heathrow, save for the puddles of blood seeping into the scattered sand on the floor. *He might be just below the counter. He might be right around the corner. He might have found Susan Miller.*

I did not want to go in. But there was only one way off the island, and only one key to the boat.

I slipped my key, as silently as possible, into the lock and twisted. It cracked and popped, and dusted my knuckles with snow. I shook away the stinging wetness.

I pulled the door open and a blast of cold air hit me, tightening my chest and trapping the breath in my throat. *So cold. Cold that can kill you. Cold that can drive you mad.*

Nothing moved in response to the sound. I slipped inside.

Corram had gone to repair Crozier after I'd given up. Whatever trail I had to follow would begin there.

My breath fogged in front of me as I made my way through the dark halls. Their anachronistic lanterns and historical ambience didn't fare well in the cold, and the lights flickered in protest. Even the electric locks on the cabinets were failing, their glass doors falling open, holograms winking out, exposing the relics of the *Terror* and filling the halls with the scent of ancient wreckage. I stifled a sob in my throat and ran the rest of the way to the replica cabins.

The plank walls were spattered with red. The maps, over which Crozier once stood in fear for the survival of his crew, were soaked in Corram. The tangle of his remains stained the floorboards.

I bent to the tatter of wool trousers feathered with red frost, plucking at the crisp mess till I heard the jingle of keys and saw the red shine of them. I slipped the hook from the loop and pulled the ring of keys free. The wool fell back to the floor with a stiff whisper. I shivered. I'd never felt so cold. The metal of the keys stung the skin of my hands, which had grown so rigid that I struggled to bend my fingers. Even my neck felt stiff as the ice crept in.

I'd freeze before I could find Susan Miller. Or the five missing women. Or the two missing kitchen staff. *What is happening here?*

I needed a coat, or more layers. My room wasn't far. A few halls away, nearer the library. My own clothes were suited for the neotropical Arctic, but Mrs. Franklin's Victorian layers were made for a mission in the ice.

I held the keys to my chest and made my way toward my room, peering carefully around corners, listening for Crozier's quiet shuffle. Every sound seemed magnified, the groaning malfunction of all the displays like the seizing of an ice-bound ship. My head whipped over my shoulder constantly, eyeing the intersections in the maze of halls.

I arrived at my door, but the lock was choked with ice. I couldn't even get the key inside. A panicked whine rose in my throat, and

I thought I heard movement in a nearby hall. My hands shook as I stuffed stiff knuckles into my pocket, grasping for my lighter. I fumbled a flame to life and held it to the ice, holding the fingers of my other hand close for warmth.

The sound nearby intensified—a stumble, perhaps, or something brushing a wall.

Tears welled in my eyes and froze there as the flame worked so slowly. Finally I was able to chisel the key into place. I wrenched at the lock till the ice popped and my door sang open with a crack that sent fine snow drifting from the ceiling.

I locked the door from the inside and peeled away insipid Lucy's black dress, and hurried into the many layers of Lady Franklin's gown. The wig that I had so often cursed for its insulating volume felt like a security blanket—warm and protective.

It was harder to move in the large dress, and the fabric swished in a way that stirred my anxiety, but the trembling in my limbs slowed and my thoughts cleared, as if the cold had numbed even my brain.

I listened at the door, hearing only the whisper of my own breath against the cold wood panel. The frozen door chimed open as if it were made of glass.

The corridor stretched empty in either direction, lights flickering and failing in the cold.

I rushed as fast as the big dress would allow, the rustle of fabric like the sound of shuffling papers.

No.

There *was* a shuffling of paper. *The library.*

The stanchions lay in a warped tangle in the hallway.

I slowed, as if my feet caught in sheets of ice, and I froze in front of the library doorway.

A man stood there, tossing through maps, a slender bone held like a pipe between his teeth. His acrylic beard ran red.

Sir John Franklin turned to me, his motions a stutter of frozen biomatronics.

The bone fell from his mouth.

I shook within, and froze without, exhaustion and terror rooting my limbs.

Sir Franklin's hand jerked up and clutched at where his heart would be, were he human.

"My love, I am lost," he said.

A script. From his diary. It's only a recording.

"My love." He took a broken step toward me.

Terror melted whatever had frozen me in place, and I backed away against the corridor wall. My satin skirts brushed the paneling, and I remembered, then, who I was. Lady Jane Franklin.

Sir Franklin's arms stretched toward me, and before I could bolt, he stumbled forward, pinning me to the wall between his hands. The synthetic skin of his knuckles was creased with dried blood and the plastic fibers of his beard were clotted with it.

"We're so hungry, my love. So cold."

I pushed ineffectively at one of his wrists as he leaned in and pressed his cold silicone lips to my forehead. The blood in his beard, still warm, pained my face. I could not draw enough breath to retch.

"There is nothing to eat," he whispered against my forehead, his enamel teeth brushing against my skin. "It's the only way."

The heat of adrenaline filled my body. No one knew how many men from *Erebus* and *Terror* were eaten by their crewmates, in the end. No one knew what degree of madness drove them there, or resulted afterwards. But would he eat his own wife? My chin trembled, but I spoke, lips grazing the tacky, wet hair that shrouded me like a veil. "I will find you. We'll send ships. Stay where you are. I am coming. Stay where you are!"

The bot pulled away, then stilled. His hollow eyes searched mine; then he turned back to the library, back to the books and maps. He picked up a chart and tore it in two. "We are lost."

I let out my breath in a staccato of clouds that fogged my vision, and I felt the tunnel of unconsciousness closing in on me. I focused my gaze on the floor, trying to will my legs to hold me up, to take me away.

The bone that had fallen from Franklin's mouth lay in a bloody scrap mound beneath the table. I couldn't tell who it had been. I did not—could not—care, anymore. Shame gave me strength, and I ran.

I clutched the boat key like a rosary as I raced down the hall toward the visitor's center.

The dome above the visitor's center glowed with blue cold, snow whipping against the glass. I paused, confused, wondering if I'd somehow hit the glass illusion controls when I'd fallen against the counter earlier. The lack of sunlight turned the room eerie. A creeping frost emanated from the cairn. Something jarred the stones inside, sending more rock tumbling. I slowed, trying to remain silent on the sandy floor. My eyes locked on the dark hollow behind the counter, I backed toward the main door.

The heel of my shoe stuck to the clumped sand where Crozier had stood with the bleeding torso of Mrs. Heathrow, and it made a wet sound as I pulled away.

The tumbling of stones silenced.

Crozier stood up from behind the counter, his whole costume soaked red, the leg from the injured sailor's exhibit slung over his shoulder like a club. His glass eyes reflected the cold light in a way that made them seem all too sentient.

He lunged forward, forgetting the expanse of desk between us, and sprawled across the countertop. His hands raked at the surface as he tried to pull himself over, his touch activating and cancelling every command in the building. The com system came alive, and broadcast his low groan through the halls, a predator snarl that set my brain alight with the instinct to flee.

I burst out of the door into the Arctic air and cold stung my face, constricting my blood vessels in a sensation of squeezing pain. The breathless chill left my raw throat ragged. *Cold.* It was as if the animated blizzard had burst its bounds and filled the whole island with its rage.

The lane to the dock had never seemed so long, and though the summer sun still hung in the sky behind its snow veil, I knew it must be nearing night. The weight in my limbs, the heaviness of my eyelids, all signaled sleep. Sleep. It sounded wonderful. It sounded warm.

I forced my feet forward over the path down to the dock.

The ferry bobbed in the berth, and two dozen bright red faces turned to me as I raced toward them, wide skirt billowing in the sudden, frigid wind.

The Past Perfects were there, huddled in the dock house, their cold faces turning to me for answers, panic written in their expressions.

"Get aboard!" I shouted as soon as I was close enough to be heard.

Something in my alarm stirred them, or perhaps it was my face painted red with the blood from Franklin's beard, and they all rushed the ferry, stampeding up the gangplank just as I reached the dock.

I pulled the moorings free and followed aboard, my feet slipping on the icy slope of the deck as I made my way to the bridge. I closed myself inside, stopping the worst of the wind, though it still whistled around the thick glass windows.

THE TERROR BAY RESORT EXPERIENCE

Too much snow stirred in the air for me to see if anything had followed me down the path. A glance behind me showed the guests had huddled together in the center of the passenger cabin, their red faces and blue lips flashing like alarm beacons.

Corram's keys stuck to my hand in thick, dry blood, but I singled out the one for the boat and pushed it in place, bringing the vessel to life. The sound of the warm engines roaring unlocked some of the tension in my chest, and I laughed a sob over the controls. The buttons and levers were alien to me, but the basics were clear, and it was only a two-hour ride to the mainland. I'd radio for help once I'd put sea between us and the island. I drew in a shaky breath as the boat pulled away from the dock and a strip of water spread between the hull and shore.

My eyes were held, locked on the shrinking stones of King William's beach, so I didn't see the white line of freezing fog that crept up on our starboard side.

Fingers of frost spread across the windows, and as I finally turned to crane my sights toward the mainland, I saw the water moving high and slow in waves thickened with cold. The heavy water dashed against the ferry. The boat tipped and righted itself just as another wave came and broke across its bow. Screams sounded from the passenger cabin.

I wrenched at the controls, turning the vessel into the surf as I'd seen Corram do on stormy days, though he'd never have taken tourists out in bad weather.

The waves came larger, and heavier—slower. And where the water thinned by the shore, they stopped altogether in razor mountains, frozen, like in the grainy pictures framed in the resort halls. The relentless force of water pushed the frozen crust higher in jagged peaks that loomed around the ferry like a cage of monstrous teeth.

The frozen expanse spread back from the shoreline, into deep water, enveloping the ferry. The hull screamed in the squeeze of unstoppable ice.

There was nowhere left to steer. No open water in which to guide the boat. The bow lodged against a crest of ice, and the sound of straining metal echoed off the crystalline walls surrounding us. We were stuck fast in the spreading ice, which continued to buckle and rise all around us.

The controls popped and darkened, lights fading in the glow of sun-stricken blue. I rocked the throttle, trying to free the rudder, but it groaned one last time before shuddering into silence.

I pushed the button for the radio, but not even static sounded on the dead line. My hand shook there, holding the button down, my stiff neck craned over the narrow microphone as my throat tightened. "We … We are lost."

The words hung in the air as solid condensation, then fell to the floor like snow.

I lowered my hands from the controls.

Wails sounded from the cabin behind me. I turned to the window that overlooked the passengers. They lay sprawled together in the center of the room, their bags and belongings tossed like so much debris among the seats.

I unlocked the bridge door with a trembling hand and stood on the narrow stairway that led into the cabin. "We're stuck," I said. "I'm sorry. I tried. There's nothing more I can do."

"Where did all this come from?" one of the women sobbed. Another clutched her close as they all stared out the windows at the frozen world that encased us.

"What do we do?" another asked.

"We wait," I said. "Someone will come for us. Someone always comes." *I will find you. We'll send ships. Stay where you are. I am coming.*

THE TERROR BAY RESORT EXPERIENCE

"But when will they come? How soon?" A small woman asked. Her face bled from where it had struck something in the turbulence.

"They better come soon," another said. "I'm hungry."

My gut clenched.

On the edge of the ice, between two peaks of frozen sea, a dark shape moved.

SKYDIVERS

There is not enough wind, stories above abandoned Manhattan, to rock the skycage. Perhaps there's not enough oxygen left to produce wind. But my dive tank is full, and my camera battery is full, and 405 Lexington Avenue—Scrapertown, the last holdout of human life in the city—is about to flush its filters.

The sprayers hiss and the fans roar to life as they chum the air with aspirated silicon, carbon dioxide, and all the waste a nest of humans produces. In a few hours, Manhattan below will be covered in a fine, sticky powder raining down over abandoned streets. Whatever the skywhales don't eat, first.

Small skyfish gather at the spouts, darting in and gulping at the mist before flitting away, circling around, and gulping more. Their tempered glass bodies catch what little light filters through the thick smog. The delicate clockwork of pumping pistons visible through their scales, processing the richness of our human waste. *Something in what we leave behind is good for them, at least.* I train my camera lens on them while I wait for the whales. I can feel them coming, their sonar thrumming the hollow of my ears. The joints of my dive cage rattle. A whale leaps out of the smog, not ten feet from my cage, and I forget my pinching mask and the metal bars digging into my knees. I raise the camera and start filming.

Soon they're everywhere, sucking silica from the clouds, filtering it through stringy shields of carbon fiber baleen. Dim light glows off their silver mesh skin and flares in my lens. The cage shakes in the waves of their song. Rust rains from the bars where the toxic air has corroded the metal. I can't hear it, but I feel it vibrate in my lungs, in my teeth. I'll extract the sound in the studio, let the waves of it wash over me.

Their sleek bodies dip in and out of the cloud banks as they arc from sprayer to sprayer, feasting on the rich clouds of waste. They're barely bigger than my cage, but the crash of their song makes them feel like giants.

The cage jerks and I fall to the side, the camera knocking against the tarnished bars. The chain grinds above as it reels me up, back to the skyway that arches between tall buildings.

The whales drift below, sliding in and out of view. The fans groan to a stop and the hiss of the sprayers fades. The skywhales swarm around the spouts, their sound waves reaching a crescendo that aches in my joints. Vapor blasts from the ports in their backs as they turn back to the toxic clouds.

The bay doors grind shut beneath the swinging cage, pinching out the last of the light. I rip the mask off my face, gulping oxygen, feeling it rush cold over the lines of sweat where the rubber chaffed my cheekbones. The button on my radio sticks when I squeeze it. "Why'd you bring me in?" My camera shows a full twenty minutes left—enough to catch a feeding frenzy, maybe even a mating. All the things I need the world to see.

SKYDIVERS

The radio crackles, "There were too many this time, Jess. Too much noise. The camera and cage were going to pop, if you didn't first."

I switch the camera off and clip it to my suit. Climbing out of the skycage is harder every time. My knees creak like the rusty winch as I straighten. I set the heavy camera on the pallet table, strip off my gear and drop it in the chem bath, and step under the swinging metal disc of the shower. Every movement echoes off the corrugated steel of the skyway. Rivets massage the soles of my bare feet.

The water always hits like a whale song, making me gasp and exhale at the same time, every fine hair on my body spiked with cold. The blast of water pounds my stubbled hair flat.

Mike is waiting with the silver blanket in the hall, eyes cast aside modestly as he wraps me up. "How was it? Get good footage?" He takes the camera from me, hefting it to his shoulder as I rub warmth back into my arms.

"It was average. Could have been something special if you hadn't chickened out." My words lose their edge as I force them past chattering teeth.

Mike just smiles. "Your job is to film. Mine's to not dump you in the air 50 stories above Manhattan."

He's good at his job. Better than the interns hired by the Exxop Conservation Agency that funded my last film. One of the benefits of going indie is hiring your own assistant. I'm not sure if it still counts as "going indie" if your employer defunds your project and buries the work in a street-level warehouse. But now they can't tell me what to film—or what truths to cut. They can't tell me how to show the skywhales to the world.

Mike unlocks the studio door and turns his back while I pull on my clothes. I don't bother with my socks or a bra; my shirt is inside-out and backward, tag tickling the underside of my chin, but I'm anxious to see the footage.

"Well, now your job is to make me some tea while we see what we've got."

"These are some good frames. We can use these. But we're going to have to dive again." Mike taps a key, slowly advancing through the video.

I rest my forehead on the table, against the warm side of the mug, as Mike pauses on an image of a whale gulping at a cloud plump with acidic fumes as clear water vapor mists from the blowhole on its back. "What about the narration script? Do we have all the words we need in the audio library?" I can feel the vibration of the whale song between the bone of my forehead and the table.

"Almost. We don't have 'silicaphilic' or 'carboncephologic'. We're going to have to splice them, or get an impersonator. There's a man on twelve who sounds *exactly* like Attenborough."

"Splice. We're going to have enough trouble competing with the ExCA as it is. We can't afford for some troll to call us out on a fake Attenborough. Are you sure he's never said 'silicaphilic'?"

"I'm sure. But he's said 'cilia' and 'philic'. We can make it happen."

"When's the next dive?" I'm already itching to get back in the sky. When I close my eyes, I still feel like I'm in the air, the bass wave of the whales rolling through me.

"Tomorrow, if you're not too sore. There's a slot open at two, after the chemists take their cloud samples."

The parts per million of dissolved carbon dioxide in the water vapor is lower than it's been since we shut down the roads and came inside …

The chemists had been happy to sit for my camera. *It's getting better out there.*

I check my watch. If I go to sleep now, I can still get eight hours before the next suit-up. "I'm fine. We have to get this done. If we fuck it up, it's over."

"Calm down, Jess. We'll get the shots."

"Don't ever tell me to calm down. You need to let me dive cageless."

He looks away and shakes his head. "Not a chance."

"They don't use cages at the ExCA. It's just them and the whales—up close. They can see everything, every last piece of how they fit into the ecosystem."

"They also have full suits and a pro fly system."

"And a backbone, apparently."

"Jess—"

"I'll take the cage tomorrow. But if we don't get the shot, next time, we do it my way."

The next dive's footage isn't much better. A few clearer shots, some audio—but not what I'm looking for. Not *the* shot that will change people's minds—make them understand why the whales are worth saving, that a new TV with skywhale fiber technology isn't worth more than what the live whales do for us, for the earth.

Barrel-deep groans and shrill piping whistles fill the studio. The whale song, rendered audible, reverberates through the small, dark room. It sounds like an old modem in mourning.

"Well, they are mating." Mike zooms in on a tangle of whales.

"But you can't see it."

"You can kind of see—right there."

"It's not good enough, Mike. If I hadn't been squeezed into that cage, this footage could have made history. Now it just makes … noise."

Mike sighs and pinches the skin of his forehead. I know I've won.

"Get a better helmet, first. With a proper air supply feed." He rubs his hands over his face.

"We made a deal."

"Well I'm making a new deal." He looks as tired as I feel, after long nights in the studio.

I pause and let him think he's won a small victory. The new helmet is back in my room, and has been for weeks. It'll obstruct my peripheral vision with its bulky air supply feed. I've held off on using it in favor of smaller models with a better view. But if it means I can dive cageless, it's worth it.

"Okay."

The helmet is only new to me. Nothing in the towers is new anymore, except tech ground together from harvested skylife. It smells as if it got good use from its previous owner. But it also smells like triumph.

Michael stands behind me in his suit and mask as he weaves cords around my arms, chest, and thighs—tying them together and clipping them to the chain. The backup and the backup's backup. I'll be lucky if I can lift my arms to raise the camera.

He insists on staying in the skyroom the whole time, being there to haul me in manually if the remote fails.

He hands me the camera and I strap it to my arm. His voice

crackles through the earpiece in my helmet. Something about signals. My radio only clicks when I squeeze it, the toxic clouds having seeped into its seams and dissolved something vital. I hold up my fingers in an "okay." We'll use the old code. One click for stop, two for lower, three for all the way up.

The bay doors slide back. They always make me think of the old streets—of the sewer vents that I was always afraid would open under my feet. Now they can't open fast enough for me. Wisps of smog slither into the skyroom, wrapping around our ankles.

Mike braces himself and grips the crank on the winch as I climb down onto the one step hanging from the edge of the hatch.

The noise of the sprayer and fan is muffled inside the fiberglass shell lined with reeking foam that squeezes my head. It will be worth it, to fly with the whales.

I step off the steel rung and dangle in the air. The silent city peeks out between wisps of haze fathoms below my swinging boots. The slick bodies of skywhales come rolling out of the cloudbanks. I raise my camera, arms straining against the tight straps that circle my chest and shoulders. There are three of them, darting around each other in a playful braid, filtering toxins from the air with their dark mouths. I film their play, my own excited breath fogging around my face.

Two whales press their noses together. The third shoves between them and swims away into a swirling mass of clouds.

I peer around my camera. Behind the entwined whales, I see that the clouds aren't swirling with their own internal wind, but are being stirred by a frenzy of skywhales.

I set my camera to thermal and press it to my face, zooming in on the dark bodies writhing in the mist. I click my radio twice. I sink lower into the smog. A cluster of whales churns around a dangling figure—a man in full skysuit. He hangs limp on the end of his line as the whales pummel him, knocking him with their tails. His thermal signature fades to the temperature of the chemical clouds.

To the right shines a bright hot figure with a camera held to its face, filming the fight.

I squeeze my radio button three times. Instantly, the winch begins to grind. Cords dig into my armpits and groin as the chain heaves me upward.

I spill onto the skyroom floor, helmet knocking the steel like a drum, drawing my knees to my chest as the hatch scrapes closed. I wait just long enough for the fans to clear the air before I tear the helmet off my head. My scalp aches where the foam pressed against the grain of my hair, chaffing me in my own sweat.

"What's wrong?" Michael frets at me, squeezing my arms and legs.

I pull at my suit straps, gasping to catch my breath. "They were filming an attack."

"Who was? A whale fight?"

"No, an attack on a skydiver—it looked staged. The ExCA was filming the whales beating a diver to death."

Mike shakes his head. "That can't be right."

"See for yourself. I filmed it."

Mike purses his lips, stalks the room in silence. The skysuits steam as we pull them from the chem bath.

"I'll take these to storage. Get them sealed up for the next project." Mike drapes the suits over his arm.

"What do you mean the next project? We're not done with this one."

"Yes, Jess, we are. This is way out of our league now."

"No. It isn't out of our league. It's *more* important now." I grab my skysuit from his arm and carry it to the hook on the wall.

"Jess, it was hard enough just competing with the ExCA. We can't *fight* them, too."

"Like hell we can't."

"It's not safe anymore."

"It was never safe, Michael. And it was never about being safe. Those whales aren't doing anything but cleaning up the crap we've dumped in the sky. They deserve better than to be vilified and killed off."

"You can't win this one, Jess."

"Yes I can. We can."

Mike runs his fingers through his hair, splitting the curls into a halo of frizz. "How?"

"We're not making a film about whales anymore."

"But you said—"

"We're making a film about the ExCA."

Mike squeezes his skysuit, wringing drops of vinegar from its folds. I take it from his hands and hang it next to mine. "Mike, when people see what I saw—"

"They'll feed you to the whales."

"Don't be an idiot."

"Take your own advice for once." He stalks out of the skyroom. My gut squeezes like it does when the winch slips.

Mike scrolls the footage forward and back, replaying the tangle of whales around the fading diver. "How do we know it's the ExCA?"

"They're rigged on a fly system. Who else could it be?"

"But why would they do that? Aren't they supposed to be

conservationists? Why would they condemn the animals that they're trying to protect?" Michael zooms in on the man filming.

"None of the work they hired me to do would have protected the whales. They only ever wanted drama shots. They wanted people to watch, but they didn't want them to see."

"That why you left?"

"That's why they fired me." I pan the screen over to the dead diver. "Apparently this was the shot they wanted. Not playful whales cleaning up our mess."

"I didn't even know the whales would do that to a diver." Michael looked sick.

"They don't! Don't you fall for their bullshit. They must have provoked them somehow. Hurt them. I've never seen a whale hurt a diver on purpose. I'd bet my camera that man was dead before he left the skyroom. Bodies don't just go cold. It takes a while, and he's already blue."

"On purpose?"

I reached over and squeezed his hand. "They're wild animals. Accidents happen, but they're rare. Don't worry."

"Well, I'm worried."

"Worry about the whales. About why the ExCA wants them to look dangerous—why they would want people afraid."

Michael flips through the script on the desk. "We're going to need to hire that narration impersonator."

"Why?"

"Far as I know, Attenborough never said 'motherfucker'."

The cold of the skyroom, the screech of grinding chains, my body processing an excess of adrenaline—all make me shiver.

The post-dive trembling where my body protests, reminds me that my feet belong on the earth. Mike wraps the thermal blanket around my shoulders, forgetting to look away as I shake in front of him.

"Did they see you?" His hands on my shoulders are as reassuring as solid ground.

"Yes."

"What?"

"It's okay, they bought it. They thought I was just some party kid skyjumping. They even gave me a safely lecture on knots. It wasn't anyone I've worked with before."

"You had your helmet on, right? Your face was covered?"

"Yes."

Mike sighs and rubs the blanket over my shoulders. He brushes his thumb over the spot on my temple where the in-helmet camera pressed against me. "Were they filming whales?"

"I didn't see any whales. They were hanging a new rigging system—I think they have plans for that spot tomorrow."

"Well, let's see what you got."

In the screen room, Mike zooms in on the ExCA cameraman's hands fussing at my chest, winding the cords into a knot. "That's an awful knot."

"Which isn't quite a crime."

"It is if you fall. That's not the right tie for skyjumping."

"That's hardly worth mentioning, Mike. But that setup looks like a fishing net. Do you think they're poaching them and selling them for scrap? Using their filming license to fish?"

"We've only got three dive days left, Jess. You need to let this go. Take a few dozen sky samples, sell them, and we'll fund another term in the skyroom in a few months."

I shake my head. "I just have to get closer. If you lower the cage from skyway 75, I could watch from above—they'd never see me. They weren't rigging that high."

"We don't have clearance for 75. And we'd have to roll out the whole chain. And there are skysquids at 75 level. So—no."

"I could use the cage."

"If there was an emergency, I couldn't pull you up before it was too late."

"I'll take an extra air tank. If you're not in the skyroom, I can take all three tanks."

"Why won't you just let this go?"

I load yesterday's footage and crank the volume. The whale song fills the studio. "Did you see this week's skysample report? It's getting better. Wherever the whales are, the sky heals. We might even get it back, someday. But not if skywhales are called dangerous and slaughtered to protect a few rich skyjumpers, and their parts harvested for new tech toys." My face is heating, wetness on my cheeks like I've been wearing a helmet too long. For the whales being ground up on recycling belts. For the people trapped in skyscrapers pumped full of oxygen while our toxins are sprayed out into the atmosphere—where suddenly there's life again. Where somehow nature turns our filth into richness. And again we're killing them.

Mike pulls me forward and kisses me on the forehead. He smells like vinegar chem baths, like pure oxygen and silicone. He pulls back and covers his eyes with his hands. "You'll have all three tanks, and the cage. And your helmet. And don't use that idiot's knot."

SKYDIVERS

Shadows drift behind the wall of clouds. The sound of the winch faded stories ago, and still the cage drops. I cut through layers of stratum and watch the toxins bead in condensation on my suit.

I keep the camera set to thermal and zoom in as far as it will go, pointing it past my feet at the space below.

When I see their shapes take form—three divers circling a cluster of whales—I squeeze my radio button once. The chain jerks to a stop. The cage rattles, swinging on the end of the line. There's still no wind, but suspended on such a long line, it seems even my breath is enough to rock the cage.

I focus on the figures below. The whales writhe in a knot among the three divers. One diver holds a camera to his face. Another chums the air with a hand sprayer. The third pokes a long, bright rod into the mass of whales and a white-hot jolt of lightning fires into their slick skin. The air itself shakes with their tortured song. The chain, the cage, my teeth—all rattling so hard I know they'll be on the audio.

The man with the rod pulls his zipline and circles the pack, jabbing into the whales and releasing a spear of current.

One of the whales falls away from the group, its tail thrashing ever more slowly as it sinks into a system of cord nets below. It lies stiff against the snare, drifting in the chemical wind churned by the writhing whales.

The steady whir of ziplines grows louder. My cage shakes. I lift my face in time to see the third diver, his chum sprayer tied to his waist in a clumsy knot, pull at the latch of the cage.

I rip my camera from my wrist tether and strap it to the bars of the cage, pointing down. Thick gloved hands grip my shoulders and pull me up out of the cage. I wrap one hand around the bars and swat at the diver with the other. The man pushes himself against my back and curls an arm around my waist.

"You're not using your safety knot," he shouts through the thin wall of my helmet. "You know you might fall." He reaches up and pries at the edge of my helmet. The air tube springs free, spraying clear air that cuts through the smog. My helmet comes away in his hands. My eyes burn. My lips split.

"I see you've got Dan's old helmet. It didn't do much for him, in the end, either."

My lungs ache. The skin around my eyes blisters. My fingers slip from the bar. Just as they slide free, I reach and squeeze my radio button three times. The cage rockets upward with all the speed of Michael's anxiety. The diver drops me, his fingers raking up for the vanishing cage. It disappears into the clouds before he can reach it— all the way up, past the reach of the diver's fly system.

I fall toward the knot of angry whales. Their skin feels like chainmail over rubber and they smell of oil. I grasp for a fin and hold on. My face swells with blisters and my eyesight dims, tinted with yellow. A blast of air from the back of a whale bathes me in oxygen, and I suck it in, feel the soothing coolness on my raw face. A bright arch of lightning slams into me. My muscles fight to contract all at once, contorting me. Tendons strain in my shoulders. The whale screams a soundless concussion in the air and shakes me loose, the whole mass of them now crashing into each other. Debris from their hides catches the light as it falls away through the smog. I fall with it, through yellow cloud banks into the net filled with dead and dying skywhales. My radio hisses a garbled panic.

The cage made it. Michael has the camera—the footage. He'll see the whales. He'll see the killers. He'll see me fall away, a skydiver flying with the skywhales. Falling with them. He'll show the world.

There's a twitch beneath my back, a jump and squirm of a whale thrashing. I reach out a hand and grasp its fin just as it pushes through a hole in the net. It blasts me with oxygen.

We drift through a layer of chemical mist so thick that it caresses the sores blooming on my cheeks. I time my breaths with the puffing exhalations of the skywhale, drawing in the oxygen it emits from its trembling crown. Its sides heave against my clutching arms. Water pours from a tattered gash below its fin.

We break through the mist and the whale shudders. My skin stings and prickles at the cold and I can't help but gasp. I tense, ready for the street-level chemicals to strip the soft flesh inside my lungs. But it doesn't. The air tastes like water. It tastes like the skywhale's breath. I breathe again.

The whale's sides slow. It no longer blasts air, but barely breathes at all, its tail pumping weakly as it slows the descent toward the street. We land in a brittle nest of crumbling, oxidized struts.

The whales' sides began to heave faster again, air vapors blasting from it in a stream. Water pours from its wounds and disappears into the rubble beneath us.

I hold on to the whale, squeezing it, whispering comfort. Whispering thanks.

The skyfish arrive before the skywhale's great engine has even stilled. Bright neon and silver flashes dart around us. My hand twitches to reach for my camera, forgetting for a moment what happened. Hoping that it is now safe in Mike's hands. That he'll take it and run.

The fish kiss at the whale's closed eyes, probing at its wounds, burrowing, flicking their fins in the fresh water. The whale is still.

My lips burn. My throat clenches, stinging from screams and chemical burns. I shoo the fish away and press my lips to the skywhale's wound. I draw from the whale—water still warm from the heat of its silent engine, its flavor sharp and clean. It washes the pain from my mouth.

Skyfish tickle my cheeks, trying to slip past my greedy lips.

The whale's body shifts and I pull away, afraid I've misjudged, that I've hurt it somehow. Fish pour into the wound again and again the whale lurches. A snapping scrape sounds from beneath it. Something else is moving—something in the broken filigree of debris that cradles us in the street.

The ruins shift, closing in on the fallen whale.

I batt away at the tickle by my ear, at my lips, in the corners of my eyes. I'm covered in whale blood, full of its vapors, and the scavengers are swarming. They can't tell me apart from the bounty of the dead whale.

I press my forehead to the whale's gritty skin and slide from its back, placing my feet carefully in the thatch of debris.

There are rusted cars, twisted dive cages—things unidentifiable. Between their ribs, flashes of bright green. I reach through the stout beams of a long-dead whale and run my fingers over the soft green below. Cool, damp—a tickle, a memory of forest roots. The green smell rises around me again as I press and water squeezes between my fingers. Moss. Living and green. Growing on the ground, fed by the blood of dead skywhales.

Air to breathe. Water. Growing things. Earth as it once was, reborn thanks to the whales, and an absence of humans. Earth taking back what we've left behind.

What if we could live with it? Take care of it this time?

But the men above with their lightning rods and greed and lies— they can't live in this world, and this world can't live with them in it. Not unless they're stopped. Not unless everyone knows what I know.

I lift my head from the mossy floor and look around. Tall buildings tower on all sides of the street corridor. The street levels and lower floors all empty. Abandoned, boarded, given up to the ruin of the earth. But one of the buildings is mine. I could not have fallen far. Somehow, there must be a way in, a way up, a way back to Mike, to my studio, to my camera. To the story I've been trying to tell.

The fog splits above me and another shadow falls. Another whale, sinking, raining water over the thirsty street.

I hurry through the rubble, out of the way of the falling whale, against the current of small, hungry fish and rustling creatures rushing toward the lifegiving feast.

There, on the corner of the street, a broad doorway gapes, the number 405 in bronze rusted green-black. Home. Work.

I have work to do.

The brittle lock breaks easily, boards falling away like driftwood. The stairway is cluttered with dirt and decay, but my blood is full of fresh air and my legs grind like whale pistons up and up.

I hear Mike before I reach the studio door, raging and weeping to the sound of dying skywhales.

His face, when he sees me burst through the door, turns the color of skywhale flesh.

"There's air," I whisper with breath that smells like ancient forests. "Tell everyone. There's air in the street."

The Time That is Left

The sky stretched large over the lake. Maddie found it difficult to tell how far away the storm was. It was close enough that the air smelled electric, but too far off for her to hear its rumble. She eyed the dark horizon, disoriented. It made the morning feel like evening, like time had warped, to see darkness in the east. But there was still a long day ahead.

"Mads, do you have our waters?" Allie asked.

Maddie took her eyes from the horizon and checked the bag in her kayak's cargo. "Yeah, I've got them. Do you have Dad?"

Allie held up a nylon sack that bulged in the shape of their father's urn.

"It's going to be weird going there without him." Maddie couldn't look at the urn. It unnerved her to think of someone as big and real as her father so diminished.

"We're not," Allie said, waving the bag in the air between them. "You know what I mean."

"I think it will help, to see a familiar place. To see the island hasn't changed, that some things never change." Allie tucked the bag carefully into her own kayak.

"Well, I hope you brought a *change* of socks this time."

Maddie triple-checked her bags and hauled her kayak through the reed-studded sand toward the water.

"Only freaks wear socks to the beach." Allie dragged her craft behind her sister's.

They'd had to leave a lot of gear back at the cabin. And the third kayak.

Their father would have carried their tent and bedding, all the food. Now they carried him. They'd divided the load as best they could, but there were no extras, no comforts. *It's only a short trip,* Maddie reminded herself. Just long enough to scatter their father's ashes in the place he loved best—at the fishing dock on St. Martin Island in the heart of northern Lake Michigan.

A gale warning hovered in Maddie's notifications, but it wasn't set to go into effect until the afternoon. They could beat it if they rowed hard.

More concerning were the rip currents that threaded like ribbons past the break, promising hard work and strained shoulders.

"We're going to get rained on," Allie said, finally noticing the ominous sky.

"If we hurry we can get the tent pitched first."

They waded their boats into the shallows, climbed in, and aimed their bows toward open water.

Waves kicked up and caught the sun, arcing aqua and falling back to a darker blue, laced with foam. The scent of wind and stone and algae, of gulls and fish and driftwood, washed away the scent of exhaust and human industry. Maddie filled her lungs for what felt like the first time in years.

THE TIME THAT IS LEFT

"That's coming in quick," Allie said, breaking her rowing rhythm as she stared at the sky instead of the rough water.

The wind had already knocked Maddie's hair loose from its tie and the spray off the wave caps was so thick it might as well be raining already.

They had rowed against the current for three hours and should be over halfway to their landing, but Maddie felt, deep in her internal compass, that something was off. That the current had carried them too far off course.

Allie must have felt the same unease, as she pulled her boat in close to Maddie's.

"Hold onto me; I'm going to check."

Maddie stowed her oar, grateful for a break from rowing, and gripped Allie's kayak while she fumbled in her vest for her phone.

Allie held her phone in one hand and pulled at her rowing glove with her teeth. She leaned over the side of her kayak and spit into the water.

"What's wrong?" Maddie asked.

Allie stared at her glove, then touched her fingers with the tip of her tongue before shuddering. "It's salty."

"What?"

"Salt water."

Maddie shook her head. "You must be really sweaty. Gross."

"No, look." Allie pushed her hand toward Maddie's face. Maddie let go of Allie's boat to get away from her sister's hand, just as a wave hit them broadside.

Allie shrieked. Maddie steadied her own boat, then reached for Allie's, but Allie was bent over, arms tucked down by her feet. "Dammit, Maddie!"

"What?"

"I dropped my phone in the hull." She pulled the dripping phone up from between her feet. She shook it and blew in the ports, pressed the button to try and bring it to life. The screen flickered grey and then blackened. "Fuck."

Allie tossed the phone back into the hull.

"Wait, get it back out, we might be able to save it." Maddie pulled her sister's boat closer.

"No point. I was going to trash it soon, anyway. But you should check yours. See where we are and where this storm is."

"But what if your doctor calls?"

Allie tensed, her lips pursed shut.

"Fine. Whatever. They can call me if they need to reach you." Maddie patted her vest pockets, trying to remember which one held her phone.

Allie held on to Maddie's boat. "They're not going to call. I already talked to them."

Maddie's hands lost their grip on her pocket zipper. "And?"

Allie shook her head. "Can we talk about it later? When we're not lost and drifting into a storm?"

Maddie nodded, a knot rising in her throat. She pulled her phone free and opened her map. Nothing loaded. The pink dot that should mark her location flickered, surrounded by a screen of grey that warped like static. None of the islands appeared, not even Washington Island, which should have loomed behind them.

The knot in Maddie's throat unraveled into tendrils of panic.

"No reception," Maddie said, her voice coarse. Her eyes stung. She licked her lips and tasted salt.

Allie looked to the sky. The thick layer of clouds had moved in, blocking the sun and creating a milky ambient light that cast no shadows. "What are we going to do?"

"Keep rowing. This part of the lake is full of islands. Even if we miss St. Martin, we're bound to find another."

Maddie caught her breath when the kayak dipped between swells, then held it as she crested each wave and the roar of wind knocked into her, blasting spray across her face like stinging buckshot. Allie clung to the end of the rope tied to Maddie's kayak, her own boat distant enough that they wouldn't impact, close enough that they wouldn't lose each other in the erratic currents. Maddie paddled as if she could beat the waves down, using the storm's surge to try and regain her sense of direction. The storm had come in from the southeast. She kept the waves at an angle to her right, hoping that would keep her in line with her northeast destination, knowing still that they were blown far off course.

A wall of water rose in front of her, bottle-green in the storm-light. A dark shape moved through the arched wave, massive, twisting, and it lunged for Maddie just as her boat skirted the break and the water fell away beneath her, taking the dark mass with it. She shook stinging water from her eyes and searched for any sign of the shape. She scanned for a fin, a tail, a wake. Allie's kayak still trailed behind Maddie; her paddling weak and half-hearted.

A rugged shape jutted out of the water to her left. A scream rose in Maddie's throat, but she choked it down. The shape didn't move with the water. The waves crashed against it. It was some kind of land or platform—something they could hold onto till the storm passed.

Maddie rowed toward it with renewed energy, her eyes scanning for the shape in the waves. Twice something nudged the bottom of her kayak, a sharp bump that she couldn't attribute to rough water. She pulled harder, moving herself and her sister closer to the rocky outcrop.

It was all jagged limestone and gnarled trees. Maddie waited for another swell to push her close to the rocks and the ropey tree root she hoped to grab. Her shoulders burned with the effort, and she was sure she'd torn muscles with endless hours of rowing through waves. Allie had given up, exhausted, and slouched in her kayak, holding on to the rope that tied their boats together. Their father had done the same for them when they were younger. They'd always arrived at St. Martin with their kayaks tied like train cars, their father, the engine, pulling them to the station. Allie had been the first to row the whole way herself, and had even helped to pull Maddie once. But illness sapped her strength. The lump in Maddie's throat returned and she wanted to wake her sister up and ask her what the doctor had said.

Maddie shook her head free of worries and salt water and focused on the tree root. She grasped it as the waves lifted her, and she summoned all the strength left in her shoulders to pull herself up onto the rocks. She jumped free of the cockpit and grabbed the rope tied to her boat before the swell of waves dropped away. She anchored herself against the stones and pulled, hauling Allie's kayak close to the shore.

"Allie! Grab the root, and I'll help pull you up."

Allie lifted her head and slowly made sense of the plan. Maddie's heart ached at the sight of her sister's weary face. Only a few years ago, she'd have surfed her boat through those waves like they were a playground.

Allie grabbed the tree root, and Maddie hauled the weight of the boat while Allie pulled herself, and soon they were both lying, tumbled out on a jutting sheet of limestone.

Maddie caught her breath and pushed herself to sit. "Well, it's not St. Martin."

Allie sat up beside her, scanning the rocky shoreline and the tall pole trees that crowded up to where stone met water. "What if it's private property? I don't want to piss off some rich Yooper on their private island."

Maddie half smiled, but she couldn't peel her eyes from the vegetation. The shrubs weren't the wispy brush she was used to, but lush broad-leafed ferns that arced tall over spreading vines. The tall poles of trees were not the wind-blown spruce she was used to camping under but scaled palms with jagged canopies.

"Wherever we are, we should get out of the wind," Maddie said. She flexed her stiff legs and pushed herself to stand, pulling Allie up beside her. They grabbed their kayaks and dragged them over the stones to the tree line. Maddie saw her own confusion reflected in Allie's face as the strange vegetation came into focus.

"Okay, this is definitely some rich bastard's island retreat. Like some kind of botanical garden." Allie pushed a broad frond out of the way so Maddie could pull their gear through.

"Yeah, well, let's hope he's got piña coladas."

They found a level break in the brush, the ground padded with moss and mushrooms and more flowering vines.

Maddie's arms shook as she bent their tent poles into the sockets.

The rain had slowed to a soft shower, but the tent nylon was soaked. Their sleeping bags were soaked. Their shoes and clothes and even the bag containing their father had been drenched by blowing water. But it was a blessedly warm night, and Maddie didn't think any amount of damp would keep her from sleeping.

Dawn came filtered through steaming air and with a symphony of countless insects. Maddie woke to swollen shoulders that seared with pain as she tried to sit.

Allie was already awake, sitting next to her, pale and drawn.

Maddie lifted a shaking arm to her pack in the corner of the tent and pulled out two water bags, handing one to Allie.

"Did you get any rest?" Maddie asked.

"I couldn't sleep. Did you see it out there? I have no idea where the hell we are."

"These islands will be crawling with tourists all weekend. And now the storm has passed, we'll be able to navigate back on course." Maddie felt sure she could figure out their location, get them back on track. She felt less sure she could endure another day of rowing.

"No, Maddie. Those palm trees, the salt water. I saw the biggest fucking black cockroaches I've ever seen when I went out to pee. We're not on the lake."

"Allie, there's no way we're not still somewhere on Lake Michigan. I admit I don't know where. But we never left the lake."

"Listen."

"No, you listen, Allie—"

"No, not to me, just listen." She put a finger to her lips.

Insects chirped a cacophony. Waves hit the rocks. "So? What?"

"No birds. No animals. Just big-ass bugs."

Maddie sighed, reached for her vest and pulled her phone out of the pocket again. The screen glowed to life, but the map still wouldn't load. Neither would her email, or any social media apps.

Allie lunged for the tent entrance and threw herself outside, rushing to the bushes to vomit.

Maddie followed her, bringing more water. "What's wrong? Is it nerves? We'll be okay…"

THE TIME THAT IS LEFT

"No, it's not nerves." Allie took the water bag and drank deeply.

"Is it because of what your doctor told you that you won't tell me?"

Allie nodded.

Maddie's stomach twisted. "Should you even be out here? Allie, you should have said something. This could have waited."

"No. It couldn't have waited. We needed to do this for Dad. And later this summer, you can do it again. For me."

Maddie shook her head, eyes stinging as if they were back in the heart of the storm. She was too exhausted to hold back the sob that fought its way up her throat.

"I'm going to go pack our camp. Why don't you walk around. See if you can find any clue about where the fuck we are." Allie turned back toward the path they'd worked through the vegetation.

Maddie stumbled through the vines and ferns to the rocky shore, choking on the sobs she didn't want Allie to overhear.

The lake had calmed, but waves lapped the rocks that formed the edge of the beach. She stared out across the water. The sun was behind her, casting her shadow toward the swells, so she should be facing Washington Island. There was a definite shadow to the west. Some darkening to the horizon that must be more land. Her arms ached to think of it, but she knew if they rowed straight for it, they could reach it before dark. They could go home, and Allie could rest. They could bring Dad back out next summer, when things were better.

Maddie calmed her ragged breaths and turned back to camp, faced again with the strangeness of the trees and greenery. Enormous insects scurried away from her steps through the undergrowth. She shuddered.

Allie had their bags packed and stowed, the kayaks roped together and ready to set out.

"I see land to the west. It's probably Washington Island. We'll head that direction and figure things out from there."

"What about Dad?"

"Allie, now's not the time—"

"Now is literally the only time I've got, Maddie."

"It's not worth risking—"

"Risking what? What's left to lose?"

Maddie's tight throat cut off her voice.

"If we're going to Washington Island, we'll pass right by St. Martin. We can stop there on the way. Just for an hour or so."

Maddie took a deep breath and nodded once. "If we pass it. If we see it."

Allie dragged their boats through the vines and out onto the rocks. "Gonna be a soggy drop into the water."

Maddie stared over the edge of the rocks to the waves. It wasn't a long drop—just five feet—but enough to make a splash. Everything would be soaked again. "Better get started."

They weren't fifty yards from shore when Maddie felt the first bump against the bottom of her kayak. She turned to Allie. "Did you feel..."

"What?" Allie asked.

"Something bumped my boat. I felt it last night, too."

They peered over the sides of their kayaks, but the morning sun reflected off the choppy water in a thousand points of light and it was impossible to see through the glare.

Allie shrieked. Her kayak splashed as it reconnected with the water. The waves around them darkened and then lightened again.

"It's a sturgeon, right? It's got to be a sturgeon," Maddie said.

"I'd agree. If we were on the lake."

Maddie shot Allie a glare. "Stop it. We cast out on the lake. We never left the lake. We're still on the lake."

Allie reached into the water and scooped a big splash right into Maddie's face.

Maddie choked and spluttered. Her lips and eyes burned. "Dammit, Allie!"

"Salt water. This is the ocean."

"Look, I know I paddled pretty fucking hard last night while you took a nap in your kayak, but I don't think I dragged us all the way to the goddamn ocean."

Allie pointed to the sky then. "Still no birds. The sky should be full of gulls so close to the islands. Pelicans, too. Herons, plovers... nothing."

"Let's just move, Allie. We'll feel better once we get somewhere familiar."

"Maddie, I don't think we're lost some*where*. I think we're lost some*when*."

The sun was getting hot, and Maddie's face heated in frustration. She turned away from Allie and rowed hard, feeling the tug of the tow rope to her sister's boat.

"A salt sea in the Michigan basin? Big-ass bugs and no birds or mammals? Giant fucking fish?" Allie joined in the rowing, punctuating each point with the splash of a paddle.

"You're sick," Maddie said. "You're confused and not feeling well. I'm taking you home if I have to drag you the whole way."

The shadow darkened the water beneath them again.

"Ever seen a one-ton sturgeon? Because I'm pretty sure even the big ones are a tenth that size."

Maddie ignored her and rowed harder, her shoulders burning, her teeth gritted. She locked her eyes on the horizon and its faint promise of land.

Their father had plastered his study walls with posters of the prehistoric lake. He collected the crinoids and trilobites, the Petoskey stones lining his bookshelves full of the geologic history of how the Devonian sea had become a glacial freshwater lake.

She's having a breakdown, Maddie thought. Grief and stress and anxiety. Who wouldn't? Maddie felt her irritation melt away, replaced with a determination to take care of her sister, to get her safely home.

Her kayak lurched and spun. Hard water shocked her frame as her boat flipped. She gripped her paddle and slipped from the cockpit, reaching up to spin her boat so she could climb back in before whatever had flipped her could snatch at her exposed legs. Her hands waved in the water, but she couldn't feel her kayak. She pried her eyes open. There—its bright red hull floating just above her, out of reach. And below her, a thirty-foot body, gnarled and grey, coated in segmented plates with a jaw like a sabered beak. Razor fins lined its thick body, whipping the creature around to lunge at her again.

Maddie screamed a curtain of bubbles and hauled herself back into her boat. She choked on air that turned seawater to spray in her throat. "*Row*," she rasped at Allie.

They paddled faster, but soon Allie's boat jumped again.

Instead of screaming, she laughed.

"Allie!"

Allie steadied her boat. "Dad would think this was so cool," she said.

Maddie shook, staring at her sister. She began to wonder if she was the one having the breakdown—if this was a nightmare and she was lying feverish in a tent on St. Martin, still waiting to wake up.

Allie bent and dug through the cargo in her cockpit. She pulled out the nylon bag and lifted Dad out of it.

"Allie, what are you doing? Row!" Maddie paddled faster but couldn't look away from her sister.

THE TIME THAT IS LEFT

Allie unscrewed the top of the urn.

"Stop it, Allie!"

"This is even better than fishing crappies off the end of a dock." She tossed the urn lid into the water.

Where it splashed, enormous, armored jaws emerged, snapping at the air.

Maddie screamed and finally tore her gaze from Allie. She turned and rowed, rowed as if her shoulders weren't breaking, as if she could outlast this nightmare. The tow rope stretched tight as she dragged Allie behind her.

The soft sound of powder dropping into the water came from behind.

Maddie chanced a glance back, and saw Allie pouring their father's remains into the dark water. A sob caught in her throat. *At least we can skip the layover on St. Martin.*

Her kayak lurched again, and this time she felt it lifted and carried forward on the back of the creature before it dove below again.

Maddie gritted her teeth and rowed harder. The splash of the urn hitting the water sounded behind her, and again the creature breached and snapped at the offering.

"Amazing," Allie said.

Maddie rowed harder.

"You can't row faster than a Dunkleosteus can swim, Maddie. It won't stop hunting till it's fed."

Maddie's throat burned as she panted in the sea spray, her arms burned as she pushed them past their limits, pulling at the tow rope, determined.

Then she shot forward, the weight of the rope released. Her kayak skimmed the water with the momentum she'd built up. She stopped rowing and spun, panic turning her face numb.

247

Allie grinned at her from her kayak, the cut end of the rope still in her hands. Her paddle floated on the water out of reach. "Row, dummy," Allie said. "I don't know if you can row all the way to the twenty-first century again, but if anyone can, it's you." She stood up in the cockpit, arms outstretched to the sky.

"Allie, no!"

"Come back fishing next summer, okay? Bring a big goddamn net."

Maddie's scream stuck in her throat as Allie leapt out of her boat. She hit the waves with a graceful splash that set the water rippling, set Maddie's boat to rocking gently, until the Devonian jaws emerged again, sluicing sheets of red water over its armored plates. It breached and splashed, and the wave it cast set Maddie's kayak shooting forward.

She sobbed, and turned, and rowed, and sobbed and rowed, her eyes on the horizon and her back to the past, praying for the future, for any future at all.

The Pescadoor

Sometimes the hook slides through and sometimes it pops, depending on the worm.

Daniel pushed the hook through till its barb crowned into view, a pus-like bead of yellow forming on his thumbnail as the worm twisted. The small thing thrashed against its fate. Daniel wondered if it was instinct or hope that kept it fighting.

The boat rocked softly on the water in keeping with the worm's rhythm, as if the creature's gyrations were enough to move it all.

Daniel didn't often fish with live bait. But here, in the reservoir, it was the only thing that worked. According to the woman at the tackle shop, anyway, and Daniel was inclined to believe her. She could have sold him an expensive lure instead of a cheap bucket of larvae.

A strong line, a live worm, and a spot just south of the old church tower poking out of the water—the side with the clock face frozen at two o'clock.

Daniel stood and faced the tower, setting his feet steady in the bobbing boat. He stared at the clock and the clock stared back, reminding him that he didn't have much time before the worm stopped wriggling and became just another speck floating in a vast lake of debris. Daniel cast his line, a whish in the air, the soft scrawl in the water where it landed, and then nothing but the lap of waves against the side of his boat—and against the stone of the protruding tower, where gradient shades of staining recorded chapters in the water's level.

The water was lower now than it ever had been since the reservoir's creation and the destruction of Alvalade, where it would forever be two o'clock on Wednesday, August 31st.

The reservoir had existed long enough to look like a natural feature, and only the church tower protruding from it afforded any clue about what had come before the flood. If it could even be called a flood, when it was an act of greedy men and not an angry god.

Either way, ninety years later and the inland sea teemed with monsters. Generations of fat fish, picky eaters whose ancestors, legends told, grew large on the corpses of the families who refused to leave their homes when Wallace blew the dam. Those who did leave spoke of at least three families who stayed, including the mayor's, who believed they wouldn't flood the town at all if people were still inside. They died wrong.

Daniel would catch one of these monstrous fish, if he could. He sat in silence as the waves counted the minutes and the clock stood still. He wondered at what moment, exactly, the worm had drowned, and if he should reel the line in and re-bait his hook. But if these fish really did descend from eaters of the dead, then maybe he'd let the worm soak a little longer.

Daniel let his head fall back so the sun could pour under the brim of his hat and warm his face. Eyes squeezed shut, he focused on the soft movement of the boat, the cool rod resting in the seams of his fingers.

It was at this point that Matthew would have started talking, asking a thousand questions a minute, and scaring away all wildlife save the mosquitoes. He'd have squirmed with impatience, rocking the boat, stuck his hand in the water, maybe even dropped his hat in, sending every fish darting into the next county. Daniel smiled at the memory, till the tightness in his throat made it hard to swallow.

He'd almost asked Matthew to come this time. But he'd said no for years before he stopped saying anything at all. Daniel wasn't even sure if the number he had written on the calendar still belonged to his son. September 2016—the calendar frozen there like the Alvalade clock, Matthew's number scrawled in the margin beside a picture of pelicans on the river. The month his life vanished as quickly as this village had. And Matthew, his son, the only sign that there ever had been a life before the dam burst.

A breeze tipped Daniel's hat back and sent ripples across the water, tugging at his line.

He opened his eyes. The tug came again, stronger, but still tentative. Daniel held his breath.

When the real tug came, the rod nearly jumped from his hands. He gripped it, yanked to set the hook, then let he line free, reel buzzing, sending shocks up to his shoulders. He pulled, then, the rod bending from his efforts. Daniel stood, bracing his stance in the rocking boat, ready to lean into the fight. He anchored the rod against his hip and moved a hand to the reel.

When he pulled, the boat lurched forward, sending a splash over the bow and rings of waves echoing away toward the distant shore.

He pulled again, reeling, and it was as if he was the one being wound in—a fish-drawn chariot racing toward the deep center of the reservoir.

The angle of the fight changed as the fish dove into deeper water, and Daniel's strain shifted from his shoulders to his legs as he tried to lift the creature into sight. The line reeled and spun, slapped and pulled, but didn't' break.

Both Daniel and the fish held the line, and the only question was which of them would tire first.

The water grew darker as his boat lurched farther from shore, well past the clock tower, out over what would have been the heart of Alvalade.

The line slackened. Daniel fell back into the hull of the boat, sun-warmed water soaking his clothes. His arm hurt where he'd struck it against the rim. The rod had been knocked from his hands and it lay crooked, half over the edge of the boat.

Daniel groaned as he stood, feeling his bruises. Had the line broken? The hook slipped? The fish torn itself away?

He picked up the rod and began to reel, to diagnose the fault and try again. It pulled in easily, hissing through the water. Then it caught, snagged on something immovable. Perhaps a sunken tree. Or a flooded rooftop.

Failure and frustration bloomed in the pit of his stomach. He'd come out here to relax and achieve something—something tangible that he could point to when every other part of his life fell apart. He could be laid off, dumped, and in debt and still feel worthy if he had an Alvalade fish on his wall. He could send a picture to Matthew, maybe lure him out of the city.

He channeled his rage to his rod and pulled, hard enough to pull up that sunken tree, to pull off that ancient roof. His fists shook with the effort of his grip.

The line tugged back.

Daniel hit the water.

He gripped the rod in shock and desperation, choking on lake foam. Thirty seconds passed before he realized he hadn't lost the fish, that it was still hooked at the other end of his line, dragging him deeper and deeper into the lake.

He shouted, his anger a soft curtain of bubbles disappearing over his head toward the sunlit surface. He was deep enough that the light looked bottle-green, the shadow of his boat shrinking. His lungs ached, eyes burned, and his nose stung where water had rushed in.

He let go of the rod and watched the silver flash of carbon fiber disappear into the depths.

Stupid goddamn fish. I hope the rod snags something and traps it swimming in circles till it starves.

Daniel kicked for the surface, reaching toward the dim glow above, following the rise of bubbles leaking from his nose. His boots dragged at his progress, his clothes like trailing anchors. He was a strong swimmer, but even as he pulled for the surface, the light seemed to fade further, the water growing colder and heavier in his lungs.

Panic overrode his rage. Daniel kicked his boots off and thrashed at the water, clawing toward what he hoped was sky. He had no bubbles left in him to release, no more air in the press of his chest as he fought the overwhelming urge to inhale. *I should have called Matthew.*

He kicked harder. A crushing grip clasped his ankle and dragged him deeper.

Daniel screamed and the lake rushed in, filling him, balancing the unbearable pressure in a smothering tide.

The grip on Daniel's ankle released. He writhed in the water, his body failing, unable to propel himself as his muscles cramped. *Should have called.*

The biting pressure came again, this time wrapping both his legs. The press against his femur threatened to snap it, and Daniel screamed again, his voice a jet of regurgitated water.

His vision dimmed. *It's been years. How long before he knows? Years.*

What little glow of light there was faded, and all Daniel saw was a shimmer of flashing silver as the pressure moved from his thighs to his waist, then his chest, then the crushing force covered his face, engulfing him in pressing dark.

Pressure squeezed the water from his lungs and stomach, forcing it out through his mouth and nose in a burning stream. He pushed back against the wall closing in against his face, a soft firmness, slick flesh with bone just behind it. A palpitating cage surrounded him, working him through a tight tunnel that pressed tears from his eyes and threatened to strip the skin from his bones. The bright sting of popping blood vessels bloomed across his body, ligaments straining to the snapping point. *Should have...*

Daniel twisted in his cage like a worm on a hook, and he wondered, again, whether it was hope or instinct driving this desperate writhing. His thoughts grew fuzzy and his body numbed as consciousness began to slip away. Sharp pain brought him back to alertness. A more forceful crush against his face, the snapping of a cheek bone, and then a release and the shock of cold water. The crush moved to his shoulders, hips, knees, and then let him go, his limbs drifting limply in a soft current. *Matthew.*

Daniel had no fight left in him. He breathed the water, out and in, taking his fill and letting himself drift toward the bottom of the lake, weightless, like his waterlogged worm, one more piece of debris in a vast soup.

THE PESCADOOR

The water grew colder as the murky bottom came into view. Algae-slicked treetops as green as a summer morning danced in the current as they would have done in a breezy meadow. Slate rooftops housed colonies of barnacle tiles, and clusters of zebra mussels clung like birds' nests to branches.

Daniel settled to rest on a plane of uneven brickwork, his cold-numbed limbs sprawled around him, his mind slowed with exhaustion. He stared up through the haze of water at a glow emanating from an ironwork lamppost above him. Small fish gathered around the light like moths, flitting in and out, nipping at smaller specs that drifted past.

The fish scattered as a dull thud sounded nearby. Another thud, and Daneil felt it this time—a vibration in the water itself as something approached. The thuds grew closer and a haze of silt kicked up around him, obscuring the glow of the lamp in a particulate mist.

The last sound, a loud bang directly next to his ear. Daniel didn't have the strength to turn his head. But he didn't need to. A figure leaned in over him, dark eyes peering down over a long, green-tinted beard. The figure clutched a twisted length of driftwood that it lifted from the bricks and jabbed into Daniel's side.

Daniel groaned, and then he wept. He had given in, relaxed into death. He had accepted his fate only for fate to spit him out for further suffering.

The figure above him gaped, then pulled a rusted bell from his tattered robe and began to shake it, waving it through the water with a dull clang that must carry for miles.

"Pescadoor!" The man shouted. "We've got one! A man's come through the fish!" The old man stowed his bell and reached down toward Daniel. "She chewed you up good, didn't she?" He slid a hand under Daniel's shoulders and lifted him easily, his body buoyant in the water. The man planted his driftwood staff deep in the silt, supporting his own weight and Daniel's, as more thudding sounds echoed from all round them.

Others appeared, propelling themselves through the dark water with driftwood staves. There were other men, younger than the one holding Daniel, and women and children among them. They gathered around, clinging to their brick-braced staves.

"He doesn't look very good," one of the children said.

"No. We'd better get him to Marla," agreed one of the men.

"Come take his other arm," the old man said. "We'll pull together."

"He's just going to die like the last one," an older boy said, and a small girl began to cry.

Daniel cried, too. His aching ribs protested his shaking sobs, but he couldn't stop. He *wanted* to die. He wanted to be already dead and couldn't understand how he wasn't.

The two men grasped Daniel's arms as though he were a prisoner and they the guards, escorting him down the brick path, through the flooded roads of Alvalade. They passed homes and old businesses. A general store with its door propped open, shadowed shelves stocked with corroded wares.

In the shifting water, the buildings appeared as if they were moving, swaying with the rock and flow of tides. Small bungalows and stately homes alike took on the facade of wreckage, coated in shaggy green and living matter. Some had collapsed, bearing stud ribs like fallen whales. They lined the rough brick road, vanishing beyond the reach of light.

The men to either side of Daniel drove their staves down in unison, propelling them forward, dragging him along until the brick road gave way to a cobble square. In its center a tall fountain spewed a stream of rippling water, creating a current where silver fish looped. Beyond the fountain, a shadow loomed. As they drew closer, Daniel made out its form—a tall building, the church. It towered over them, its spire rising through the water, reaching all the way back to the sun.

If I could climb it, follow it up...

Daniel's escorts halted, driving their staves deep to keep them still.

"Marla!" the old man called. "We have a Pescadoor!"

The swollen wood of the church door groaned open, the sound like a whale's song, echoing, magnified, through the water.

A woman emerged. Her white hair was so long it might have tangled in a swimmer's feet, and it drifted above her, whipped and twisted in unseen currents. Her dress shimmered, a cloth of woven fishing line. "This one going to make it?" she asked, poling herself forward with a twisted old fishing harpoon.

"That's up to you, Marla," the old man said. "But he's better off than the last one. Bruised and broken, but awake enough to make a fuss."

"If he's fussing, he'll make it. Bring him in." She turned her back and disappeared into the church, pulling the banner of her hair in after her. The men followed, dragging Daniel.

The water inside the church was warmer, and somehow thicker. Breathing it was like drinking water that someone else had spat out, and Daniel gagged on it. A thin line of bloody bile slithered from his lips and hung there in the stagnant water. It was darker, too, cut off from the dim glow of sunlight, the stone walls around them lit only by scattered sconces with bulbs shaped like flames.

They carried him through the church to the sacristy, where an altar had been swept clear to serve as a surgery. The men hoisted Daniel onto its surface and spread his limbs, securing his arms and legs with weights fashioned from rough-spun sandbags. Marla stood on a crate to gain enough height to lean over him. She pressed her fingers to his wounds, feeling the jagged edges of fractured bones, her touch preternaturally sure of where he hurt most.

"Cheek and ribs, knee, all fractured. A few abrasions. Nothing vital, nothing critical. Overall, this one's in good shape. Yes, he'll do. The knee will slow him, but we'll wrap that right up." She busied herself at a chest out of view, then returned with spooled bandages. The gauze floated as she unwound it, as light as her ribbon of hair and just as pale.

Daniel screamed again as she straightened his knee, driving the shattered joint into alignment before wrapping it in layers of the light cloth. Hot tears stung his eyes before floating away, clear beads in the dark water. Still, her words had brought him some measure of comfort. He was going to live. He was not broken beyond repair. And as relief poured in and drowned the shock, the pain came rolling behind it, and Daniel finally let the hovering darkness sweep him away.

Daniel awoke weighted with sandbags to a bed of woven water reeds. A man sat on a driftwood stool beside him, scraping a long pole with a rusted blade. A wooden roof stretched overhead, its beams shimmed and reinforced three times over.

"You're awake. Been a long time since we had a living Pescadoor." The man curled away a long strip of bark from the stick in his hands. His hair and beard were thick and dark, as were his hands, latticed with scars. He appeared younger than Daniel, but older than Matthew.

Daniel lay in silence, inventorying the various hurts of his body, weighing whether or not he should try to sit up. A slight shift of his core and the stabbing pain in his ribs decided for him.

"What happened to me?" The question felt heavier than the sandbags at his hands and feet.

"You tried to catch the Alvalade fish, and you almost succeeded. But it turned the tide, as it usually does, and it caught you. Chewed you up and spit you out, so you're one of us, now. A Pescadoor—one who came though the fish."

"Am I... Are we dead?" Daniel drew in a deep, shaking breath of lake water that sparked the ache in his ribs.

"Don't think so," the man said. "We're drowned, sure, but we still have to eat, shit, piss. We have kids that were born down here. Life goes on in Alvalade as it always did, just wetter. Darker. And I miss steak." The man half smiled at Daniel.

"You lived in Alvalade? That was almost a hundred years ago."

"I didn't, no. I was a fisherman, like you. Marla lived in Alvalade, and the old man who found you, Peter. They don't age much. Must be something in the water."

Daniel let his thoughts wash through him, skepticism warring with his senses. *I'm in a coma. I'm knocked out in some hospital somewhere, dreaming all this.* If that were true, there was nothing left to do but wait, hope to wake up, pray he wouldn't sleep out his life in that bed, dreaming this watery world. *I hope someone finds Matthew, tells him. Maybe he'll come. Maybe he'll be there when I wake up.*

"You caught the fish, too?" he asked the man.

The man laughed. "No. I just got drunk and fell in the water. Easy fish food. Not many actually hook that thing. I bet it was pissed."

Daniel strained his shoulders, remembering the fight, being dragged in his boat, tricked, pulled in. "Yeah. Bigtime pissed." He smiled, flinched at the pain in his broken cheekbone. At least he had that. He'd hooked a monster, pissed it off, and lived. Sort of.

The man grinned in return. "I'm Jim."

"Daniel."

"Daniel, this is for you, when you're up to it." Jim leaned the driftwood pole against the side of the bed. It was just like the ones the townsfolk had used to propel themselves through the water, but with the image of a curved fish carved into the side of it.

"Thank you." Daniel slipped a hand from under the weights and grasped the pole, rubbing the grain of wood with his thumb.

"You'll be up faster than you think. Bones knit quick down here. They'll all be wanting to talk with you when you're up. We've been wanting to catch that fish for ages. Peter has a plan for it, and he's going to want your help."

Daniel nodded, unsure what help he could provide other than to advise them to avoid that fish.

"I won't tell them you're up yet, or they'll be all over you. If you need help or get hungry, ring the bell." He pointed with his chin to a small metal bell on the bedside table, then he ducked out of a leaning doorway.

Daniel used his free hand to rub his eyes, collecting grains of sand from the corners and shaking them away. He prodded the sore, swollen mound of his broken cheek. He couldn't imagine being hungry. His stomach felt bloated, strained with lake water and anxiety.

He pulled his other hand from beneath its weight and felt his torso lift gently from the woven mattress. He floated in equilibrium, gently pinned by the weights at his ankles. In the stillness, he heard the gentle thud of a walking pole pacing beyond the thin walls of the house. The sounds traveled well through the water, back and forth, someone waiting with something less than patience.

Daniel closed his eyes against the cold water and counted the vaulting steps till his consciousness drifted like a ghost ship.

I wonder if they've found my boat. Fishing. I told them I was fishing, but did I say where? No. Yes—to the woman at the bait shop. Where I paid in cash. Untraceable. But my car and trailer are parked at the launch; someone will notice it's been there too long. Someone will come looking. Will they send divers to recover my body? What will happen when they drag me to the surface? Do I remember how to breathe air… Does anyone miss me yet? Matthew…

Not yet. Maybe never. Maybe when the grass grows so long the neighbors complain to the city. Maybe when the electric bill goes unpaid long enough to send someone knocking. The system will notice a piece out of place, but they won't care.

Vanished—I'll have simply vanished.

Relief. A surprising joy, to vanish.

"Whoa, whoa, down you come, lad." Jim's soft hands sent a jolt of sensation through Daniel's body and he shook involuntarily, rattling the jagged edges of bone against bone. Jim pressed him back down to the mattress, replacing the weights at his wrists.

"You don't want to be doing that, not inside at least. In the dark, where the current can't reach, floating like that will drive you mad. Stay grounded."

Daniel blinked away his stupor, fighting his way back from the farthest reaches of his mind. "No one is coming for me," was all he could say, the last tracing thread of his dream like a gossamer line slipping from his fingers.

"Peter is coming for you. He's tired of waiting for you to wake up. Do you need anything before his interrogation? Some fish, or… or fish?" Jim smirked.

Daniel squirmed on the bed, aware of a growing discomfort. "How do we go to the bathroom?"

Jim laughed, then. "Did you ever have a pet goldfish?"

"…yes?"

Jim cocked one eyebrow. "I'll give you some privacy. I can maybe buy you five minutes before Peter finds his way in. Try and waft things out the window, if you can." He poled out of the door again.

Daniel wondered how he'd undo his trousers without floating away again, then realized there was no need. He relaxed, and let the lake return to the lake. All the water he'd swallowed passing through him like a filter. The bed was briefly warm before the heat spread, dissipating, and Daniel gagged before he could banish the thought that they were all breathing this communal toilet.

The gagging aggravated his ribs, and his face was still contorted with pain when Peter vaulted into the room.

"Good, you're awake. And I sense your functions are in order." His long nose wrinkled above his beard. He took a seat on Jim's stool and leaned in close to observe Daniel's body, head to toe. "You really did fare quite well inside the fish. Some men are entirely broken in her jaws. Sometimes we only find pieces."

Up close, Daniel could see the strings of algae tangled in Peter's beard, and the scattering of small snails that clung like beads to the locks.

"Yeah," Daniel said, "lucky me."

"You *are* lucky. And you'd better hope your luck holds out. We're all hoping it does—you may be exactly who we've been waiting for these ninety years."

Daniel stared into the old man's eyes. Ninety years under the lake—he must have been a small child when Wallace blew the dam. His parents must have been among those too stubborn to leave, too hopeful to face the reality bearing down on them. Daniel wondered if blind hopefulness was hereditary.

"Jim said you have a plan?"

The old man nodded. "You, and all your kind, came to us through the fish. In all these years, Alvalade has welcomed thirteen Pescadoors—survivors of the fish's belly. But only three of you hooked the fish first."

Daniel's face flushed in an involuntary swell of pride.

"The fish is not just a fish," Peter said, "It's a doorway. You came to us through it. The only way out is to go through the door again."

Daniel stared. "You want me to get chewed on by the fish again?"

"No. No, we can't follow you that way—probably none of us would survive it. But I do want you to *catch* the fish again. Trap it for us, here in Alvalade."

"You want me to hunt the fish that almost killed me, that's killed almost everyone else who's ever seen it?"

"Yes, exactly."

"And what are you going to do with this monster if I catch it?"

"If the fish's stomach is a portal, a doorway, as I suspect it is, then I'm going to open the door. I'm going to turn it inside out. I'm going to make a path for all of Alvalade to return to the sunlight. I'm going to unmake the lake." The old man's eyes bulged with fanaticism.

Daniel wanted to back away, to shrink from the manic fervor bearing down on him.

Peter grinned, a green crescent in his tangled beard. "Rest up. You can't fight a monster with a broken leg. When you are well, we'll set the trap. You can have your revenge, your legacy, and we'll all have our freedom. You'll be the greatest fisherman that ever lived, the hero of Alvalade. And I will eat peaches again. Ha!" He patted Daniel on the shoulder and spun out of the room, his beard and tattered robe swirling behind him.

Daniel pulled his hands and feet from the weights and grasped his walking pole, gritting his teeth against the pain of movement.

The tower. I need to get to the tower, climb it to the surface, get away from this nightmare.

He levered himself upright, trying not to bend, relying on the driftwood staff to steady his shaking frame. He stood, breathing heavily, tasting the close waters of the house in the back of his throat.

Daniel peered out of the doorway before making his escape. Peter had vanished into the dark water, and Jim was out of sight, though presumably close enough to hear the bell if Daniel rang it. Daniel placed his staff gently against the threshold and pushed himself out into the soft current of fresh water.

Floating was easier than walking, though his arms grew tired driving the pole into the sand and pushing himself forward. It was easy to drag his bandaged leg behind him, kicking off with his good foot, making his way down the brick road, past the rows of old houses. The windows had all gone dark, the streets empty. Glowing lampposts provided the only islands of light, and Daniel followed them, hoping he'd chosen the right direction. It wasn't long before the bricks gave way to the cobbles of the square.

Daniel sat on the edge of the fountain to rest. The fresh water pouring from the fountain revived him like fresh air, and Daniel crawled closer for more of it, to bathe in the filtered stream and scrape the film of dank water from his skin. He looked more closely at the figure in the center of the fountain. A statue of a bearded man, muscular and posed, drove a patinated brass trident through the side of a giant carp. Daniel wondered if that had always been the Alvalade fountain's figure, or if it had been added post-flood, if this was the legendary Pescadoor that he was supposed to embody. His purpose, if he stayed. He couldn't stay.

The reminder drove him back to his feet, and he dragged himself through the current to the front of the church. In the dark, the facade was even more imposing. The stained glass glowed black-green in the murky water, and the shadows of the doorway were as dark as nightmare. Daniel stared up at the tower, as far as his sight could reach. He ran a hand over the stone surface of the wall, testing its grip. Slick algae coated the stones. It would be hard to climb, even with his buoyancy, and he had no idea how high the tower really was, how far to the surface of the lake. And when he reached the surface, what then? Swim for shore? And what if the fish came for him again? His shoulders ached at the thought of the climb, the swim, the fight. But it was the only plan he had.

He leaned his staff against the stone wall and drove his fingers into the narrow spaces between stones.

"They all try that, at some point."

Daniel started and slipped from the stones, falling slowly back into the silt and cobble of the lakebed.

A figure moved out of the darkness of the doorway.

Daniel saw the column of her pale hair before he saw her face. "You were waiting for me?"

"Not long. You came sooner than I thought." She sat down on the stones next to him. "I say *they* all tried that way out, but the truth is we've all tried it. It's no good."

"But I saw the tower from my boat. It breaks the surface. If we just climb…"

"That fish will pluck you off the side of the tower like a bird takes a rabbit. We've all climbed. We've all seen the fish. None of us has ever seen the surface. It's like the tower goes on forever. I guess you talked to Peter? Scared you right out of bed, didn't he, the ass." Marla pulled a silver cigarette case from the pocket of her nylon robe, popped it open, and pulled a slender fish from its compartment. She slid the fish past her thin lips and chewed, a small cloud of red blooming in front of her mouth.

Hopelessness pinned Daniel to the sand. "I can't catch that fish again."

"You did it once."

"From a boat. With a rod."

"We've got dozens of boats down here, if that's all it takes. And where's your rod now?"

Daniel closed his eyes and breathed as deep as his ribs would let him, the tang of blood faint and bitter on his tongue. "Last I saw, the fish dragged it away with her."

"Sounds to me like the work's half done, then. She's hooked already. All you have to do is grab on."

Daniel slept in the church that night, spread-eagled and weighted to the altar. He awoke to the sound of hammers concussing the water, the impact of metal on stone sending ripples through the lake that caressed his cheek.

He pulled his limbs from the weights and grasped his walking staff, flinching every time the fall of the hammer echoed through the water. Opening the church door took effort, his staff becoming a lever to pry open the swollen timbers. His shoulders ached, tendons still strained from his battle with the fish.

Daylight filtered into the square in ribbons that glimmered over the cobblestones.

Peter and Jim stood on the rim of the fountain, their faces blurred by the jets of clear water, hammers swinging slowly through the resistance of the lake. Clouds of stone dust circled them on the current, small chips of marble scattering around the square.

The figure at the center of the fountain stood in pieces, its arm maimed by hammer-fall as the two men chipped away at the stone. A hole gaped in the stone fish's belly.

Daniel watched as the men worked, driving away the last of the marble and pulling the brass trident free from the sculpture. Peter weighed the weapon in his hands, hefting it and swishing it through the fountain's jets to clear away the remining stone dust. Then he brought it to Daniel.

"We figured this might help," he said, his algae-green grin flashing through his beard.

The trident's weight dragged Daniel's hand toward the lakebed. On land he'd have barely been able to lift it at all. He doubted he could swing it with enough speed and precision to spear a killer fish. He tilted his head back, letting the trace flashes of sunlight play across his eyelids.

"How does that leg feel?" Peter asked, looking Daniel over with slow, yellow-tinted eyes.

Daniel flexed the muscle in his leg. It hurt, but not as much as it should. He gritted his teeth, then his jaw slackened in surprise.

Peter nodded, algae beard waving. "Hurts heal fast here. Another day or two and you'll be dancing on that knee. Three days till we hunt the fish."

Daniel hefted the trident again. "I don't think this is going to work."

"We'll polish it up, give it a nice clean edge," Jim said, taking the trident from Daniel. "Get it battle-ready."

"I don't mean just that," Daniel said. "I mean any of this. The whole plan."

"This boy came for the tower as soon as he could move," Marla said, her voice close behind Daniel's shoulder. Daniel started, stirring the silt at his feet. He hadn't heard her sneak up behind him. "He's hungry for the surface. He'll do whatever it takes, in the end."

"You'll have to trust us, lad. We know our town, our lake, our fish. This is all I've thought about for nearly a century, and I've thought it all through, every which way. I'm not promising it will work. But it's our best chance. And yours, too." Peter reached for Daniel's face, his hand slipping beneath a trailing strand of hair to his ear, where the old man's long fingers pinched, then pulled back. A small snail waved from its shell, trapped in Peter's grip. Peter brought his fingers together with a snap, then scattered the bits of shard and mucus to the current. "The sooner we do this, the more of you will be left to return to your family."

Family.

Daniel's hands shot to his face and neck, raking his fingers through his hair. He found three other snails that had taken refuge there, drawn by his warmth and the stillness of sleep. A cry of disgust rose in the back of his throat.

"You belong to the lake. To Alvalade. To us. If you want out—if you ever want to see the sun again—you have to take us with you." Peter laughed.

Marla stepped closer and took Daniel's shaking hands in hers. Jim bent to retrieve his fallen walking stick.

"Quit raving, old man," Marla said. "Even the best plan sounds foolish coming from a fool's mouth."

"Ah ha—even our matriarch admits it's the best plan!" Peter continued to laugh.

"Take him to the library, Jim. Let the lad see for himself, or let him put forth his own ideas. He's the Pescadoor after all. He knows that fish better than any of us, inside and out." Marla released Daniel's hands as Jim handed him his staff.

"Follow me," Jim said, and turned toward the far end of the town square, the trident in one hand and his walking stick in the other.

Jim stopped in front of another stone building not far from the town center. Its limestone walls had survived as well as the church had, and were just as popular with colonies of green growth and clinging life. Its wooden door had long since rotted away leaving nothing more than a dark stain on the stone at the threshold.

Jim and Daniel entered the building. Tall windows afforded them some light, by which Daniel took in the wrenching scene of the flooded library.

Stately wooden shelves had swollen and toppled, spilling mounds of bloated books that water and time had eroded into feather-like cushions with only the vaguest hint of art or text within them. They lay in drifts, their stories lost to the lake.

"What can we hope to learn in here?" Daniel asked. The space felt like a graveyard to him. Tension rose in his throat, a smothering he hadn't felt since he'd been pressed to the fish's insides. He backed toward the exit.

"Not down here. Come on, keep following."

Daniel shook his head, but took a slow step after Jim. Behind a row of fallen shelves, a staircase rose, winding around the perimeter of the room to a circular loft above. The loft was lined with even more shelves, the floor strewn with more waterlogged volumes. They circled the loft to another staircase.

As they rose, the room grew lighter, the water clearer. A spiraling staircase cut through the ceiling of the level above, clinging to the stone wall by rusted brackets.

"Step lightly here," Jim said. He poled off the floor and floated, more swimming than walking, up the spiral stairs and through the narrow opening. Daniel followed.

His eyes stung and he clenched them shut, clapping a hand over his face to block the light that shot through his skull like a harpoon. Jim's hand closed around his wrist and drew his arm down.

Daniel blinked his way into the light, willing his sluggish pupils to contract.

They stood under a vast glass dome. Its pinnacle glowed just beneath the surface of the water, but its crown sloshed green, bubbling. A pocket of air had been trapped below the dome when the town flooded, its chamber now a wild terrarium. Tangled roots trailed from the floating vegetation and the chirp of frogs echoed around the enclosed space.

The narrow strip of floor that circled the base of the dome

was lined with alcoves, each housing a corroded bronze bust. The roughened, green faces all stared inward toward the very center of the open space where the hanging roots had been woven into a viny ladder.

"Go on," Jim said, pointing the top of his staff toward the trailing ladder.

"This is what Marla wanted me to see?" Daniel handed his staff to Jim, let the leaning banister at the loft's edge bear the weight of his bound leg.

Jim nodded. "The oasis. Swim out to the center and climb up."

Daniel pulled himself over the narrow bar that separated him from the gaping chasm of three open stories to the library's book-strewn floor below. He floated there but felt as if he should be falling. His gut cramped with anticipation and his skin slicked with cold. He tore his eyes from the dark pit beneath him and looked up, to the glow that promised warmth, air, summer breezes and the buzz of insects.

Daniel reached through the water and swam, pulling himself across the cupola to the ladder, and guided himself up its woody structure. The island of vegetation above him bobbed in the water as it took his weight. A hundred frogs scattered from its surface into the water, disturbed by the sudden shift in their world. Daniel kicked his feet and swam as much as climbed, not wanting to upset the balance of the enclosed world above him, the closest he might ever get to home again.

The closer he came to the surface, the more his eyes stung, head ached, jaw clenched as the water seemed to grow thinner, the pressure lessening its grip on his body. Finally, he reached the top, light-headed, his knuckles bare inches from the sloshing surface of the water. It was skimmed with a green film of growth. Daniel reached out his hand and brushed a window in the surface, then flinched back, his eyes searing from the bright light that cut through that breach. He panted in pain.

No. No, I belong in the light. The sun can't hurt me. That's my home up there.

Daniel tucked his chin to his chest and hauled himself up, through the clinging film of green and into the air of the oasis.

His arms shook, hands straining to keep hold of the roots. The weight of his body pulled at his muscles, an impossible force. Daniel gasped in the air and choked. Lake water spewed from him in a fountain, gagging him, as air rushed in to fill the pockets of his lungs. He coughed, shaking the web of shrubs till all its small creatures fled from it.

Daniel's lungs screamed, clamping shut on the emptiness inside, and he threw his head back in agony as he struggled to breathe. Heat seared his face, hot light bathing his features till they burned. He clawed at the roots, trying to pull himself into the shadows of the low bushes, into some shelter from the aggressive star boring down on him through the thin veil of water and glass above.

A familiar smell assaulted him, one that made his guts turn to water. He felt his body give, draining itself into the vegetation. Cooking meat. Smoking flesh. Daniel cracked his eyes and saw wisps of smoke trail past his eyelids. As he squinted, the tight flesh of his swollen cheekbone split, and blood ran down his neck into the sponge of moss beneath him.

Something strong gripped his ankle.

The Fish. Daniel panicked, kicking out, thrashing at the thing that trapped him. His lungs still refused to draw air and his body twisted in on itself.

The thing at his ankle pulled, dragging him. He let go of the roots. He let go of the struggle, of the fight to survive this lake, and once again he released himself to death, exhausted and angry that it had teased him, only to come back for him so quickly.

The grip moved up his leg to his body, firmly pulling him from the oasis back into the shelter of the lake. The flesh of his face hissed as it hit the water.

Daniel's body spasmed as his lungs sucked in a long draw of water. The cold lake soothed his burnt face.

"That's what Marla wanted you to see," Jim said.

His voice was close, right in Daniel's ear, and Daniel realized that it was not the fish that had him, but Jim. Jim had pulled him from the oasis, from the choking dome of oxygen and burning sun, right out of the jaws of death and back into the life-teeming lake.

Daniel opened his eyes as far as his burnt skin would allow. Schools of tiny minnows flitted around them, gaping to swallow the reddened water clouding from Daniel's wound.

Jim guided Daniel's limp body back to the landing and supported him till the heaving need for water in his lungs calmed.

"It took me a long time to get used to the idea that I belonged here," Jim said. He handed Daniel his staff, and Daniel hugged it to his chest, leaning on it. "But you are one of us. You belong in the lake, now, and unless Peter's plan works, this is where you'll stay." He held out the trident, then, and Daniel saw that Jim's hand was burned, too, where he'd reached it out of the water to save him. It looked as rough as the ruined bronzes surrounding them, all of them as still as statues until Daniel moved, and took the trident from Jim.

Marla had her bandages ready when they returned to the church. Still, she hissed when she saw them, clucking her tongue in sympathy.

"You really went for it, my boy," Peter said, laying a gentle hand on Daniel's shoulders.

"He climbed clear out of the water," Jim said. "Flopped up there like a fish till I dragged him back in."

Peter shook his head. "We'll make an offering to the frogs as an apology."

"I told you this one was thirsty for the surface. He'll do anything to get back to land. This is the one, Peter." Marla had finished bandaging Daniel's face. She stood in front of him, and he stared back into her eyes. He could tell they had been brown, but a silvery iridescence flashed in them when she turned away.

"Take him home and let him rest," Peter told Jim. "Bring him to the pool in the morning. We have planning to do."

Tadpoles in the water, thousands of them, the puddle squirming as dark as an oil slick.

"Scoop gently, like this," Daniel said.

Matthew dipped the edge of his bucket into the small, muddy pool by the creek and pushed it though the mass, cupping a flopping heap of the creatures into his pail. He shrieked and dropped it, scattering them across the dirt where their twisting slowed, slowed, stopped.

"Careful!" Daniel scolded.

Matthew wept. "I want to go in. I want to go in! I want to go to the library."

THE PESCADOOR

A racket sounded outside of the house, deep concussions and reedy whistles. Daniel sat up, reaching for his walking stick. When he stood, his legs held solid beneath him, the broken knee no longer sore, just stiff from its wrap of bandages. He walked from the room, digging the toes of both feet into the sand.

Outside, three children sat before the stoop, each with an instrument built of scavenged debris, and they bent themselves heartily to their performance as Daniel leaned out to see them. Jim sat in a crooked chair to the side, carving a piece of wood and smiling.

Daniel opened his mouth to say something, but he could hardly hear his own thoughts over the din, let alone his voice. At last, the song wound to an end, each child trailing off at different beats.

Jim set his tools in his lap and clapped. Daniel stared, till Jim raised his eyebrows, then Daniel followed his lead, applauding, the small faces before him lit with pride.

"Sorry. I've never been very good with children. Thank you," Daniel said. "That was very nice."

"That's your song," said the girl holding a drum made from an old pot and fish leather. She'd been the one crying before, when he'd been found on the lake floor.

"The hero song. Peter wrote it. We learned it in school." The little boy with a carved wooden tube lined with reeds waved his instrument in the water like a sword.

"Mam said you'd come get the fish soon and then we don't have to have her seaweed soup anymore," the smallest of the three said. She banged her sticks together to emphasize the last word.

Daniel's stomach growled loud enough to be the fourth instrument in their small band.

"'Bout time you got your appetite," Jim said. "Let's get some breakfast and head to the pool." He set his project aside and stood, shooing the children from the porch.

"We want to go to the pool!'

"No, you have school. Off you go." Jim prodded them with his staff, and they scattered.

"There's a school?" Daniel stepped off the porch and followed Jim.

"Of course. They have as much to learn as any kid up there does."

Daniel nodded, then stopped, digging his feet into the silt. "Wait, there's a *pool?*"

Jim laughed. "Well. There was a pool. Now there's a hole in the ground where the current doesn't reach. Peter's built a replica of the lake there—like a modeled map. The children treat it like a dollhouse, but it's a war map. We track the water levels, the shoreline, new wreckages, and places where the fish has been spotted."

Daniel hurried to catch up to Jim. They stopped at a small storefront, the glass of its windows long gone and its door hanging at a crooked angle. Inside, the space was dark, but Daniel's eyes adjusted quickly to the shadows.

A woman stood behind a long counter, a white knife in her hand. Its handle was carved in swirling grooves, the serration of the blade knapped like stone. She glided it through the thick stomach of a fish, separating its soft flesh from a delicate cage of bones.

"Dottie, the lad's ready for his first lake meal." Jim reached into his coat and pulled out a handful of carved wooden spoons and placed them inside a suspended cloth to keep them from floating away.

The woman nodded, lips pursed in a thin line. "I'll get him something mild," she said, disappearing into a deep pantry behind the counter. She reappeared with a wrapped bundle. "Take him outside, though. I won't forget your first time and I don't ever want to see the like again."

Jim smiled and took the parcel, leading Daniel back out of the shop.

"Thank you," Daniel called over his shoulder as they left.

"You won't, not this time," Dottie said.

Jim led them to a boulder on the edge of a grassy stretch of sand and untied the cloth. Inside were raw piles of fish as soft as pudding. "You like sushi, Daniel?"

"I did…"

"Well, this is something like that, except not the nice fish you're probably used to. But if you're hungry enough, it's good. And you get used to it." He handed Daniel a soft pile.

Daniel wasn't sure he was hungry enough, but he was hungry. He popped the handful in his mouth and swallowed without tasting. His throat rebelled against the texture and fought him, but he held it down and reached out for another handful. Jim grinned and handed him more. Small fish had accumulated around them, sucking up their drifting crumbs. Jim grabbed one of them from the water in front of him and popped it in his mouth. "The crunchy ones are like a side of chips," he said. Daniel stuck with what he could swallow easily.

When they'd finished, Jim tucked the oily cloth into Daniel's pocket. They set off for the pool.

It was almost a mile's walk there, past abandoned parks and flooded houses.

The grounds around the pool were firm, unshifting, as a fine layer of sand coated the slate flagstones that almost felt like walking on earth again. Peter's voice echoed from the cavern of the pool, muttering to no one.

Jim and Daniel descended the stairs set into the corner of the pit, joining Peter around the perimeter of the map.

Daniel gaped. It was a perfect replica. He recognized Jim's handiwork in the small carvings that made up the church and library, its dome a membrane of an old mixing bowl. The town itself occupied a much smaller footprint in the vast lake than Daniel had expected, with most of the map an empty spread of sand dotted with the outline of small boats, and exes carved from fishbone dyed red. At the far end of the pool, a pile of rubble marked the place where Wallace had blown the dam, letting the Alvalade river flow into the valley.

Daniel scanned the expanse. A concentrated cluster of red exes surrounded a particularly large shipwreck just east of the church tower.

Peter leaned over this area and pulled a fresh ex from his pocket, placing it firmly in the sand. "You," he said.

The strength in Daniel's legs wavered. "Are all those exes… Were those Pescadoors?" There were hundreds of markers, reaching every stretch of the lake that had water deep enough to swim.

Peter shook his head. "Not all of them. Most don't come through the fish, not even in pieces. But those are souls taken by the fish, whether they came though or not."

Daniel gave those souls a moment of silence, stewing on the hundreds of questions that poured in like a flooding river. Finally, he asked, "Are you sure it's just one fish?"

"We're sure," Peter said. "We used to not be sure, thinking it was different generations of the same monstrous line, but one Pescadoor, seventy-odd years ago, he came close to defeating the thing. Speared it hard, right by its tail, with the harpoon Marla now uses as her walking stick. It got him, poor soul, but he carved a wound that left a hearty scar on the beast. You can still see it, like a gulch along its left side."

THE PESCADOOR

"So, what do we do?" Daniel asked. "Walk up to that shipwreck and ring the bell? Invite it to tea?"

"We can't approach it there," Jim said. "We've tried that." His face flushed.

"We need to distract it, and we need to wear it out. We'll create a diversion, a feeding frenzy that will tire it and fill its gut, slow it down. While it chases its food, we'll chase it, hopefully unnoticed till you can get a good shot." Peter circled an open area with the tip of his walking stick. "There are no attacks here because this is spawning ground. The water is cloudy, with low visibility, and small fish are everywhere—easy prey that doesn't fight back." He carved another line leading into the circle from the south.

"If we approach from here, and stay concealed in the spawning mist, we can lie in wait for the fish. When she gets sluggish, we strike." Peter smacked the sand with his stick, sending a cloud of silt into the water and planting a crater in the map.

Daniel stared at the mark, imagining himself into the scene. "Spawning mist?"

"Best not to think about it too much," Jim said.

Daniel sighed, his long breath of water disturbing the lingering cloud of silt. "This is reckless."

Jim lowered his head, agreement writ across his face. Peter's face glowed, his desperate energy driving him to a manic determination.

Daniel looked between the two of them. "This will probably kill me," he said. "But I'm fairly sure I'm dead already, or as good as. I'll try it."

Peter whooped and spun a circle, causing a cyclone that toppled the tall model church.

Jim didn't move, save for his fingers, that wrung in a tight knot in front of him. "I'll go with you," he said.

Peter stilled, his excitement stalled. Daniel stared in surprise.

"You never caught the fish," Peter said. There's no need for you to go."

"It improves our chances if I go," Jim said. "I can watch Daniel's back." He lifted his chin to turn to Peter. "You could come, too, you know."

Peter huffed. "It's not in the legend. According to legend, the hero spears the fish. Daniel will do it."

"You wrote the legend, Peter, and the song. It's all made up. *You* made it up. If we really want this done, the least we can do it work together." Jim turned and headed back toward the pool stairs. Daniel followed, still struggling to find words. He found his tongue just as he caught up with Jim.

"The plan is doomed, Jim. I'm doomed, and I know it. I welcome it. I've surrendered to death twice already this week—I'm ready for this game to end. You don't have to do this."

"You've been here a week, toyed with by death. I've been here twenty years at least. I don't even know how long—it's always two o'clock. I'm ready, too." Jim gripped Daniel's forearm and pulled him along. "Still. If you're dumb enough to hope, I have an idea."

Dottie scowled. Her hair was tied back in a bandana of woven green linen. The girl from the stoop circled her ankles, banging the fish leather drum. "I can't work that up overnight, not alone. And it's going to take more than a pocketful of rough spoons to buy that kind of labor."

Daniel's gaze moved between Dottie and Jim. Jim's pleading look made him appear almost childlike, a young boy begging for sweets before supper. "We'll help, Dottie. We'll all work together, and I'll pay you fair, I promise. Hell, if the plan works, I'll build you a new house."

"And if it doesn't? If you get eaten and leave me with your debt?"

"They're not going to get eaten, mama, Daniel is the hero from the song! I'll make your fish suit, Daniel. Mama showed me how to sew." The girl held up the apron of her dress, which had been patched with rough squares of mismatched fibers.

"I'll leave you everything," Jim said. "If the fish gets me, all I have is yours—the house, the shop, all the materials in the shed. There's a bushel of Cyprus in there. Would be a good business for Robbie, someday."

"Robbie's busy fishing."

"Well, for Ellie, then, whoever. Or sell it. But we need the suits, and we need them tomorrow. They give us a better chance, and we need all the help we can get."

"Maggie, go get your sister. Tell her we have work to do." Dottie unfolded her strong arms and jabbed a finger toward Jim. "Tell Marla what you told me. If you fail, the shop is Ellie's."

Jim nodded, a small smile hinting at the corners of his mouth. "Now, you're the boss, how can Daniel and I help?"

Dottie led them to an array of wood frames behind her house where rows of fish skins were tied, stretching. She handed each of them a rock with one edge knapped to a sharp blade. "Make sure there's no more meat on these skins. Scrape off anything that rots, then untie them and bring them in to us. When we have enough stitched together, we'll take your measure and fit you out." She disappeared back into the shadow of her house, where Ellie had joined her and Maggie at a long table set with spools of sinew thread and fish-bone needles. They pulled piles of skins from a reed basket and began whipstitching the small skins together into larger spans of fabric.

Daniel turned back to the frames and the fresh skins curing in the current. "Jim, if the fish is coming to the spawning ground to eat other fish, how is dressing like fish going to help us?"

"The spawning ground is for easy prey. There will be hundreds of smaller fish there. And bigger ones there to eat them. We're big enough to look like a hassle—she'll see us as fellow predators, not as prey. That's my theory, anyway."

"You're just as mad as Peter."

Jim laughed. "Just as mad and just as desperate. You would be, too."

Daniel ran the stone blade over the fish skins, scraping away soft slivers of meat that drifted into the water around them. Shoals of fish circled through the frames, gobbling up the scraps and nibbling on the tattered edges of the skins. At their feet, crawfish clipped at anything that drifted to the lakebed, occasionally nipping at the sand-softened skin of Daniel's feet.

By the time they'd finished cleaning the skins, Dottie and her girls had pieced the rest into a sheet of silver fish-scale fabric. Dottie draped the cloth over Daniel as Maggie and Ellie began joining the new skins together.

The fish leather felt oddly soft against his skin, and lighter in the drifting currents than his other clothes were. Water seemed to flow around it, rather than soaking in and dragging at the fibers.

Dottie pinned and clipped the fabric, muttering to herself, till she'd plotted a pattern for something that Daniel thought resembled some kind of monstrous mermaid. Then she set Daniel the task of winding thread from skeins to spools while she sewed the more complex pieces.

By the time they had fitted Jim, there were no more menial tasks to complete, and Dottie dismissed them, and they poled away into the fading light of evening, leaving the girls to finish their needlework. Robbie passed them, returning home, a busheling bundle of fish tossed over his shoulder.

"Looks like a good catch, Robbie. Well done, lad," Jim said. Robbie nodded. "Sorry we've left your mum in a state. Had a large project in mind."

"Thanks for the warning," the boy mumbled, altering his course for the shed instead of the house itself. Daniel recognized him as the boy who'd proclaimed him doomed at their very first meeting. A naysayer, or maybe a comforting voice of reason, Daniel couldn't decide.

Jim and Daniel made their way to the church, where Marla somehow already knew of Jim's pledge to Dottie. Marla checked Daniel's injuries and confirmed him fit and healed.

"Do you feel ready for tomorrow, lad?" she asked.

"Yes. I'm still not certain that I survived the fish the first time— that this isn't some kind of nightmare, or purgatory. Danger doesn't matter, if it is. Nothing matters."

Marla swung a hand through the water and struck him across the face.

Daniel fell back, falling slowly through the water to the flagstone floor of the church. He cupped a hand to his cheek, the same cheek that had been broken just days ago.

Marla stood over him, glowering. "Alvalade matters. Wallace didn't think so. The sacrifice of our families, our homes, didn't matter to him, and they don't matter to you sportsmen who fish our graves for empty prizes." She brough her foot down, slowly but with the pressure of the whole tower above them, on Daniel's chest.

"Whether you care or not, I want you to fight tomorrow like it matters. If you ever want to see the sun again, it matters. It matters to everyone who's spent a century here in the dark, and I swear to you, if you fail and survive, I will use your bones to make a cage for the next Pescadoor who dares to look me in the eye and tell me nothing matters."

To see the sun again. Son again.

Daniel squirmed under her, her gaze pinning him as heavily as her foot. His chest burned, pressure growing in his face from the restricted blood flow.

Marla removed her foot and Daniel scrambled back like a crab evading a bird of prey.

Jim stood by, fingertips pressed to his lips in shock.

"Rest well," Marla said. "Tomorrow, it's freedom or death. Either in the fish's craw, or in mine."

Daniel stood as still as possible while Dottie's needle circled him, whipstitching him into the sheath of fish skin. His clothes lay draped over Marla's arm, sure to be scraps to mend the holes of the whole village for years to come, if he should fail.

Peter smiled and wept, tears like crystal beads drifting around him. The rest of the village stood by, wrapped in hope or skepticism, each face displaying their prediction as clearly as if they held up signs.

When Dottie tied the last knot, she stepped back, and her band of children launched into another rendition of the hero's song. Peter danced along, spinning in the current, his green-tinged beard like a ribbon wrapping him as he turned.

When the song had finished, the whole lake fell eerily silent.

THE PESCADOOR

Daniel felt the thud of his own heartbeat in his ears, another drum, beating a marching song.

"I will lead you to the spawning grounds," Peter said.

"And then you'll leave us there," Jim muttered, just loud enough for Daniel to hear.

They made their way out of town, off the edge of the brick roads onto pure silt and water-weed fields. The fog of the spawning ground was visible long before they reached it—a distant haze like a thunderstorm on the horizon.

Daniel walked with the trident as his staff, its heavy bronze pole like an anchor, hoisted with every step. Jim used two staves, each tipped in a rusted metal spike, shafts carved with ridges for better grip.

As they grew closer to the grounds, the sand became rockier. Chunks of limestone and granite turned their ankles and chimed against the metal of their poles. Peter shushed them. "No unnatural sounds," he whispered. "The fish knows the noise of men."

Daniel's face curled in disgust as they entered the edges of the spawning cloud. Silver bodies darted overhead, trailing billowing streams of excretions, turning the lake into a soup of reproduction.

Peter stopped and turned to them, hands outstretched. He squeezed his eyes closed and whispered into the current, his words carving a clear path through the mist of fish spawn. Daniel couldn't hear him, but the stream carried the clear pattern of an incantation. Then Peter raised his arms, eyes popping open wide, and brought them down, lifting himself off into the water and swimming away. His white robes disappeared in the mist in moments, leaving Jim and Daniel alone in the open lake.

"Over here," Jim whispered, gesturing to a spot where large rocks created an outcrop under which they could shelter. They knelt in its

285

shadow, and Daniel traced fossil patterns across its surface. Rough coral and the rings of crinoids—evidence that Wallace's disaster hadn't been the first time the valley had flooded. A Devonian Sea had been here, once, a thriving body of water, full of monsters that would make the Alvalade fish look like kittens.

The cloudy water felt viscous in Daniel's lungs, slowing his breathing. Fish darted like bullets through the mist, sending ripples of current that spread like wind.

"So, we just wait?" Daniel whispered.

"I don't think we have to wait," Jim said. His eyes cast upward, forehead nearly scraping the stone overhead.

Daniel followed his gaze. A shadow moved in silhouette above them.

"That could be Peter. Or a boat." It was impossible to gauge size or distance in the milky water.

Jim shook his head. "Watch."

Where the shadow moved, fish scattered.

And then the shadow plunged. It dove through the spawn, rocket-fast, sending panicked schools of fish spinning off in galaxy arms.

Daniel lifted into a crouch, but Jim held him down. "Wait till she's tired."

They watched the fish feast. A generation of bluegill, bass, and pike disappeared down its throat, entire bloodlines halted in one swallow. When its sides bulged and half the spawning fish had fled or died, the shadow began to slow. Its lunges became halfhearted, and it drifted closer to the bottom of the lake, toward the large rocks where Daniel and Jim waited.

The shadow grew as it moved closer, the fish revealing its true size as it neared.

Daniel's throat felt dry despite the water pooling there. Jim's grip on his arm grew tighter, then released as Jim moved his hand back to his spear.

They crouched, ready, as the silver belly of the fish emerged from the mist directly above them. She sensed them just before they moved. Her body jackknifed, twisting on itself to bring her jaws closer to their hiding place.

Daniel lunged from beneath the rock, trident angled to thrust. He drove it toward her belly, but the tines skidded over the mucous coating her tough scales. She shot forward over his head and he ducked, spinning slowly, just in time to see his trailing fishing rod drag past him, bumping along the lakebed rocks. He dove for it, wrapping one hand around the braided carbon handle.

Once again, the fish pulled him like a doll through the water. Daniel struggled to right himself and dug his heels in amid the rocks and fossils that littered the lakebed. The fish strained at the line, then stopped, and turned to face him. Their eyes locked, hers a silver yellow, the black centers an abyss—a promise of death too long delayed.

Daniel lay the rod down, slowly, letting it rest against the rocky silt. Then he raised the trident and brought it down hard, burying it deep into the ground, its tines pinning the rod in place.

The fish charged.

Daniel ducked, weaponless, dodging the raking jaws that opened wide enough to swallow the whole world. Jim shouted behind him, and Daniel spun to see him braced, one spear raised, meeting the fish's charge head-on.

Daniel screamed as the fish writhed, and Jim and his spear vanished.

The fish ascended, mouth working at her prey. Blood rushed

from between her lips. Daniel's heart dropped, his chest a hollow drum, and rage rose to fill the space where hope had been.

He swam forward, plucking Jim's second spear from the sand.

"You're tied, you bitch! Like a dog to a stake," Daniel shouted.

She turned back to him, jaw still gyrating. Her sides bulged with prey.

Daniel traced the line from the rod to the fish's mouth. Twenty feet, at most. She'd be cursed to swim in circles, just as he'd wished on her when she'd pulled him in.

A shaft of wood shot from between her lips. Blood and floating scraps of flesh billowed out as she opened her jaw wide. Jim's hand followed, clawing at the slick membrane of the fish's mouth.

Daniel raced toward the fish. She was too busy to notice him, too annoyed by her escaping meal to care about the one coming for her.

Daniel drove his spear into the fish's eye, its tip sinking into that black abyss.

She thrashed, and the spear's shaft caught Daniel in the gut, knocking him heavily to the rocks below. His back scraped along a jagged edge, tearing his fish leather suit to shreds and skinning the flesh from his shoulders. His own blood tainted the water, a red flair, easy to follow.

But the fish did not follow. She twisted and shook, thrashing at the end of the line that pinned her to the rocks. Jim's spear still waved from her mouth, Daniel's buried deep in her eye.

Daniel rolled onto his stomach, clutching at his ribs, now freshly broken, trying to make his way back to the fish, to reach into her gut and drag Jim from the depths himself.

The fish slowed, her thrashes turning to twitches. Daniel ground his teeth in a violent grin. He'd seen these death throes a hundred times in the bottom of his boat. The beginning of the end, the exhaustion before the final heaving puffs of the gills.

Daniel swam close, not trusting her stillness, poised to dodge any final twist she might take.

Jim's fingers lay slack just inside her mouth.

Daniel reached for them, brushed the insides of the knuckles, and grabbed the wrist. Jim's grip tightened on him, and they held fast as Daniel hauled on the arm, digging his feet into the corners of the fish's mouth. The fish twitched weakly, her fight exhausted.

Jim's head soon appeared, then his shoulder, then his other arm fought its way free, and Daniel grabbed that too, pulling till all of Jim slipped out of the sticky mess of the fish's gorging gut.

Not all of Jim. Most of Jim. Daniel held on to him as they both sank to the lake floor, Jim's bloody torso trailing shreds of what had been his legs.

"You got her. You got her..." He whispered in Daniel's ear as they settled in the fog of silt.

Daniel propped Jim in his lap. Jim's face was as pale as the fish's belly. His eyes roved, as if searching for him in the dark.

"*We* got her. She's dead, Jim. Your plan worked, and we got her."

Peter appeared through the fog of spawn and blood. He placed a hand on Jim's forehead. Marla's hands gripped Daniel's shoulders from behind. Daniel looked up to them both, but they weren't looking at him, or at Jim. Their eyes locked on the bobbing limp figure of the fish overhead.

"It's time," Peter whispered. He pulled Dottie's carved bone blade from his robe and launched himself into the water beside the monstrous fish. Marla followed him. He slid the blade in below the fish's jaw, drawing it along the seam of her belly till he reached her tail. "It's time to unmake this lake," he said. He gripped each side of her wound and pulled, opening her to the wild waters that stirred up around them. He folded her flesh back, pushing, wrapping the skin of her belly around her back, cracking her spine. The glut of her last meal, gallons of fish and Jim's twisted legs, washed away on the rush of water.

Daniel struggled to stay upright in the current as it pulled harder.

Peter made one final drive at the fish, and with a pop, snapped the last of her inside out.

The water around them roared. Marla's shrieking laugh sounded, then vanished into the tide.

Daniel felt himself pulled from the lake floor. He gripped Jim harder as silt and rock and fish blew past. A bright shine flashed before his eyes, and Daniel grabbed for it, the trident, still pinned in the limestone bed. He gripped it against his shoulder, hands clutching Jim's arms, as the lake raged in a hurricane around them. Water spun in a cyclone, a whirlpool whipping everything toward the drain Peter had opened in the fish.

Daniel's ears popped as the pressure changed, and his chest spasmed as he choked on the water. He heaved, lake pouring from him in a tide that seemed endless, as if he himself contained the whole of the Alvalade reservoir inside him.

When it finally stopped, when the roaring subsided and only a thin string of bile dangled from Daniel's lips, he took a long shuddering breath. Air. He breathed air.

Daniel straightened, his ribs screaming, and looked around. He stood in a muddy wasteland. Thousands of fish flopped lazily in thick mud. Boulders and boat wreckage protruded from an algae slick landscape. In the distance, Alvalade stood, its brick roads weaving through the mud to the towering form of its stone church.

Jim lay silent at his feet.

Daniel knelt to him, brushing mud and debris from his face. Jim's skin peeled away at his touch, the water-soft flesh falling apart like fish scales.

Daniel screamed and backed away from the body of his friend, sobs threatening to punch through the agony in his throat.

A wet sucking noise sounded behind him, and Daniel turned.

Peter stood, his body bent under the weight of his own bones. "Alvalde is free," he said, and then he collapsed, his frame crumbling like an empty puppet. Threads of green-tinged beard blew away on the breeze. Beyond him, the roofs of Alvalade fell. Houses disintegrated into soaked sticks, the library's dome collapsed, releasing its oasis to the wide world. The church tower cracked, and the stones gave, the clock chiming all the way to the floor where it stopped, finally, forever.

Daniel watched the underwater world fall apart all around him. Alvalade had waited, lost to time, and then time came rushing in on the first breath of air.

He walked for miles through the mud, leaving his friend's bones at the trident marker, a fitting headstone for the hero of Alvalade. He walked the brick paths threaded between the piles of rubble where once fish was served, music was played, and wounds were healed. He passed out of the far side of town, to the edge of the shore, where his truck and trailer stood, empty, dusty, warm from days of sun.

Daniel peeled the tattered strips of fish leather from his skin, leaving Dottie's last masterpiece in a pile where the dock had been. He crawled naked into his truck and waited. Soon, others would come. Rangers and hikers, fishermen and campers. The press. The news. The story would reach far and wide, to the city, to Matthew. Aghast and curious, puzzled, and anxious to hear what happened. For the story of a lost town, a lost lake, a lost father, and the biggest fish you ever saw.

The Ballad of Lady Lithium

Lithium. It sounds Elvish. It doesn't taste it, though, and the man who brings it to me does not look like a bearer of gifts. But it does cast a spell, of sorts, and for once in a long while, I sleep.

All I can hear is wind and waves and the sound of my own breathing.

I wake on wet sand, golden with rivulets of rich black flowing through it. The surface is smoothed by a fresh tide and the stones and zebra mussels are stuck fast in its wet suction. As am I. I pull my hands free and push myself up, crab-walking away from the foam that chases my toes.

The waves are small, cresting a gentle nod, but a bright ribbon of rip current crosses them just where the water turns dark. The narrow beach is backed by brush-studded dunes, and I clamber up and over the rise, dropping the edge of the earth away behind me. Shortening the world.

Wind-stripped pines shelter a small table in the dry grass, and at the table sits a wind-stripped woman. Her hair is all trained to one side, like the branches above, the windward side of her face eroded, smoothed by blown sand, like sea glass. The leeward side ridged as tree bark.

"The water will kill you and the wind will kill you. But I won't. Come. Sit."

Her lake-stone eyes are hardly more inviting than the rip tide, but they pull twice as hard, so I sit.

She smiles and her lichen beard sways in a breeze that cuts through my clothes. My body is too heavy to shiver. I am as still as the pines.

"Have you come or were you sent?" she asks, and her teeth flash, striped and broken like the zebra mussel shells.

"Sent." My voice is not as raw as it was last night when I explained myself to the nodding admissions nurse.

"Relief? Rage? Resignation?"

"Yes." The sand drying to my skin itches and smells of algae, of the lake water rich with nutrient putrefaction.

The pine woman smiles. "Close your eyes and feel them—the ones who sent you away."

I close my eyes and feel sharp grains in the corners. I squeeze them shut tighter, wonder if my eyes would make pearls of them.

"Do you feel them? Their shoulders have dropped. Foreheads relaxed. They are breathing full into their bellies as they have not done for months."

I do feel it. Their peace. My brother, especially, sleeps unguarded, un-listening, heavily. I reach as if to stroke his cheek, but a switch of woven grass strikes my hand away.

My eyes pop open and sand falls from my lashes, caught by the wind before it reaches the driftwood table.

"Why don't they always sleep like that, if they can?" I ask. I never have. I never could.

"They don't carry your worries. And, so long as you are here, they don't carry you."

With my eyes open, their peace fades, replaced by my own twisting anxiety. "So, when I'm here, they can rest?"

"Yes."

"Does that mean that I should stay?"

"Many do. There is good soil here, to put down roots, and silence, and peace for you, too."

My eyes travel her branched crown—the boughs that reach back toward a wall of trees, a forest dense and dark and silent.

"If I stay, do I become like you?"

"For a time. I am still becoming. In time, we will become like them, and others will take their place here at the driftwood table."

To be a tree does not seem bad. To live in rich earth and silent shadows. And to know my family sleeps as they have never slept before—without me.

"And what if my family come looking for me?"

"You know better than I would whether they will or not."

I see by a flash of mica in her eye that she knows as well as I do. I stand from the table.

"Go join the forest. Find a patch of sunlight."

When I step away from her, the wind catches me again, but my clothes have dried, and it doesn't cut quite as cold. In the trees the air hardly stirs at all, though I hear it roar overhead through the canopy.

I run my fingers over the sticky bark of a slender pine. Its branches are thin, and dip under the weight of its needles. My hand comes away tacky with sap and I roll it between my fingers, releasing the scent of spruce.

"I always thought of trees as patient," I whisper to the rows of sentinel souls planted there at the edge of the world. "But you've given up."

I glance back toward the sound of rolling waves. The pine woman of the dunes is watching the water, not me. I turn back to the forest. There is no path through it, though the undergrowth is sparse and the blanket of fallen needles makes for soft walking.

The forest ends as abruptly as a song, as a cliff, as love. One second the world is perfumed shadows and the next it is all dry light.

On the other side of the forest, far from the sound of the sea, there are fields. Hills roll with them, all carved deep and rich with plough lines. Figures move through the furrows, dragging their ploughshares through earth scented with promise.

I step onto the soil, wondering if I should walk in the cut or on the mound, following the lines as a trail toward one of the nearby figures.

The man waters the earth with his sweat as he drives through the field. His hands are trowels, and his feet are wedged blades, arms thin, bent wood. He moves through the dirt with a purpose.

"Hello," I say, as I match my step to his stride.

"Don't just stand there." His pace quickens. "Get to work."

"I don't work here. I'm not from here."

He stops and turns to me, allowing the earth a moment to be still. "None of us is from here. We all work here."

"But why? What are you planting?" I scan the fields, and everywhere they dig and plough and till, but nowhere is anyone sowing. Nothing is green.

The man has grown agitated. The blades of his trowel hands beat together like anxious cymbals. "We just work. We find meaning in it, and it gives us meaning. As long as we keep going, it will keep us going." He turns back to his plough and digs the blade deeper, leaning against the rail as he drives it forward through a trench already freshly cut by the person not half a field ahead.

I reach down and grasp a clump of dirt. It's soft and damp, full of life and ready to make things grow.

"Go to the barn!" the man shouts over his shoulder at me. He waves a blade hand up the hill to a white structure on the horizon. "They'll fit you out. Get you to work. It helps, I promise. It gives you a reason to keep going."

"But what's the reason?" I call back, letting the dirt fall back to the ground.

"The work!"

They do move with purpose, as if they have forgotten all their cares but the task before them. Would it be a relief to be so focused? Or have they simply traded one burden for another? And what could grow in earth that is always turned?

Still, I climb the hill toward the barn, if only to gain the vantage of its height, to see what lies beyond the ever-turned fields.

In the distance, a shock of color. Structure spires in bright display, the puffs of pampered trees, and the drifting trails of hearth smoke.

I set out across the toiling fields.

A deep ditch marks the end of the fields, and beyond that, a smooth wide road, shiny black with tar. Across the road, lawns begin, trim and green and bordered with riots of flowers. At the end of each lawn sit cottages, all in a row, their stout chimneys all whispering trails of fragrant woodsmoke.

On the porch of each cottage sit pale women in pale dresses, their wide-toothed grins visible all down the street.

The moment my foot brushes the blacktop, they stand in unison. And as I pass the first cottage, they run toward me, skirts and curls flying out behind them.

Their grins are stitched in place, their painted eyebrows knitted with concern as their polished fingers outstretch toward my sea-soaked, forest-torn, field-stained clothes.

"You poor thing!"

"You've been through so much."

"You must be exhausted!"

"Let us carry you."

Their hands are soft against me, but as strong as viper jaws. My feet lift from the tar, though I feel something cling, tying me to earth as they pull and pull me away.

"Feet up, we've got you."

"Lean on us, dearie."

The higher they raise me, the more their hands feel like vines, and I twist to free myself.

"We're here to help!"

"Relax. Let us bear your burden."

As they move forward in unison, carrying me bodily, my head falls back. I see, behind me, that some of the women have gathered around the patch of ground where I had stood—where now a cluster of thistle grows, with dandelions and morning glory sprouting in my wake. Stiff-smiled women pull at the weeds and cast them into a sack that they carry after me, my weed-trail and myself all aloft through the smooth, clean streets.

They finally set me down where the lawns turn to dust.

They set my bag of wilting thistles beside me. And all at once, every smile turns away, and the world grows darker.

"They're real helpful, huh?"

The voice comes from the dust behind me and carries with it dark humor. I turn to the source to see a young man as filthy as myself.

"They don't like weeds in their lawns. People like us track weeds wherever we go. So, they 'help' us all the way out of town." The young man stands and offers me a hand, which I take, and pull myself to standing. Part of his hand crumbles away in my grip.

The dust where we stand borders a heap of refuse. Cast-off and broken things fashioned into rubbish castles. Figures move among the structures, and all of them look like me. Like the young man. Like us.

He leads me to a house—a home—made of bits of oven and freezer, of an old brass elevator sparkling in the sunlight. "You live here?"

"We do. We gather here. Like all of these things. And we make the best of it." He doesn't smile, not really, but he is at peace.

"Does no one come to look for you here?"

He does smile, then, but it isn't pretty. "No. This isn't a place to wait, it's a place to stay. No one is looking for us. Is someone looking for you?"

I close my eyes again, like the pine woman taught me. I feel my family's peace. The burden of their hearts and shoulders lifted, as the smiling women had lifted me.

"No," I say. "No, they're not coming for me."

He squeezes my shoulder with a hand stained with rust, and more of him falls away. "Then you're home. Everything here has been thrown out."

I wander the paths between the assemblage of structures. I see myself in the torn lace curtains, in the broken mirrors, in the sunken chairs, and the cars that move too slowly and never without a push. I belong with these things, yes.

But I'm not at home. I try not to think of the dust underfoot.

At the center of the refused city there stands a tower built all of crumpled letters. Ink runs down its sides in stain trails that mark the turning of the years, though the message never changes. Every bit of paper echoes the one below it, above it. It rustles like the canopy of trees. I circle the tower and keep it to my back, escaping that sound, that whisper of unanswered pleas.

All I can hear is wind and waves and the sound of my own breathing, as the shore comes into sight again. The far shore—not studded with bent pines, but a deep beach of bright sand with a shallow leeward sea. There is no riptide here, and the water is warm against my ankles, knees, stomach, throat, eyes.

I lift my feet and taste the bitterness of metal in my throat.

"This isn't a long-term facility. You either get better or you go to a state hospital."

"Do people get better in a week, doctor?"

"Well, no, but we need to see you're on track."

"What do you need to see?" I stare at the art on the wall, a painting of the shore. It looks cold.

"Stay stable. Work hard. Smile, take care of yourself. Make friends." He shakes his head, as if the answer is obvious. As if the answer has always been the same.

"Easy enough." I don't smile, but I'm at peace.

"No, it's not easy. But we're here to help you." His help is nine-to-five and billed by the hour.

"Can you write me a prescription for friends?"

He's not smiling, either.

"If I can convince you that I can do these things, then I can go home?" I picture my family's shoulders rise, their jaws tighten, the lines around their eyes deepening. The knife under my brother's pillow.

"If you can convince me, we let you leave. Where you go is up to you."

He does hand me a prescription, though. Lithium. My elven gift.

There are many nights yet to sleep, and many other islands, and maybe I am not pine, but willow. No one is coming for me. No one is looking. So, I swim.

ACKNOWLEDGMENTS

I would like to thank my family for allowing me to float between this world and a hundred others. Thank you to my friends and mentors, especially Rena Mason. Thank you to Doug Murano for his endless support, and to Thomas Brown and Todd Keisling for making this book beautiful. Thank you to Lee Murray, Cynthia Pelayo, Nathan Ballingrud, and Laird Barron for your generosity and kindness.

Thank you to the Post-Apocalyptic Writers Society (PAWS) for being my literary family—Kat Rohrmeier, Chip Houser, Steve Toase, Marianne Kirby, Carina Bissett, and Julie Day—you all have some heart in these stories.

Thank you to the original editors of these pieces: Andy Cox, Ellen Datlow, John F. D. Taff, Doug Murano, Scarlett Algee, James Everington, Dan Howarth, Carina Bissett, Josh Viola, Hillary Dodge, Willow Becker, Michael Cluff, Christi Nogle, Aric Sundquist, James Chambers, Gemma Amor, Laurel Hightower, Cynthia Pelayo, Curtis Lawson, Joe Morey, Amanda Gowin, and Craig Wallwork. You're all dream-makers (and nightmare distributors).

And a special thanks to the Lighthouse Inn in Two Rivers, Wisconsin. At least six of these stories were written while I hid away from the world in your lakeside rooms, fueled by room-service nachos. Literally could not have done this without you. I'll be back soon.

About the Author

SARAH READ is the Bram Stoker Award®-winning author of *The Bone Weaver's Orchard, Out of Water, Root Rot,* and the forthcoming *The Atropine Tree.* You can find her online at authorsarahread.com.

CONTENT WARNINGS
(some spoilers)

The Hope Chest: child abuse

That's For Remembrance: none

Wish Wash: violence against animals, gore, suicidal ideation

Root Rot: violence against children

Into the Wood: violence

Pelts: violence against animals and children

Bloody Bon Secours: violence

Diamond Saw: pregnancy, violence, gore

When Auntie's Due: pregnancy, violence against children

Seeing Stones: violence

Death Plate Seating for 1,000: claustrophobia

Inn of the Fates: implied suicide

Trouble with Fate: pregnancy, gore

The Terror Bay Resort Experience: violence, gore

Skydivers: violence against animals

The Time that is Left: death, illness, suicide

The Pescadoor: violence against animals, gore

The Ballad of Lady Lithium: suicide, mental illness

Printed in the United States
by Baker & Taylor Publisher Services